The 3 Musketeers

Alexandre Dumas

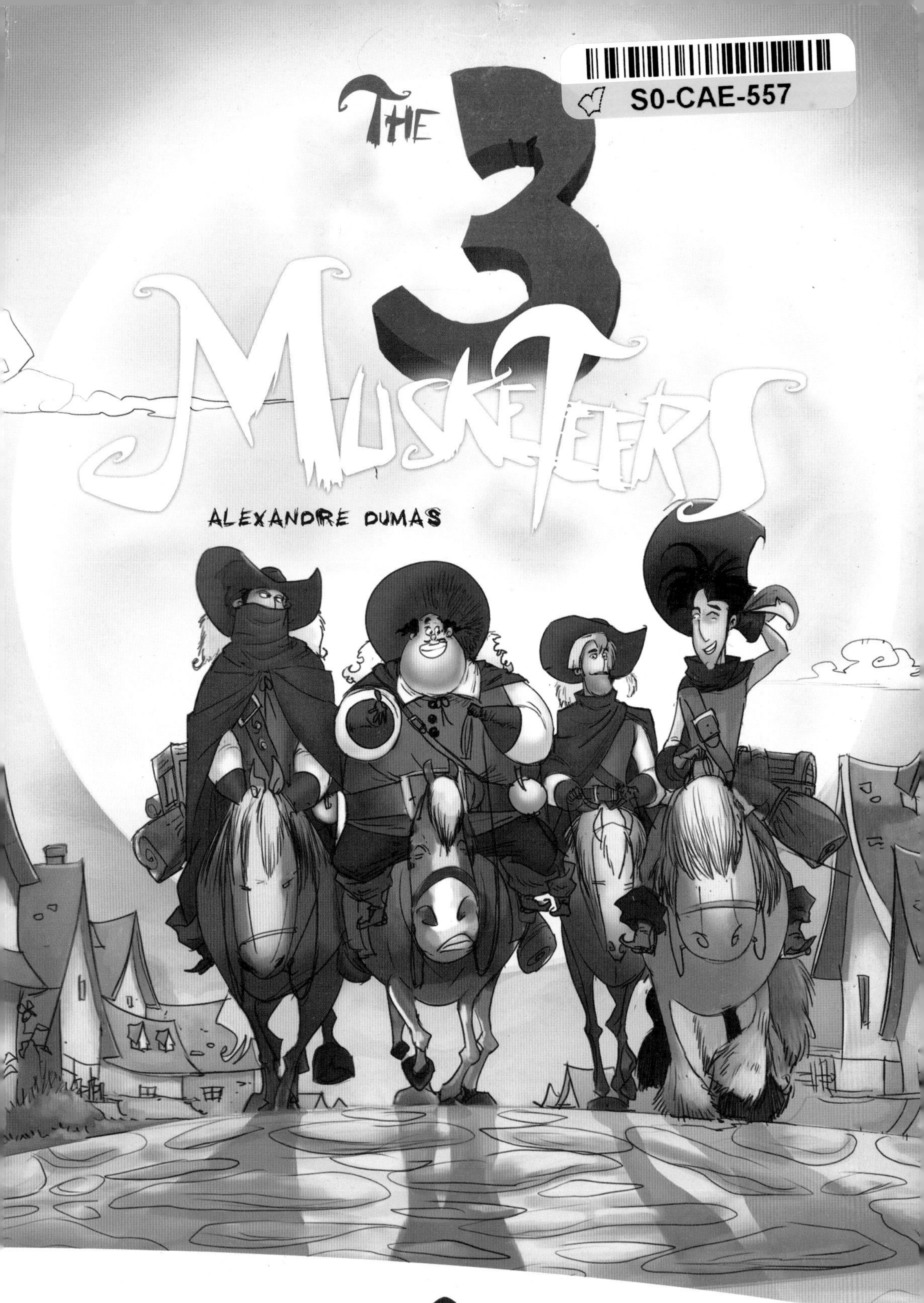

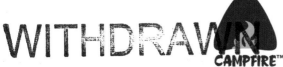

CAMPFIRE™

KALYANI NAVYUG MEDIA PVT. LTD.
New Delhi

THE 3 MUSKETEERS

Sitting around the Campfire, telling the story, were:

WORDSMITH BRUCE BUCHANAN
ILLUSTRATOR AMIT TAYAL
COLORISTS AJO KURIAN & VIKASH GURUNG
LETTERERS BHAVNATH CHAUDHARY, LAXMI CHAND GUPTA
& GHANASHYAM JOSHI
EDITORS SUPARNA DEB & ANDREW DODD
EDITOR (INFORMATIVE CONTENT) RASHMI MENON
ART DIRECTOR RAJESH NAGULAKONDA
PRODUCTION CONTROLLER VISHAL SHARMA
COVER ART AMIT TAYAL & AJO KURIAN
DESIGNER JAYAKRISHNAN K. P.

www.campfire.co.in

Published by Kalyani Navyug Media Pvt. Ltd.
101 C, Shiv House, Hari Nagar Ashram
New Delhi 110014
India
www.campfire.co.in

ISBN: 978-93-80028-57-6

Printed in India at Rave India

ABOUT THE AUTHOR

Alexandre Dumas was born on July 24, 1802 in the village of Villers-Cotterêts, just outside Paris, France. His father had been a general in Napoleon's army, but he fell out of favor, leaving Dumas and his family in an impoverished state. When Dumas was only four, his father died. His mother was unable to provide him with a decent education, but he loved to read and did so whenever he could. His mother used to tell him stories about his father's brave deeds. They inspired Dumas's vivid imagination, and he spent much time dreaming of adventure.

Dumas was not a very good student, but he had beautiful handwriting, and so he studied to work as a notary. He first began writing musical comedies, and then historical plays, in partnership with a poet and friend, Adolphe de Leuven. Historical themes, as well as the use of a collaborator, became permanent aspects of Dumas's style throughout his career.

Influenced by William Shakespeare, Sir Walter Scott, Friedrich von Schiller, and Lord Byron, Dumas wrote his first plays in 1825 and 1826. Within a few years, *Henry III and His Court* (1829) brought him great success and recognition. By 1851, he had written more than twenty plays. Around this time, he also began writing fiction—first short stories and then full-length novels. He wrote *The Three Musketeers, Twenty Years After*, and *The Count of Monte Cristo* during this golden period.

Dumas died in poverty on December 5, 1870 at his son's villa in Puys, near Dieppe, France. He was originally buried in the cemetery of Villers-Cotterêts. However, in 2002, his body was moved to the Panthéon in Paris, and buried among other notable French literary giants, such as Émile Zola, Victor Hugo, Jean-Jacques Rousseau, and François-Marie Arouet Voltaire.

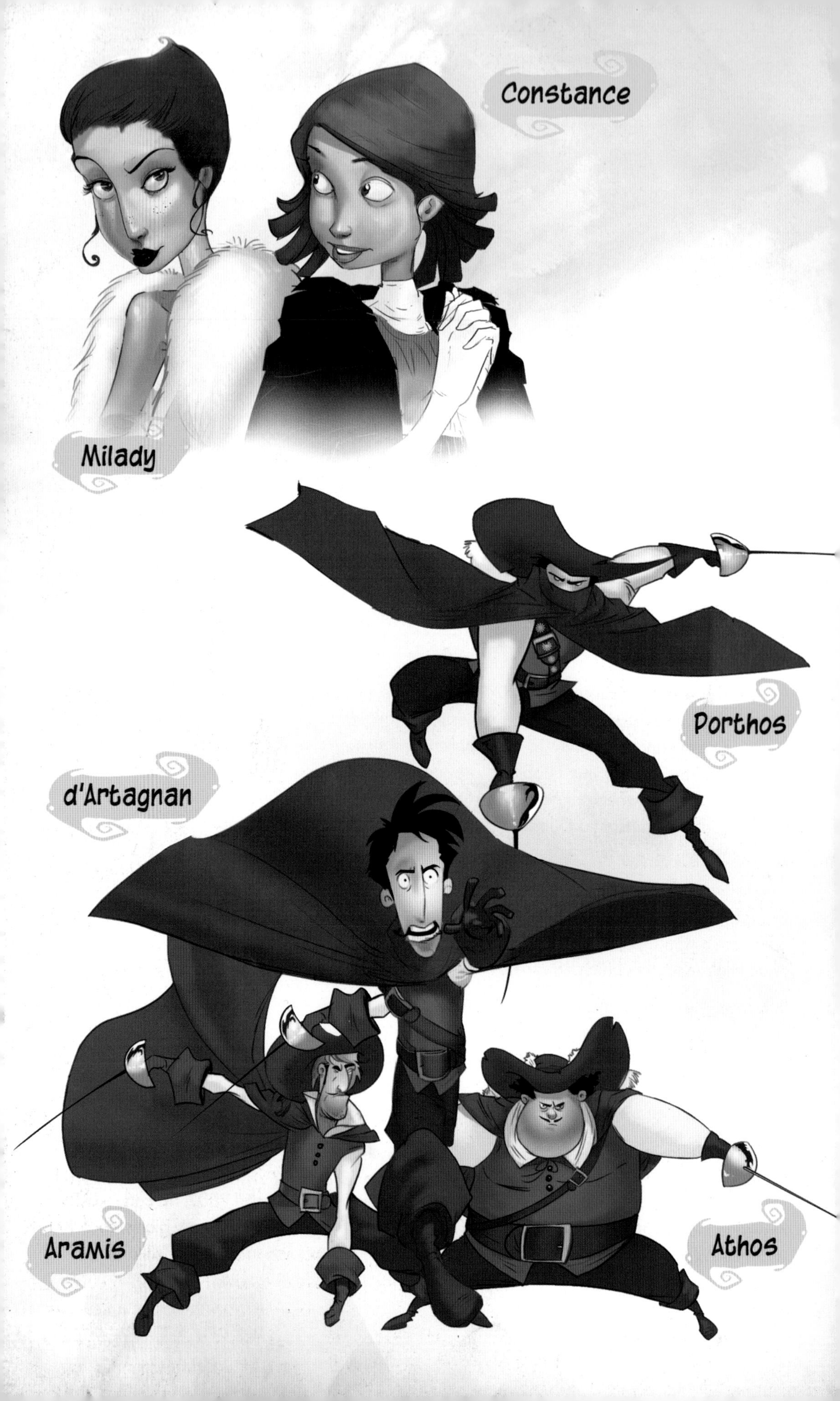
Constance
Milady
Porthos
d'Artagnan
Aramis
Athos

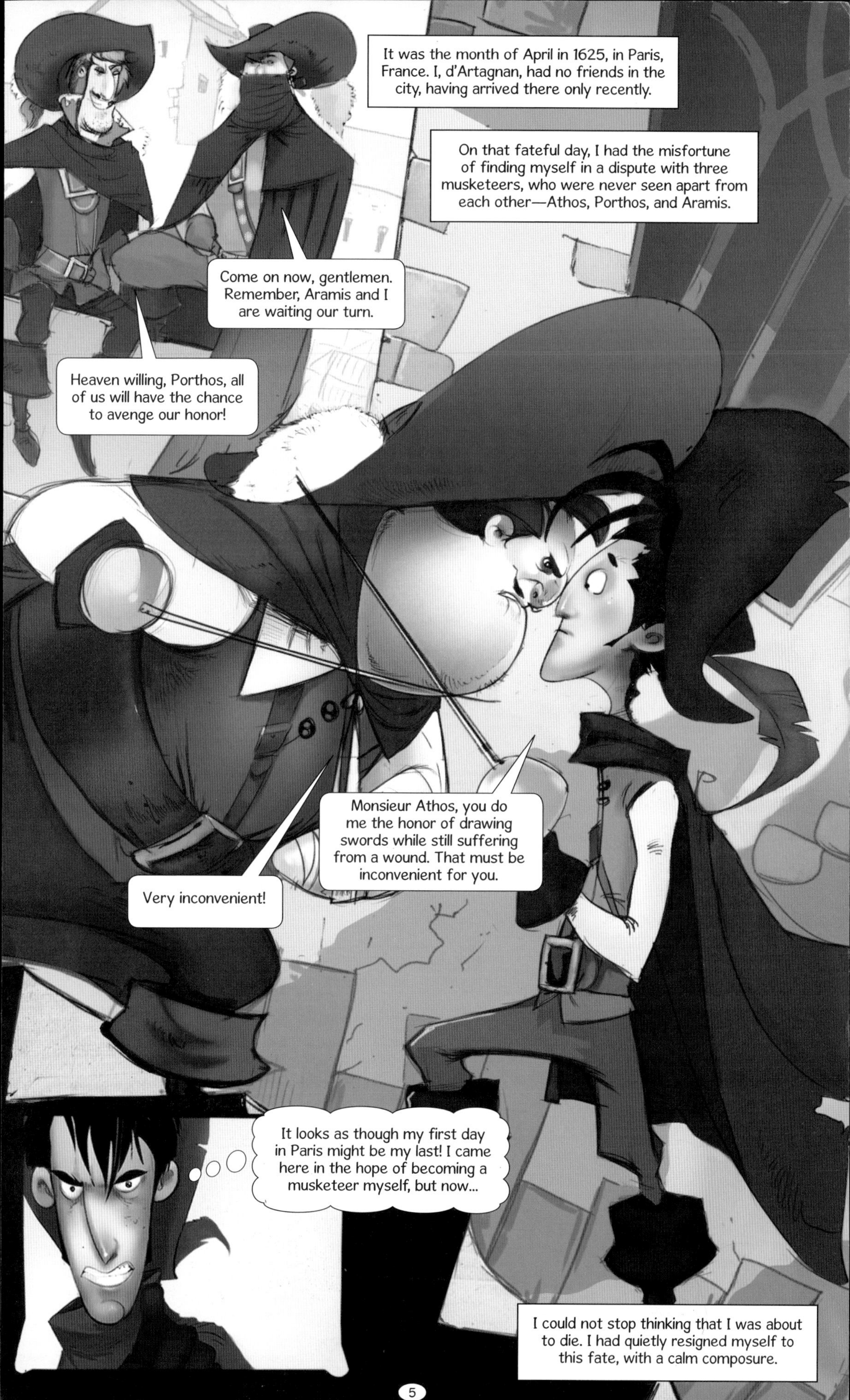

It was the month of April in 1625, in Paris, France. I, d'Artagnan, had no friends in the city, having arrived there only recently.
On that fateful day, I had the misfortune of finding myself in a dispute with three musketeers, who were never seen apart from each other—Athos, Porthos, and Aramis.
Come on now, gentlemen. Remember, Aramis and I are waiting our turn.
Heaven willing, Porthos, all of us will have the chance to avenge our honor!
Monsieur Athos, you do me the honor of drawing swords while still suffering from a wound. That must be inconvenient for you.
Very inconvenient!
It looks as though my first day in Paris might be my last! I came here in the hope of becoming a musketeer myself, but now...
I could not stop thinking that I was about to die. I had quietly resigned myself to this fate, with a calm composure.

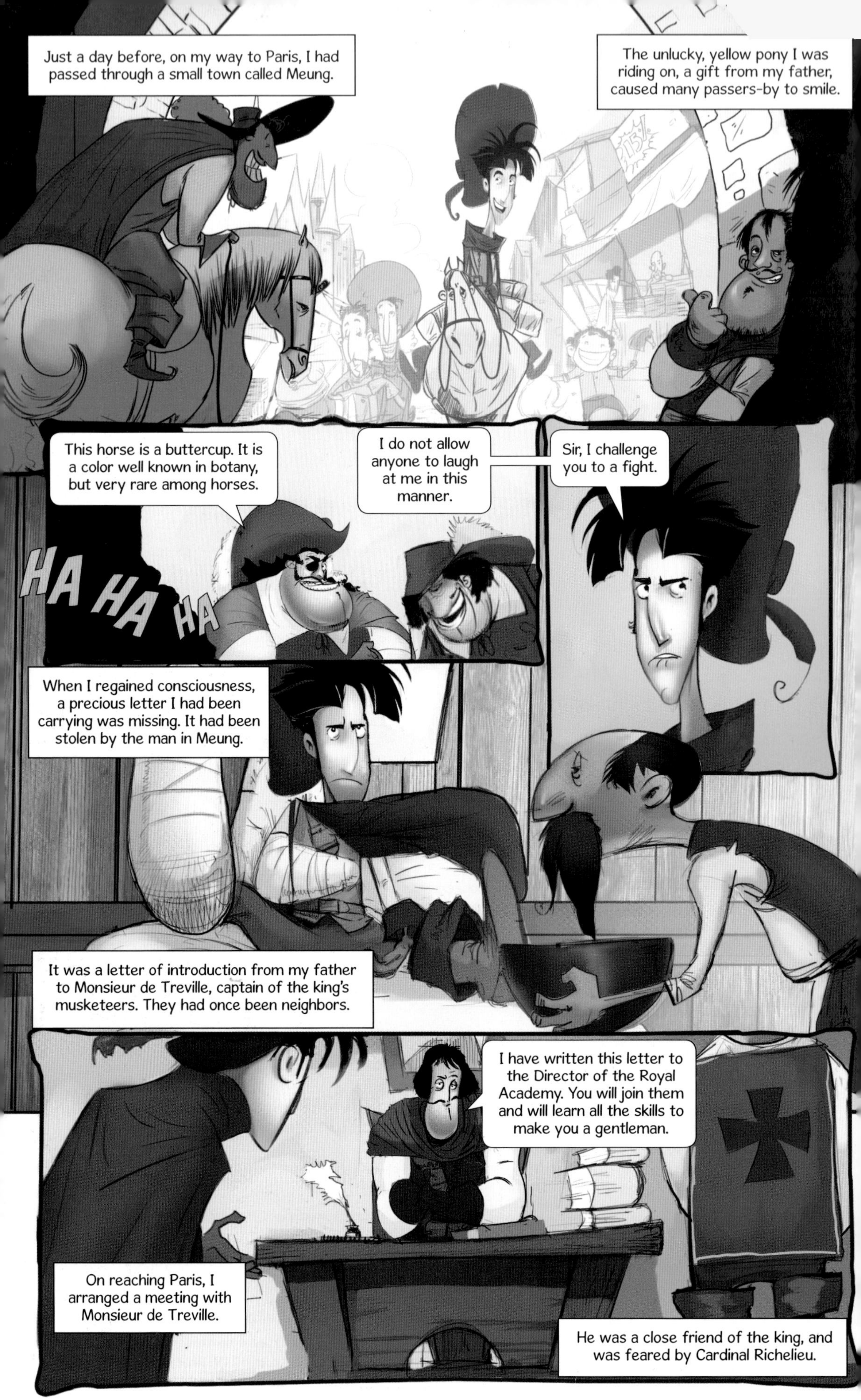

Just a day before, on my way to Paris, I had passed through a small town called Meung.
The unlucky, yellow pony I was riding on, a gift from my father, caused many passers-by to smile.
This horse is a buttercup. It is a color well known in botany, but very rare among horses.
HA HA HA HA
I do not allow anyone to laugh at me in this manner.
Sir, I challenge you to a fight.
When I regained consciousness, a precious letter I had been carrying was missing. It had been stolen by the man in Meung.
It was a letter of introduction from my father to Monsieur de Treville, captain of the king's musketeers. They had once been neighbors.
On reaching Paris, I arranged a meeting with Monsieur de Treville.
I have written this letter to the Director of the Royal Academy. You will join them and will learn all the skills to make you a gentleman.
He was a close friend of the king, and was feared by Cardinal Richelieu.

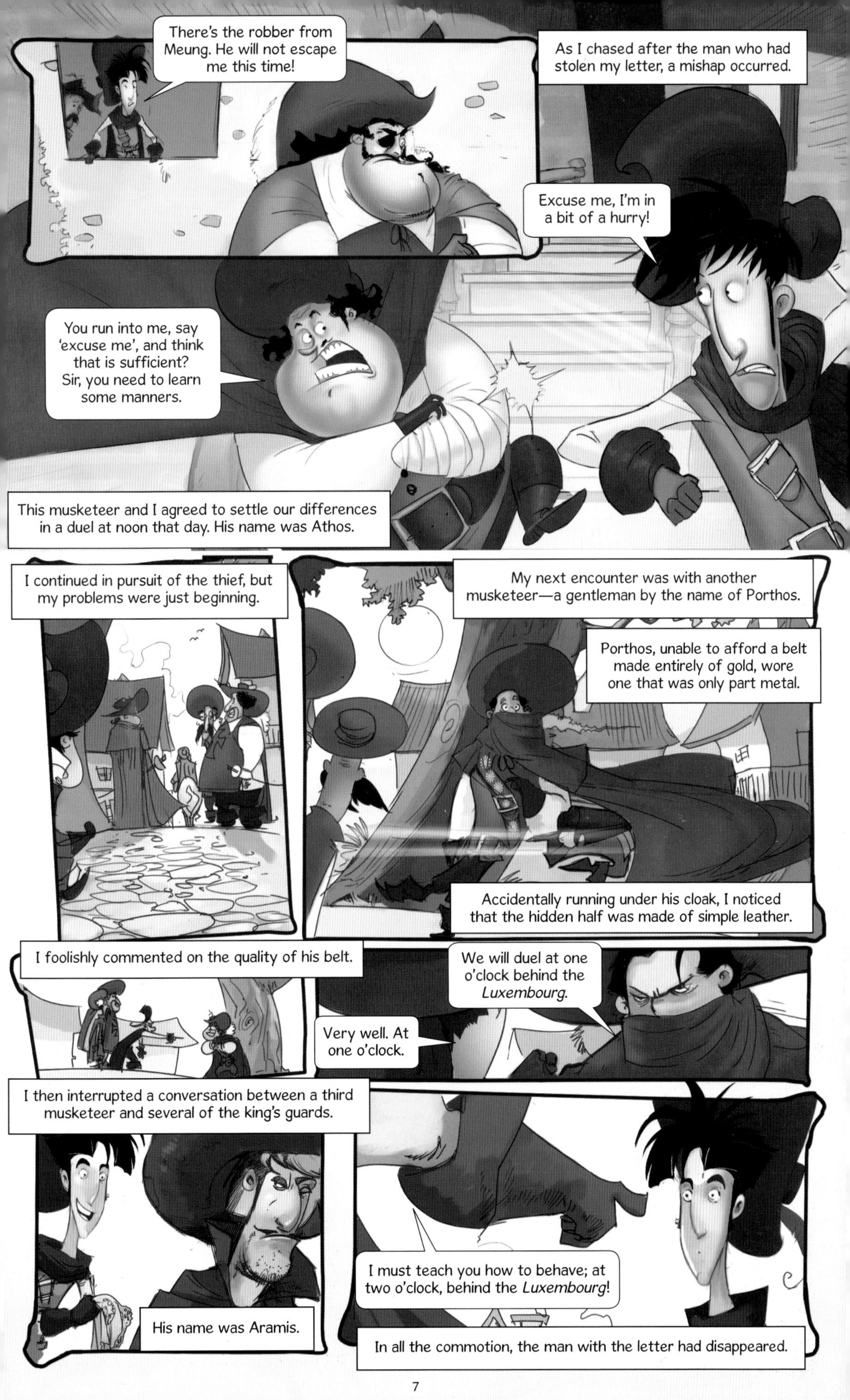
There's the robber from Meung. He will not escape me this time!
As I chased after the man who had stolen my letter, a mishap occurred.
Excuse me, I'm in a bit of a hurry!
You run into me, say 'excuse me', and think that is sufficient? Sir, you need to learn some manners.
This musketeer and I agreed to settle our differences in a duel at noon that day. His name was Athos.
I continued in pursuit of the thief, but my problems were just beginning.
My next encounter was with another musketeer—a gentleman by the name of Porthos.
Porthos, unable to afford a belt made entirely of gold, wore one that was only part metal.
Accidentally running under his cloak, I noticed that the hidden half was made of simple leather.
I foolishly commented on the quality of his belt.
We will duel at one o'clock behind the *Luxembourg*.
Very well. At one o'clock.
I then interrupted a conversation between a third musketeer and several of the king's guards.
His name was Aramis.
I must teach you how to behave; at two o'clock, behind the *Luxembourg*!
In all the commotion, the man with the letter had disappeared.

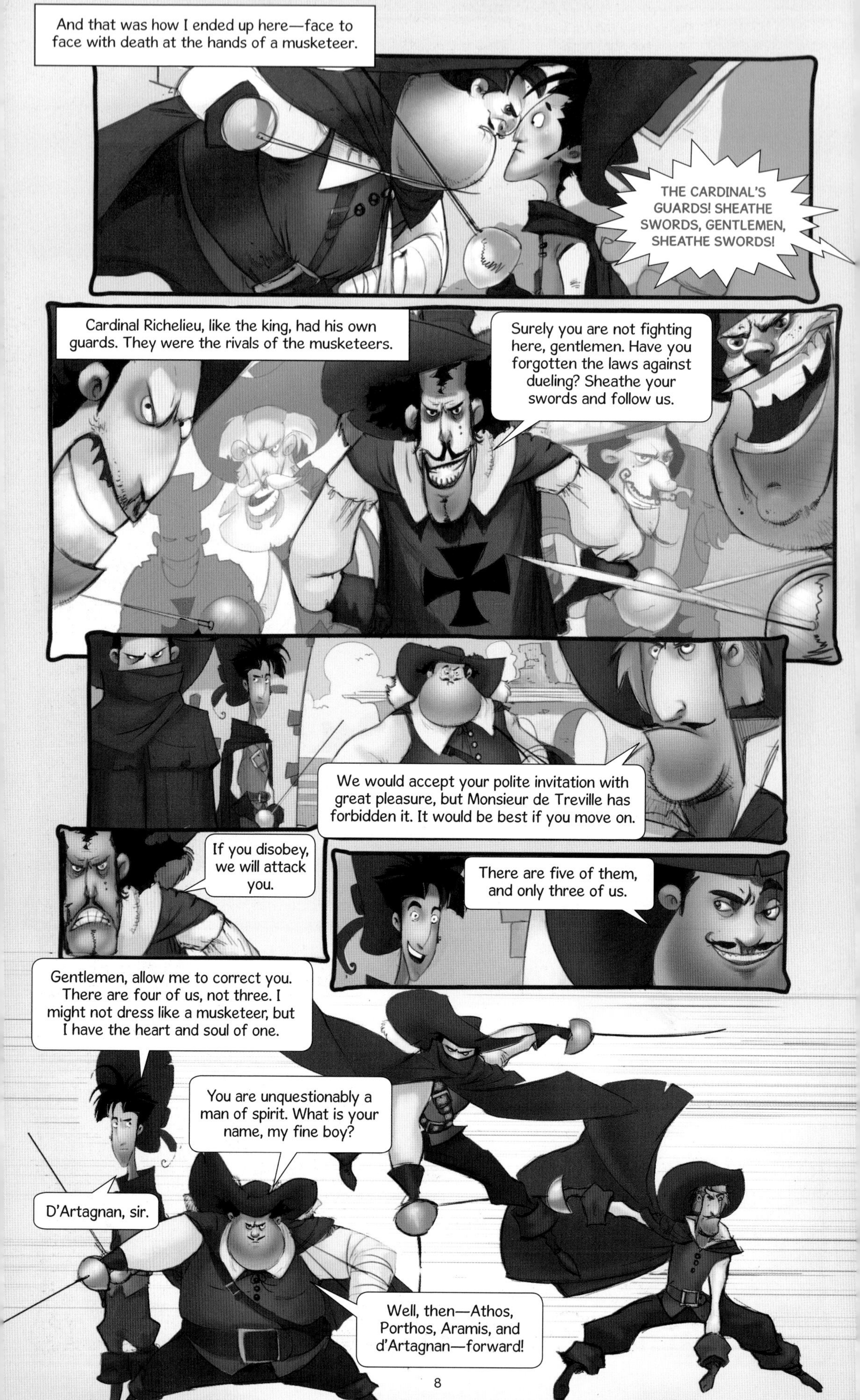
And that was how I ended up here—face to face with death at the hands of a musketeer.
THE CARDINAL'S GUARDS! SHEATHE SWORDS, GENTLEMEN, SHEATHE SWORDS!
Cardinal Richelieu, like the king, had his own guards. They were the rivals of the musketeers.
Surely you are not fighting here, gentlemen. Have you forgotten the laws against dueling? Sheathe your swords and follow us.
We would accept your polite invitation with great pleasure, but Monsieur de Treville has forbidden it. It would be best if you move on.
If you disobey, we will attack you.
There are five of them, and only three of us.
Gentlemen, allow me to correct you. There are four of us, not three. I might not dress like a musketeer, but I have the heart and soul of one.
You are unquestionably a man of spirit. What is your name, my fine boy?
D'Artagnan, sir.
Well, then—Athos, Porthos, Aramis, and d'Artagnan—forward!

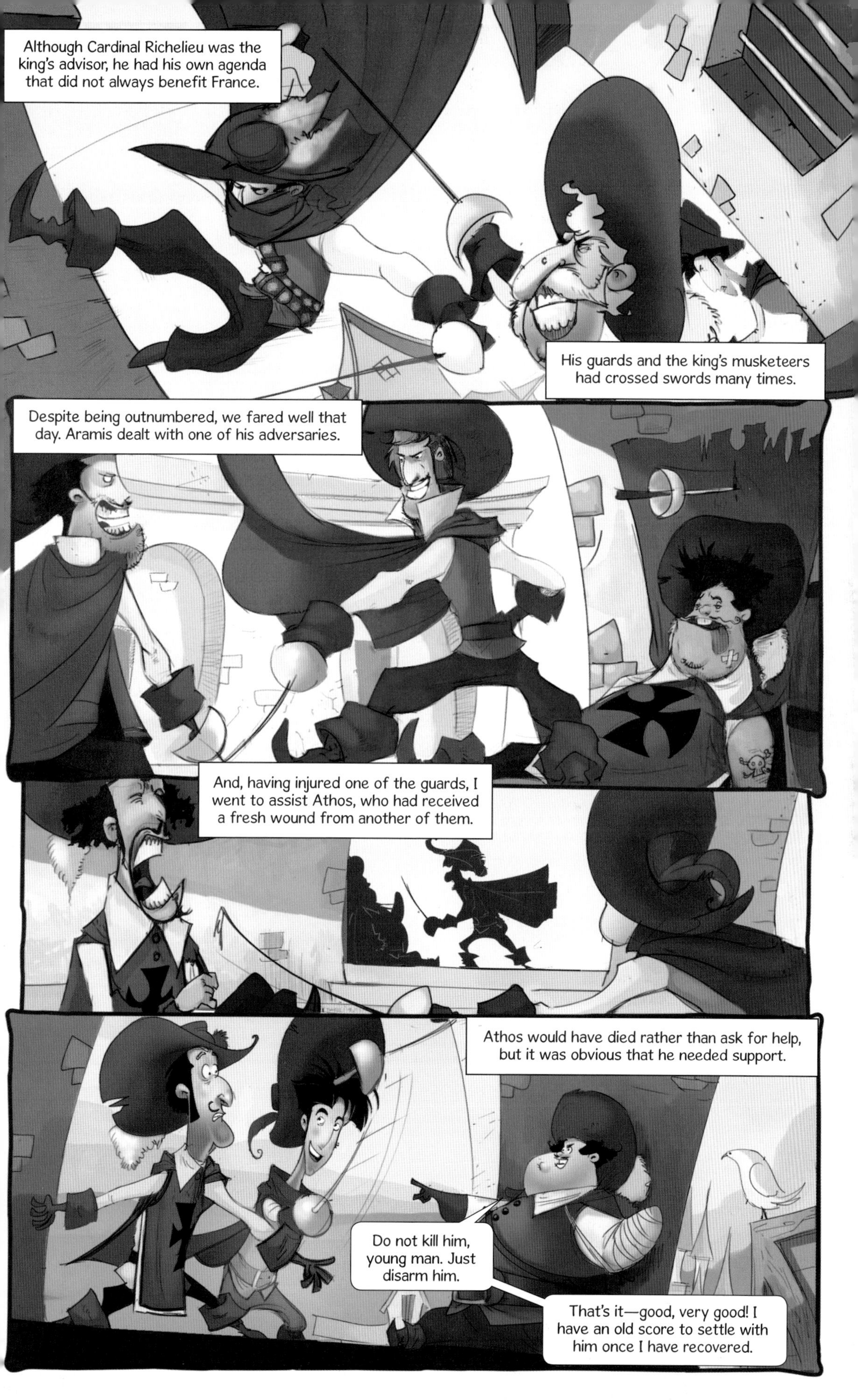
Although Cardinal Richelieu was the king's advisor, he had his own agenda that did not always benefit France.
His guards and the king's musketeers had crossed swords many times.
Despite being outnumbered, we fared well that day. Aramis dealt with one of his adversaries.
And, having injured one of the guards, I went to assist Athos, who had received a fresh wound from another of them.
Athos would have died rather than ask for help, but it was obvious that he needed support.
Do not kill him, young man. Just disarm him.
That's it—good, very good! I have an old score to settle with him once I have recovered.

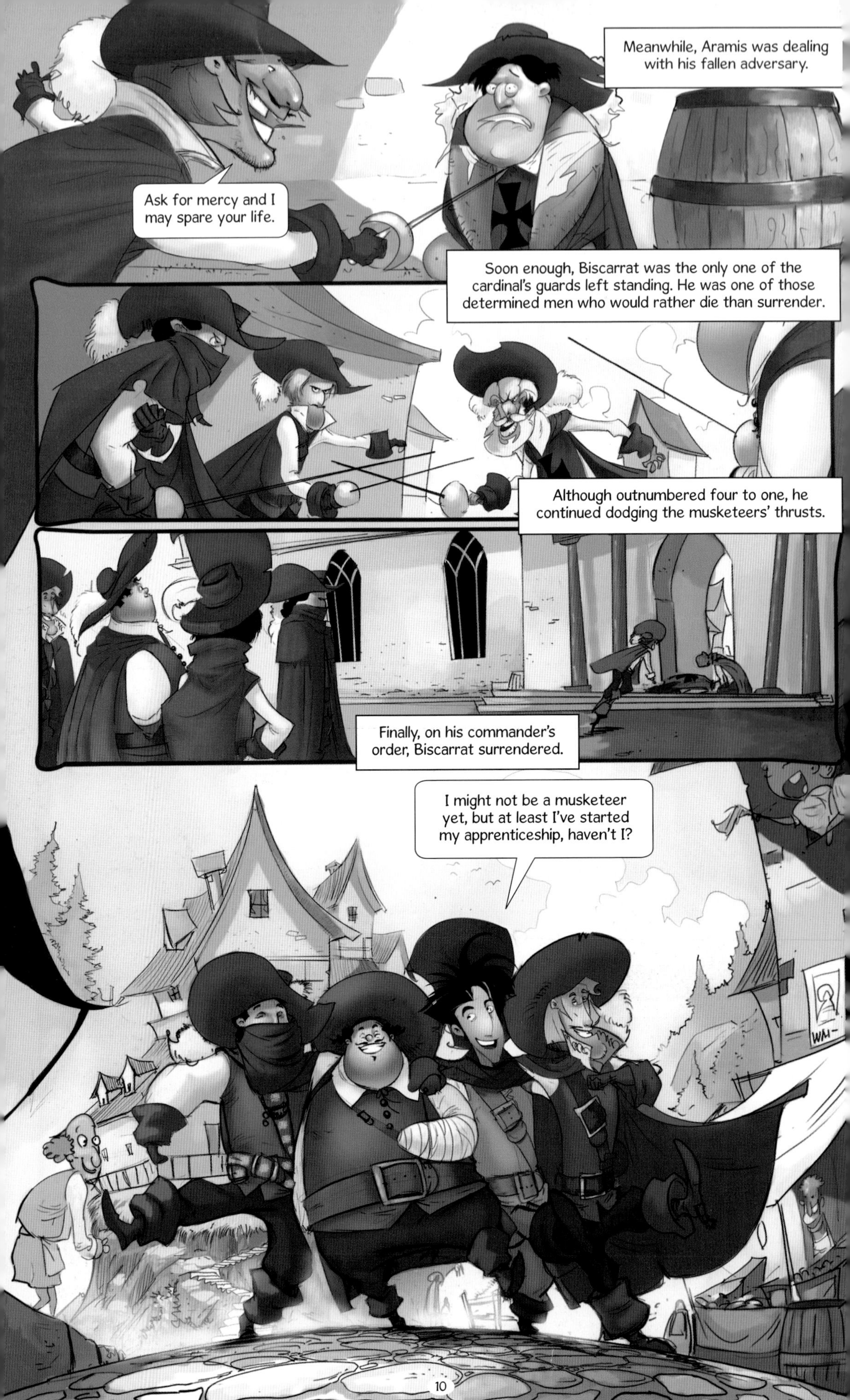
Meanwhile, Aramis was dealing with his fallen adversary.
Ask for mercy and I may spare your life.
Soon enough, Biscarrat was the only one of the cardinal's guards left standing. He was one of those determined men who would rather die than surrender.
Although outnumbered four to one, he continued dodging the musketeers' thrusts.
Finally, on his commander's order, Biscarrat surrendered.
I might not be a musketeer yet, but at least I've started my apprenticeship, haven't I?

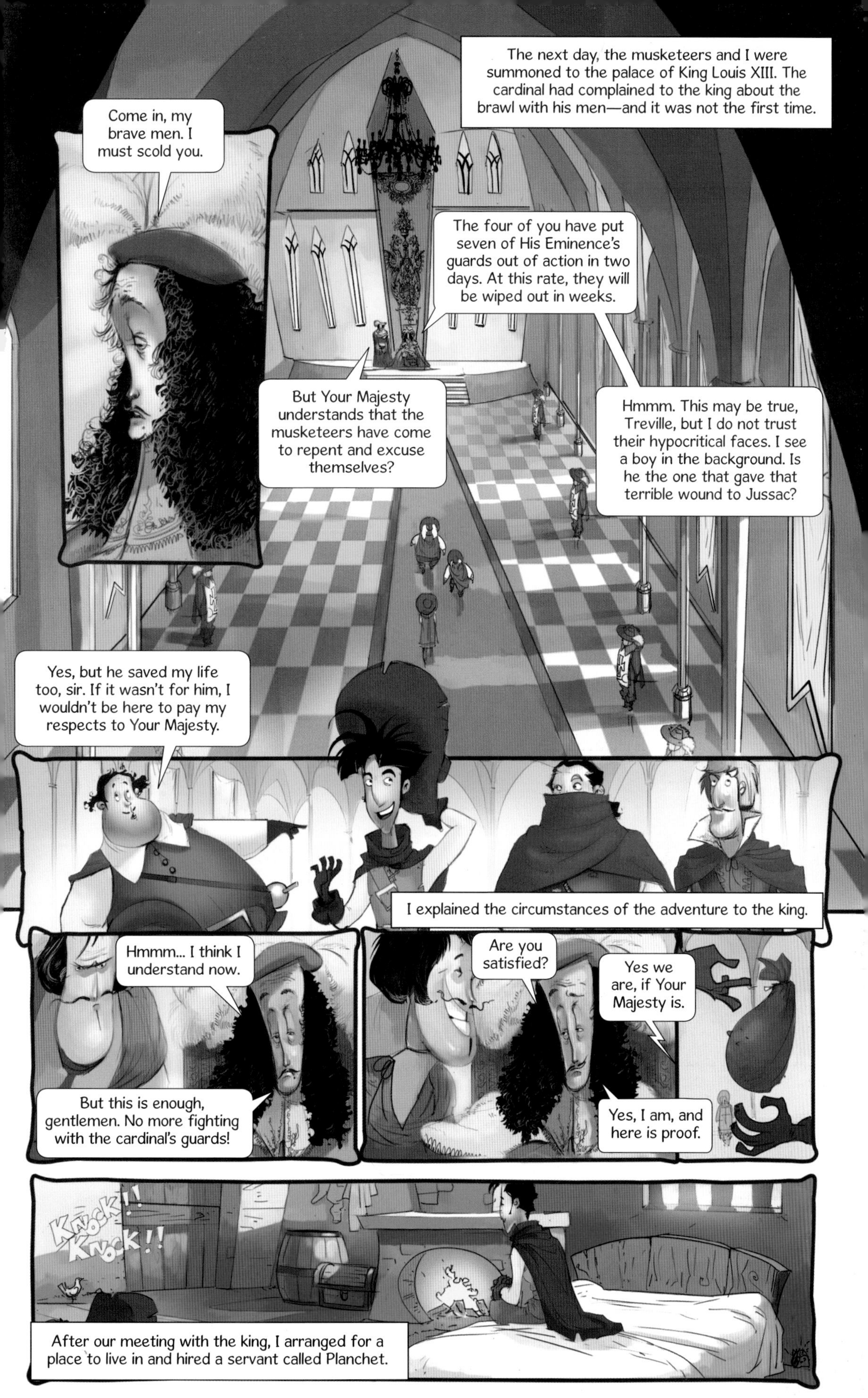

The next day, the musketeers and I were summoned to the palace of King Louis XIII. The cardinal had complained to the king about the brawl with his men—and it was not the first time.
Come in, my brave men. I must scold you.
The four of you have put seven of His Eminence's guards out of action in two days. At this rate, they will be wiped out in weeks.
But Your Majesty understands that the musketeers have come to repent and excuse themselves?
Hmmm. This may be true, Treville, but I do not trust their hypocritical faces. I see a boy in the background. Is he the one that gave that terrible wound to Jussac?
Yes, but he saved my life too, sir. If it wasn't for him, I wouldn't be here to pay my respects to Your Majesty.
I explained the circumstances of the adventure to the king.
Hmmm... I think I understand now.
But this is enough, gentlemen. No more fighting with the cardinal's guards!
Are you satisfied?
Yes we are, if Your Majesty is.
Yes, I am, and here is proof.
KNOCK!! KNOCK!!
After our meeting with the king, I arranged for a place to live in and hired a servant called Planchet.

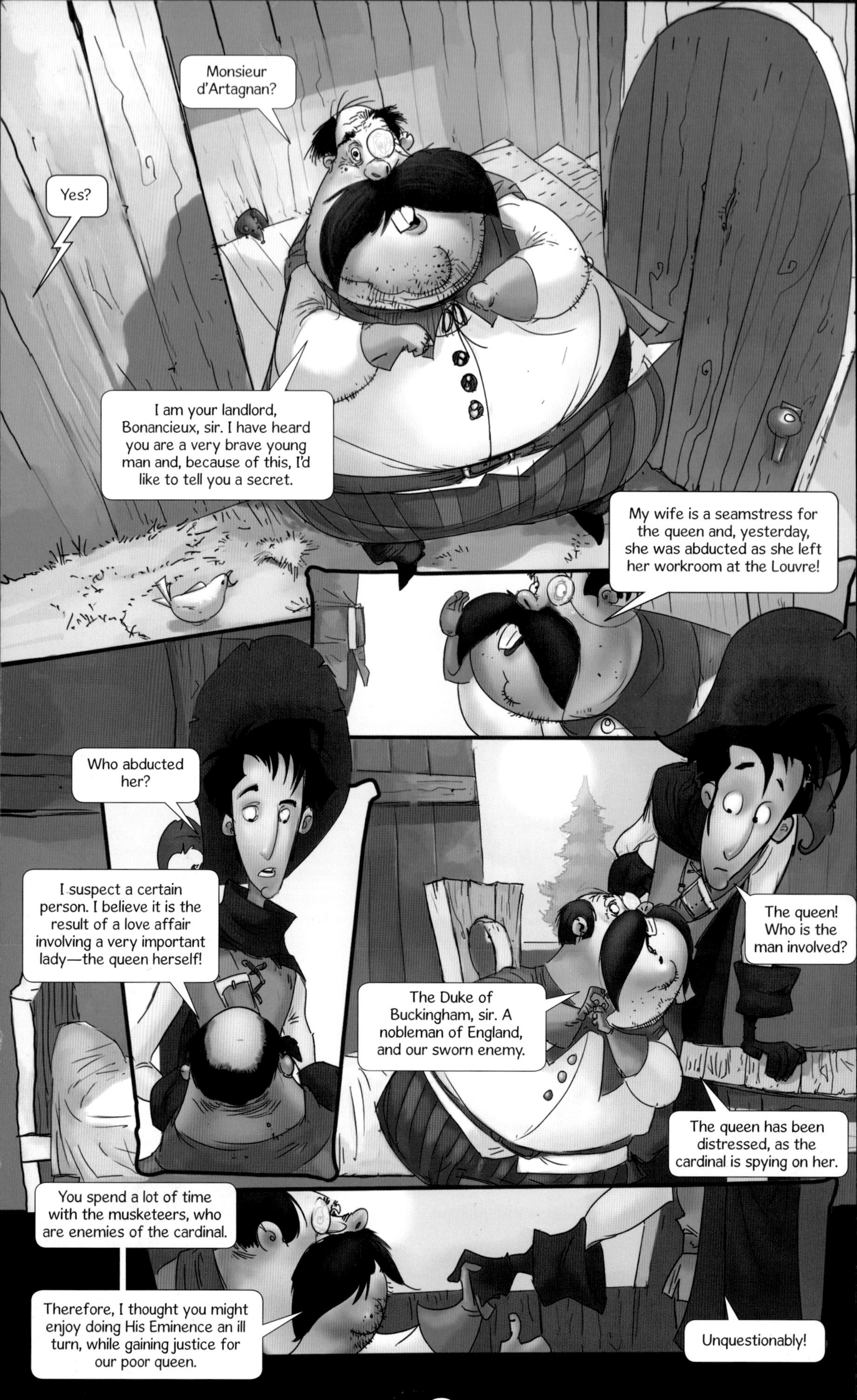

Monsieur d'Artagnan?
Yes?
I am your landlord, Bonancieux, sir. I have heard you are a very brave young man and, because of this, I'd like to tell you a secret.
My wife is a seamstress for the queen and, yesterday, she was abducted as she left her workroom at the Louvre!
Who abducted her?
I suspect a certain person. I believe it is the result of a love affair involving a very important lady—the queen herself!
The queen! Who is the man involved?
The Duke of Buckingham, sir. A nobleman of England, and our sworn enemy.
The queen has been distressed, as the cardinal is spying on her.
You spend a lot of time with the musketeers, who are enemies of the cardinal.
Therefore, I thought you might enjoy doing His Eminence an ill turn, while gaining justice for our poor queen.
Unquestionably!

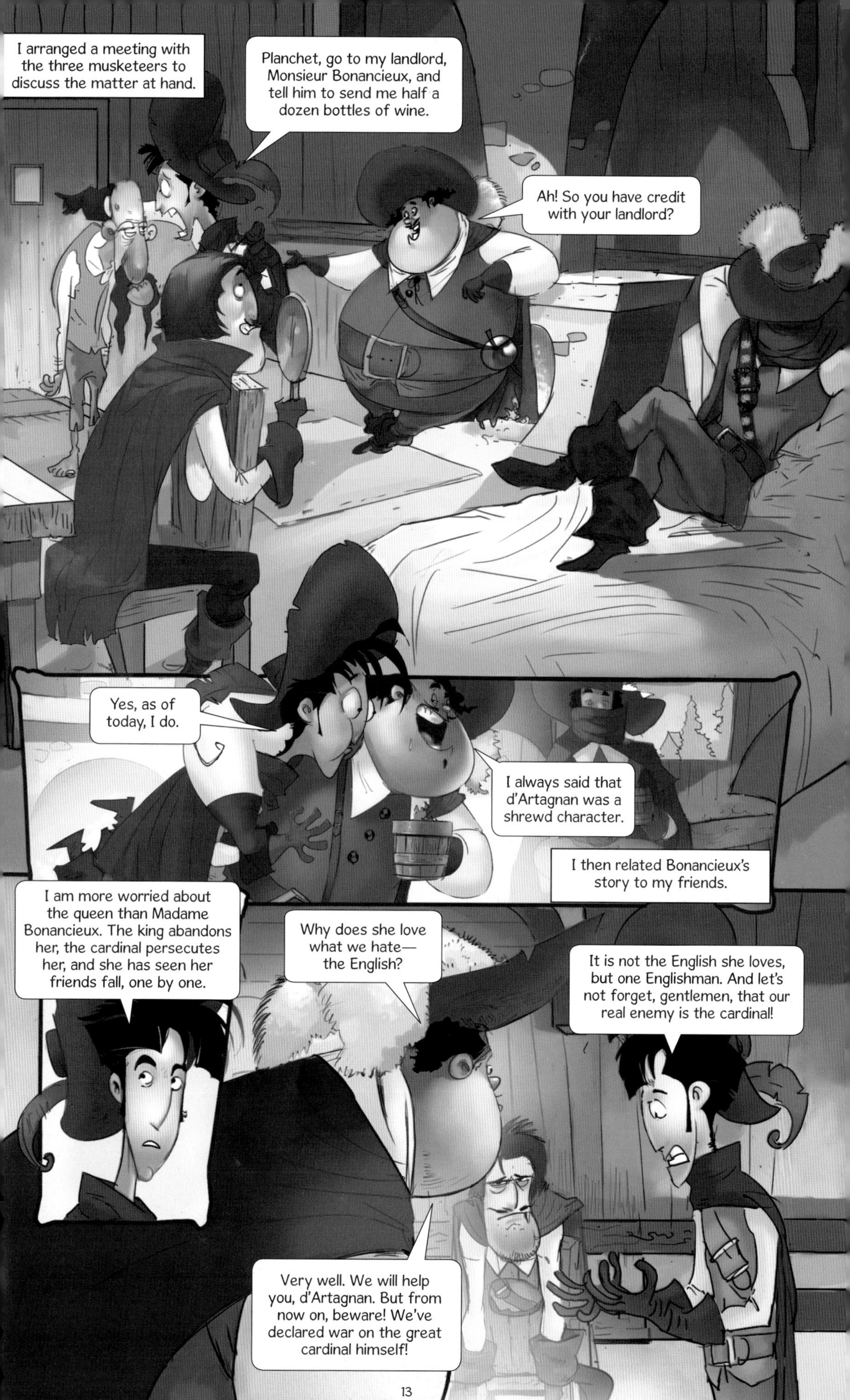
I arranged a meeting with the three musketeers to discuss the matter at hand.
Planchet, go to my landlord, Monsieur Bonancieux, and tell him to send me half a dozen bottles of wine.
Ah! So you have credit with your landlord?
Yes, as of today, I do.
I always said that d'Artagnan was a shrewd character.
I then related Bonancieux's story to my friends.
I am more worried about the queen than Madame Bonancieux. The king abandons her, the cardinal persecutes her, and she has seen her friends fall, one by one.
Why does she love what we hate—the English?
It is not the English she loves, but one Englishman. And let's not forget, gentlemen, that our real enemy is the cardinal!
Very well. We will help you, d'Artagnan. But from now on, beware! We've declared war on the great cardinal himself!

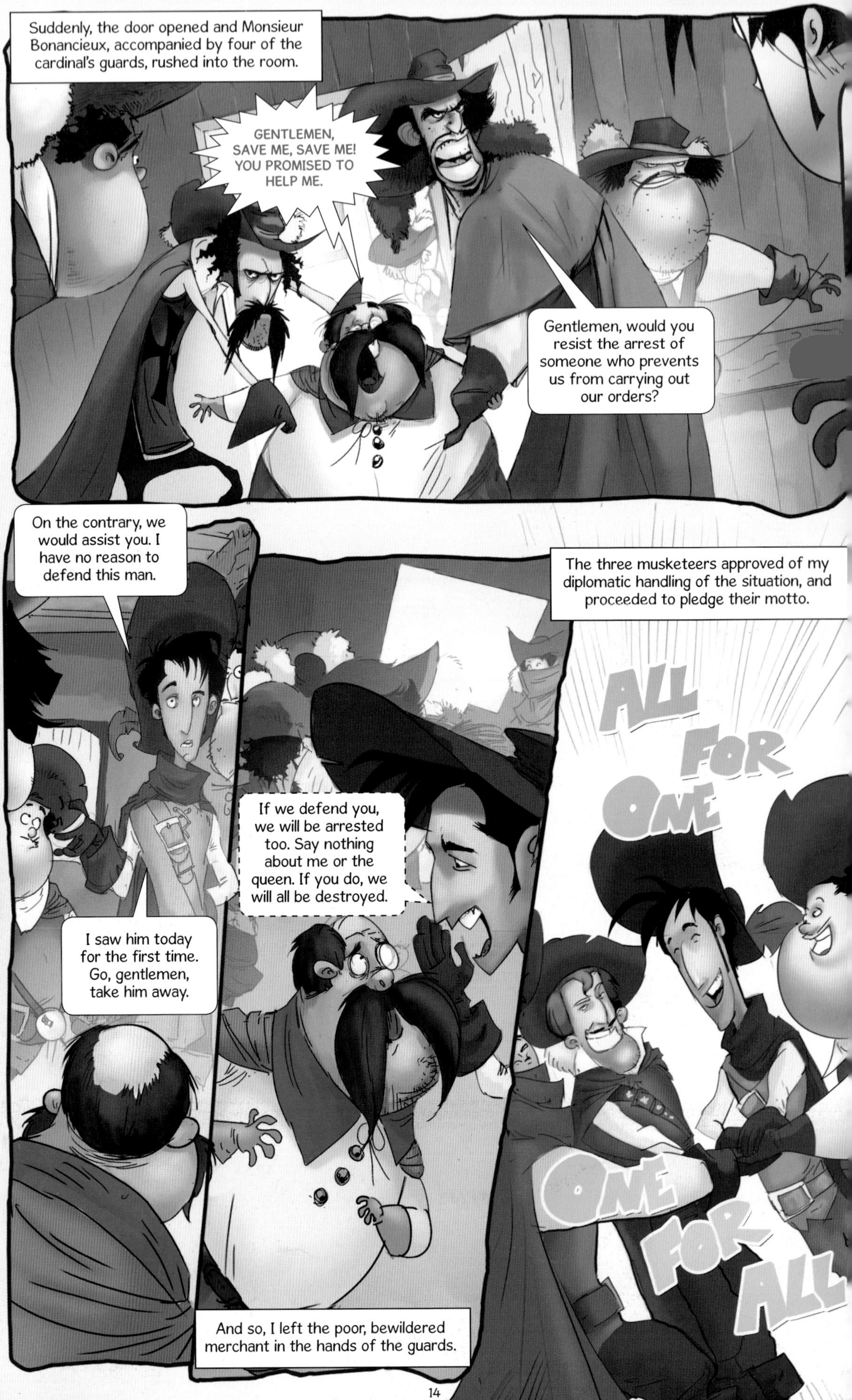

Suddenly, the door opened and Monsieur Bonancieux, accompanied by four of the cardinal's guards, rushed into the room.
GENTLEMEN, SAVE ME, SAVE ME! YOU PROMISED TO HELP ME.
Gentlemen, would you resist the arrest of someone who prevents us from carrying out our orders?
On the contrary, we would assist you. I have no reason to defend this man.
I saw him today for the first time. Go, gentlemen, take him away.
If we defend you, we will be arrested too. Say nothing about me or the queen. If you do, we will all be destroyed.
And so, I left the poor, bewildered merchant in the hands of the guards.
The three musketeers approved of my diplomatic handling of the situation, and proceeded to pledge their motto.
ALL FOR ONE
ONE FOR ALL

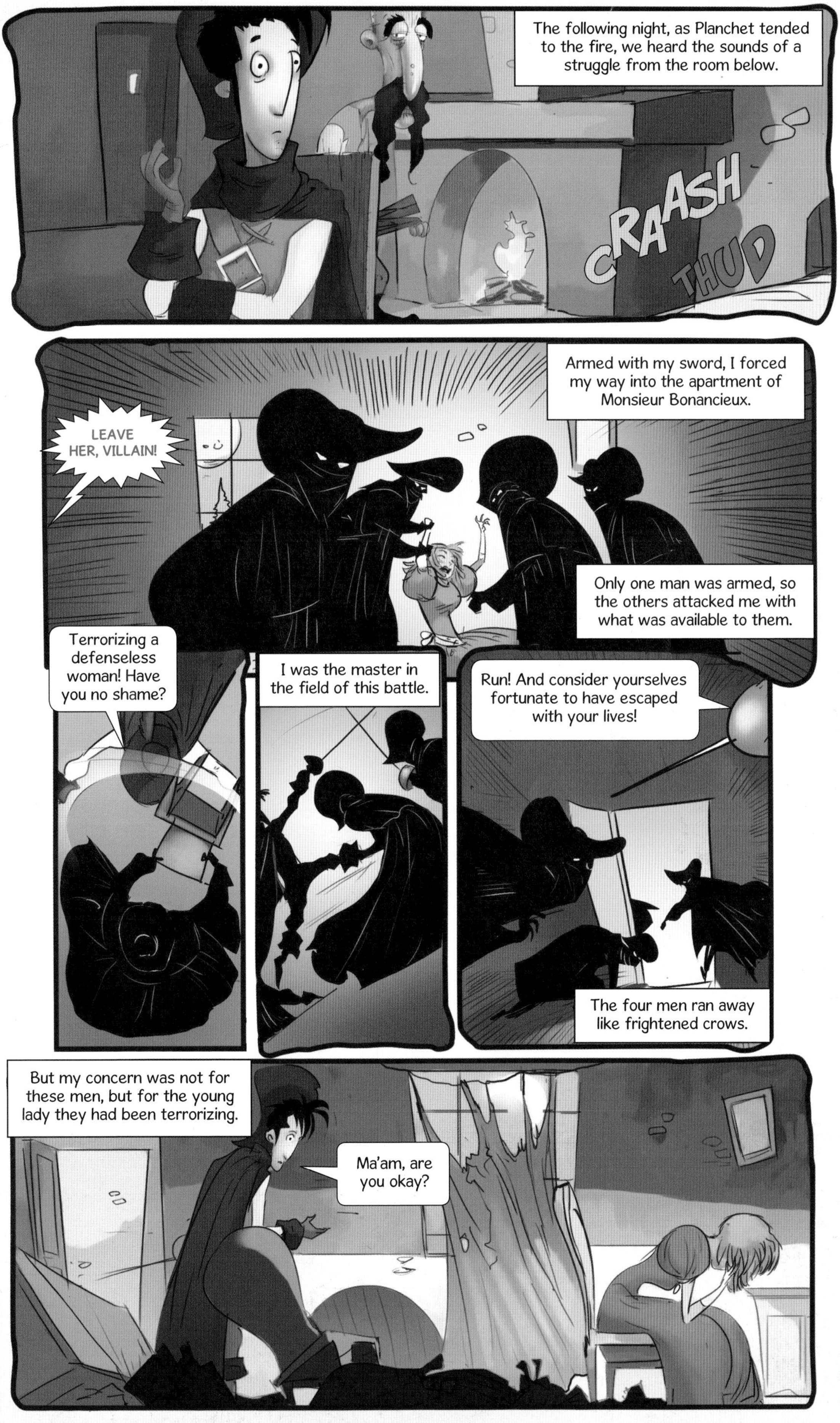
The following night, as Planchet tended to the fire, we heard the sounds of a struggle from the room below.
CRAASH
THUD
Armed with my sword, I forced my way into the apartment of Monsieur Bonancieux.
LEAVE HER, VILLAIN!
Only one man was armed, so the others attacked me with what was available to them.
Terrorizing a defenseless woman! Have you no shame?
I was the master in the field of this battle.
Run! And consider yourselves fortunate to have escaped with your lives!
The four men ran away like frightened crows.
But my concern was not for these men, but for the young lady they had been terrorizing.
Ma'am, are you okay?

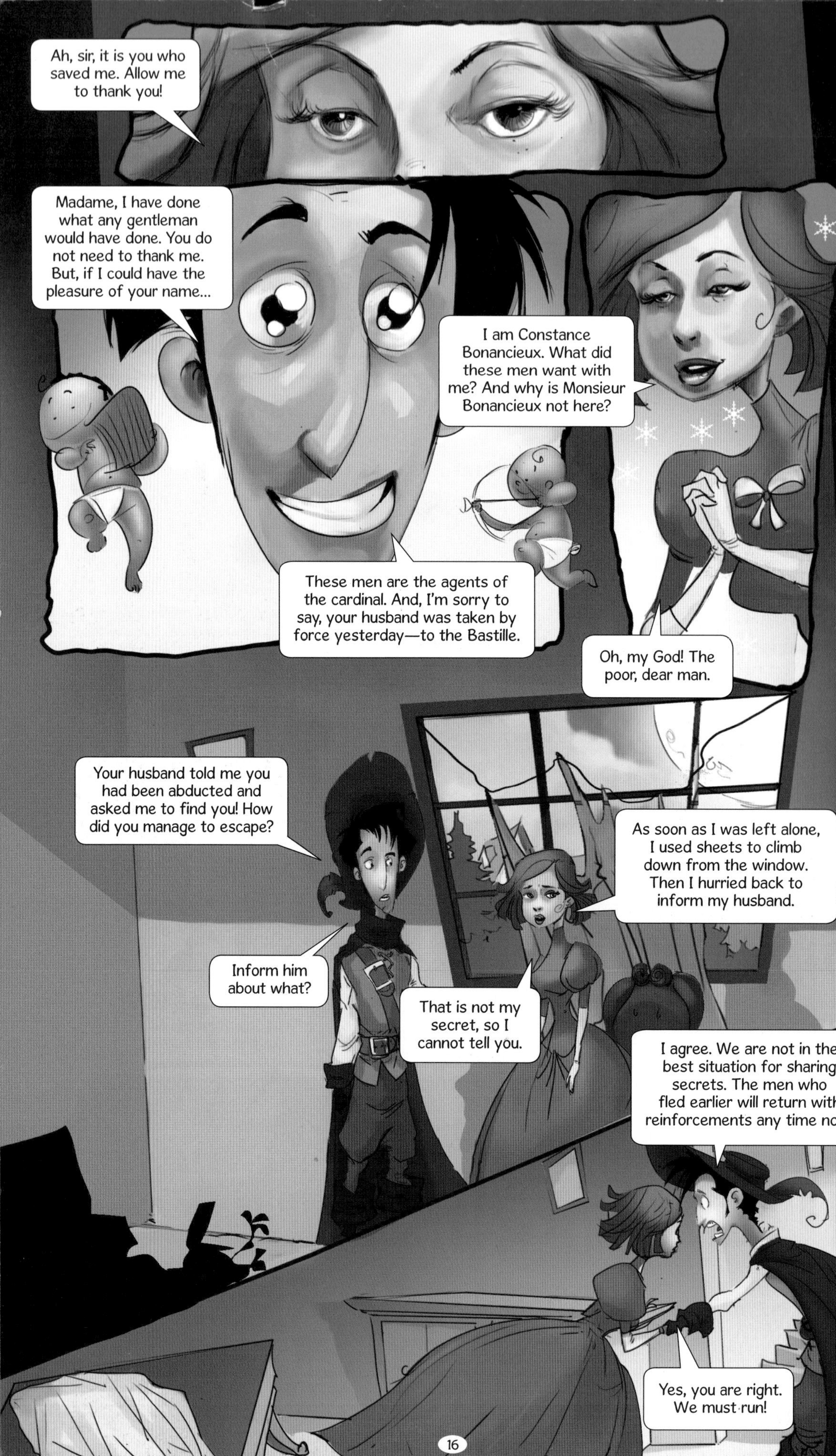
Ah, sir, it is you who saved me. Allow me to thank you!
Madame, I have done what any gentleman would have done. You do not need to thank me. But, if I could have the pleasure of your name...
I am Constance Bonancieux. What did these men want with me? And why is Monsieur Bonancieux not here?
These men are the agents of the cardinal. And, I'm sorry to say, your husband was taken by force yesterday—to the Bastille.
Oh, my God! The poor, dear man.
Your husband told me you had been abducted and asked me to find you! How did you manage to escape?
As soon as I was left alone, I used sheets to climb down from the window. Then I hurried back to inform my husband.
Inform him about what?
That is not my secret, so I cannot tell you.
I agree. We are not in the best situation for sharing secrets. The men who fled earlier will return with reinforcements any time no
Yes, you are right. We must run!

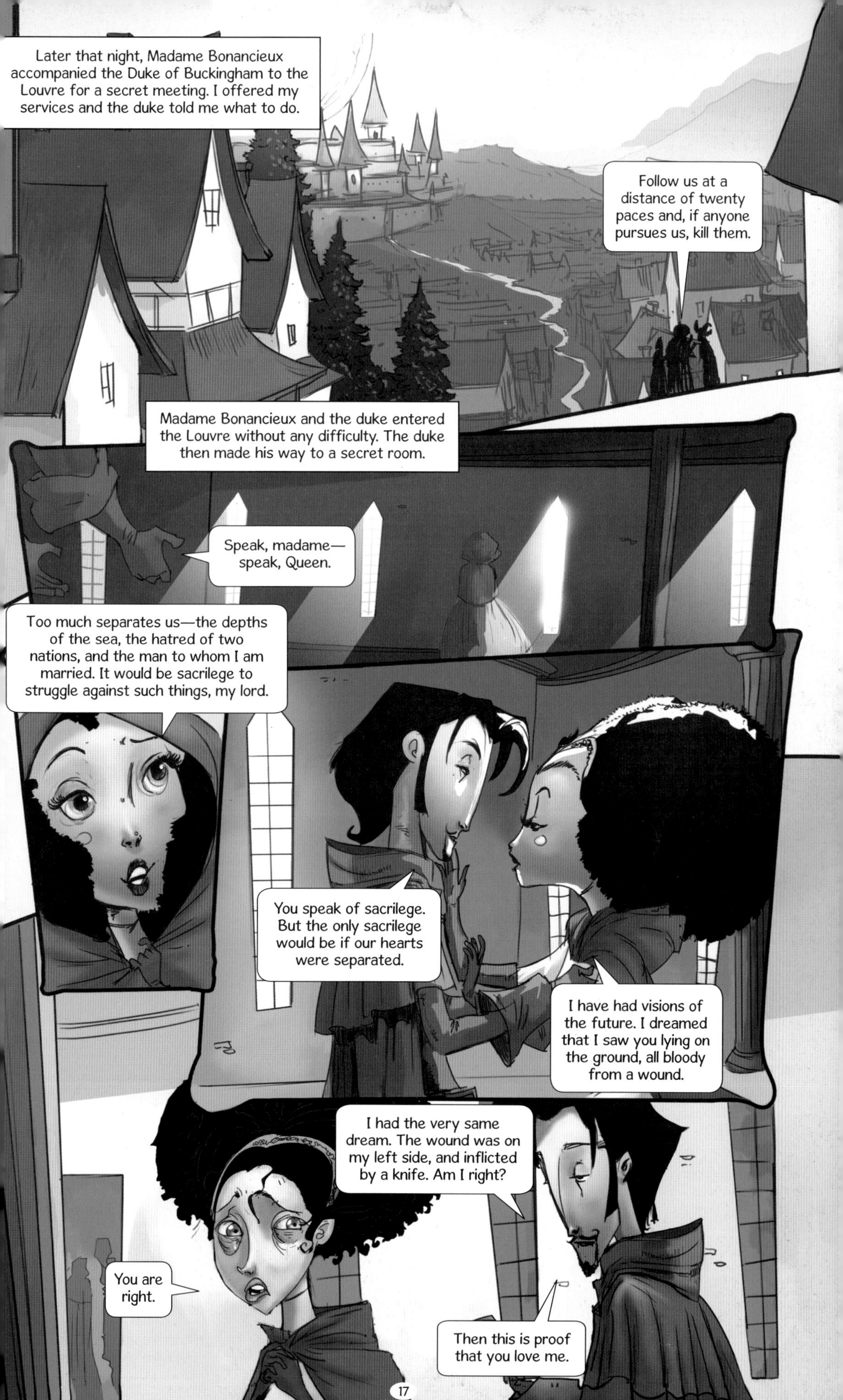

Later that night, Madame Bonancieux accompanied the Duke of Buckingham to the Louvre for a secret meeting. I offered my services and the duke told me what to do.
Follow us at a distance of twenty paces and, if anyone pursues us, kill them.
Madame Bonancieux and the duke entered the Louvre without any difficulty. The duke then made his way to a secret room.
Speak, madame—speak, Queen.
Too much separates us—the depths of the sea, the hatred of two nations, and the man to whom I am married. It would be sacrilege to struggle against such things, my lord.
You speak of sacrilege. But the only sacrilege would be if our hearts were separated.
I have had visions of the future. I dreamed that I saw you lying on the ground, all bloody from a wound.
I had the very same dream. The wound was on my left side, and inflicted by a knife. Am I right?
You are right.
Then this is proof that you love me.

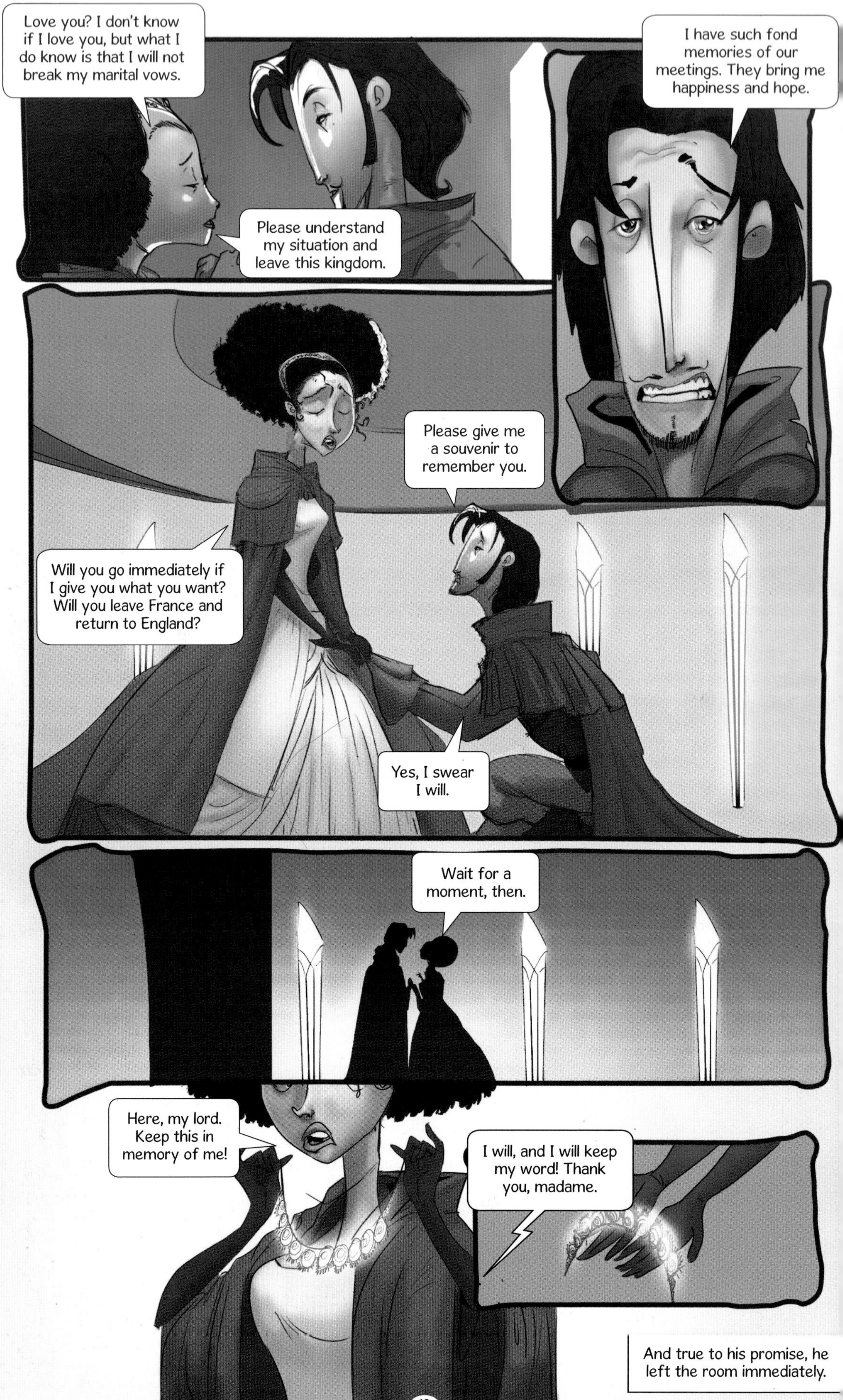
Love you? I don't know if I love you, but what I do know is that I will not break my marital vows.
Please understand my situation and leave this kingdom.
I have such fond memories of our meetings. They bring me happiness and hope.
Please give me a souvenir to remember you.
Will you go immediately if I give you what you want? Will you leave France and return to England?
Yes, I swear I will.
Wait for a moment, then.
Here, my lord. Keep this in memory of me!
I will, and I will keep my word! Thank you, madame.
And true to his promise, he left the room immediately.

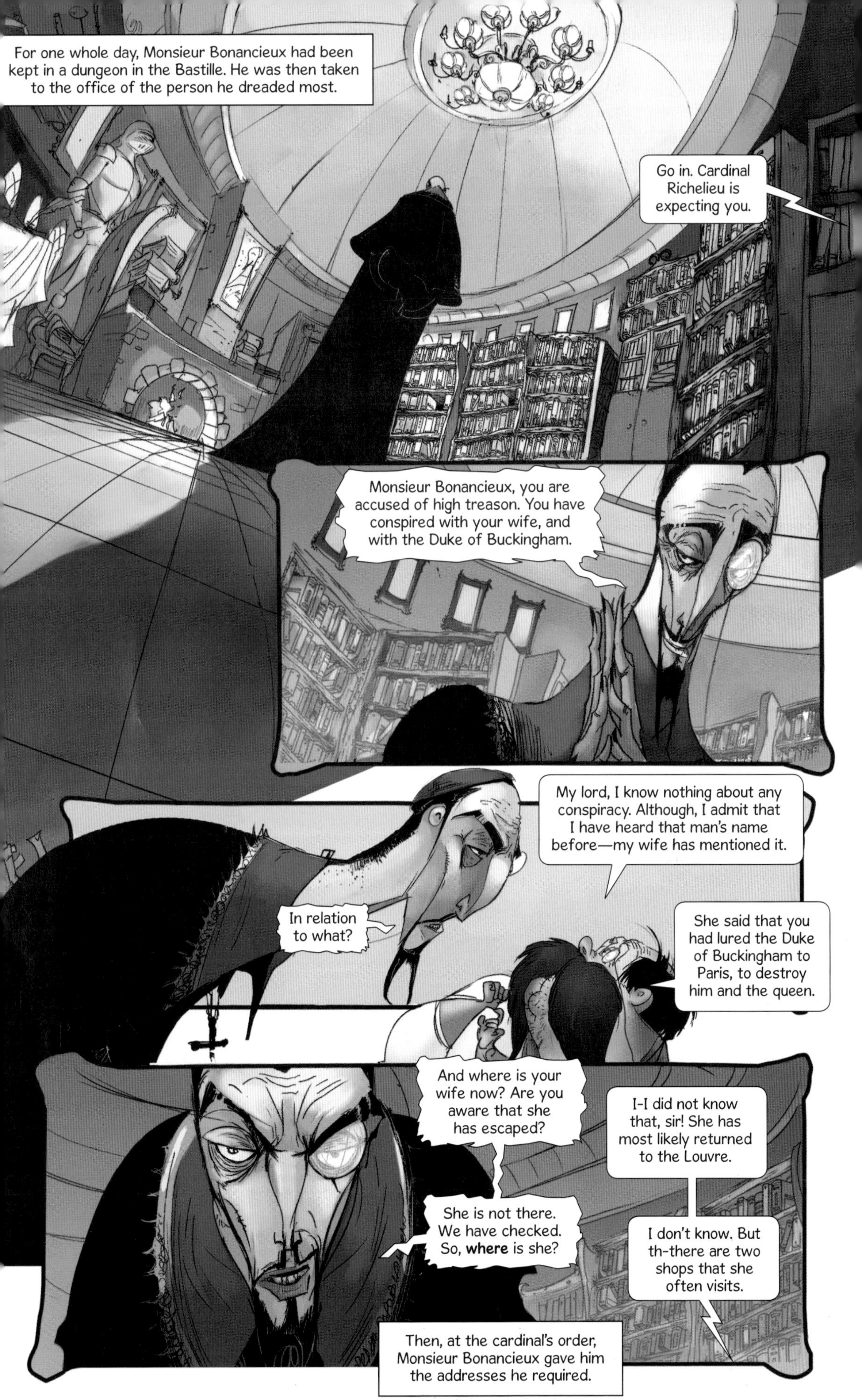
For one whole day, Monsieur Bonancieux had been kept in a dungeon in the Bastille. He was then taken to the office of the person he dreaded most.
Go in. Cardinal Richelieu is expecting you.
Monsieur Bonancieux, you are accused of high treason. You have conspired with your wife, and with the Duke of Buckingham.
My lord, I know nothing about any conspiracy. Although, I admit that I have heard that man's name before—my wife has mentioned it.
In relation to what?
She said that you had lured the Duke of Buckingham to Paris, to destroy him and the queen.
And where is your wife now? Are you aware that she has escaped?
I-I did not know that, sir! She has most likely returned to the Louvre.
She is not there. We have checked. So, **where** is she?
I don't know. But th-there are two shops that she often visits.
Then, at the cardinal's order, Monsieur Bonancieux gave him the addresses he required.

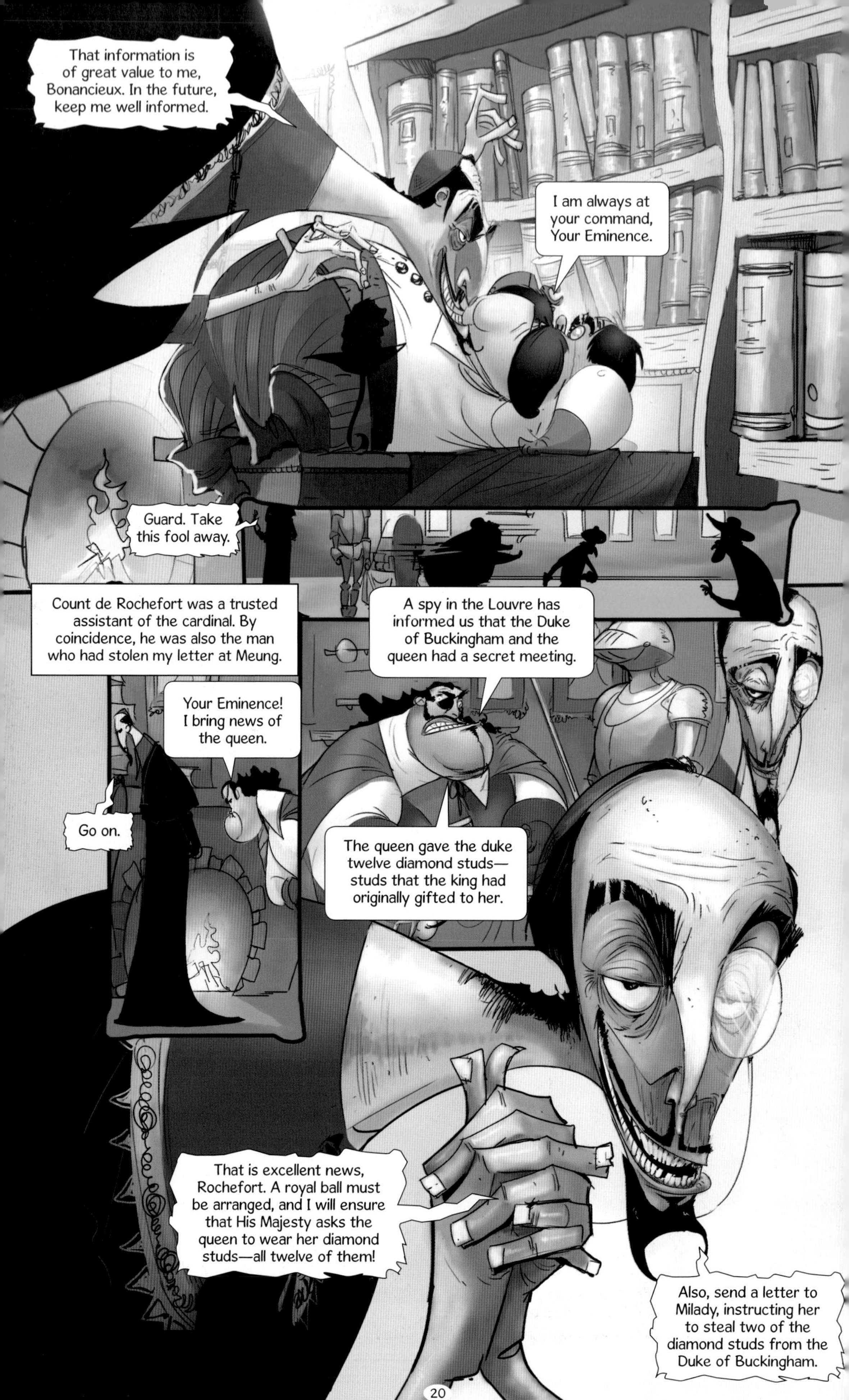
That information is of great value to me, Bonancieux. In the future, keep me well informed.
I am always at your command, Your Eminence.
Guard. Take this fool away.
Count de Rochefort was a trusted assistant of the cardinal. By coincidence, he was also the man who had stolen my letter at Meung.
Your Eminence! I bring news of the queen.
Go on.
A spy in the Louvre has informed us that the Duke of Buckingham and the queen had a secret meeting.
The queen gave the duke twelve diamond studs—studs that the king had originally gifted to her.
That is excellent news, Rochefort. A royal ball must be arranged, and I will ensure that His Majesty asks the queen to wear her diamond studs—all twelve of them!
Also, send a letter to Milady, instructing her to steal two of the diamond studs from the Duke of Buckingham.

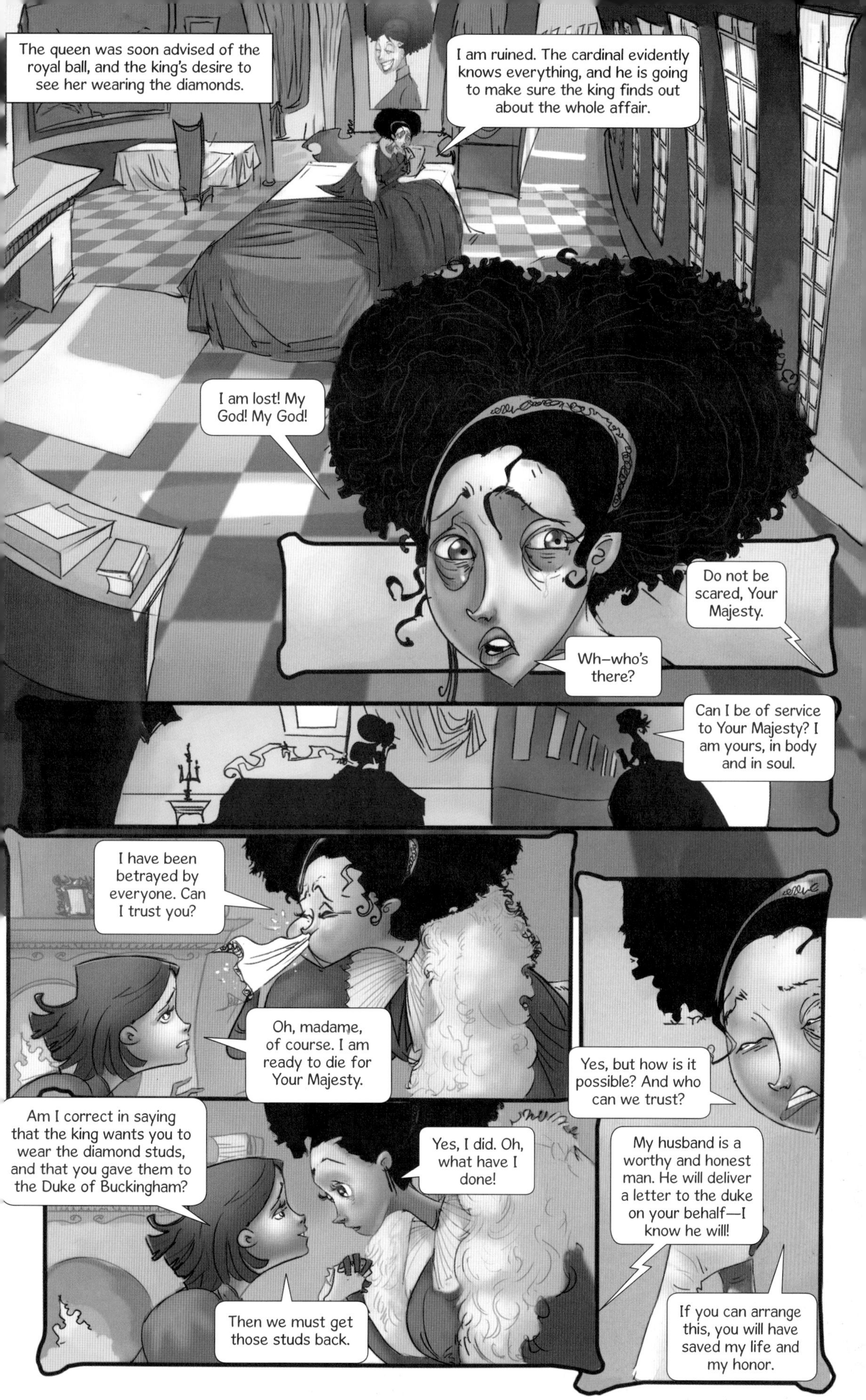
The queen was soon advised of the royal ball, and the king's desire to see her wearing the diamonds.
I am ruined. The cardinal evidently knows everything, and he is going to make sure the king finds out about the whole affair.
I am lost! My God! My God!
Do not be scared, Your Majesty.
Wh–who's there?
Can I be of service to Your Majesty? I am yours, in body and in soul.
I have been betrayed by everyone. Can I trust you?
Oh, madame, of course. I am ready to die for Your Majesty.
Am I correct in saying that the king wants you to wear the diamond studs, and that you gave them to the Duke of Buckingham?
Yes, I did. Oh, what have I done!
Then we must get those studs back.
Yes, but how is it possible? And who can we trust?
My husband is a worthy and honest man. He will deliver a letter to the duke on your behalf—I know he will!
If you can arrange this, you will have saved my life and my honor.

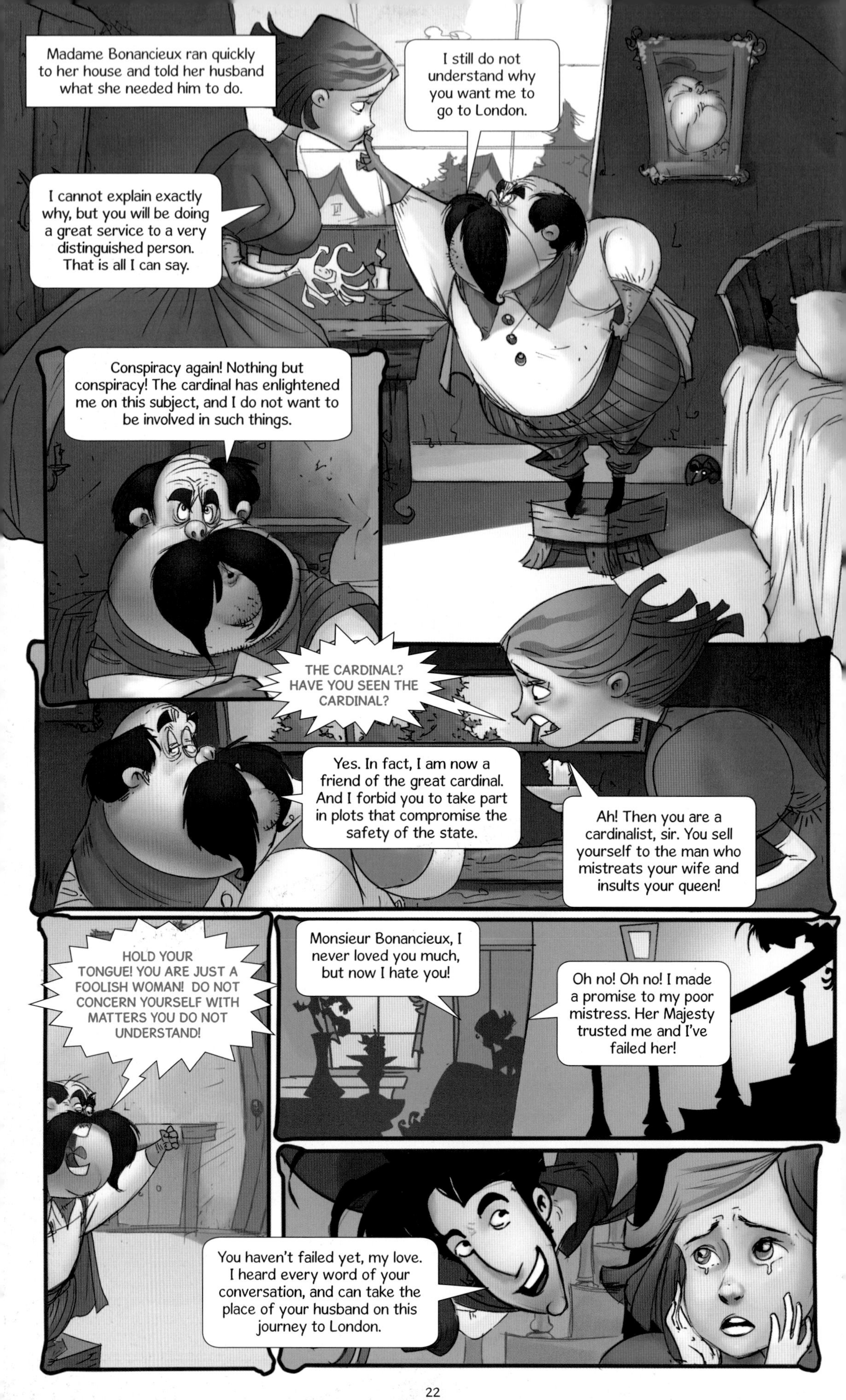

Madame Bonancieux ran quickly to her house and told her husband what she needed him to do.
I still do not understand why you want me to go to London.
I cannot explain exactly why, but you will be doing a great service to a very distinguished person. That is all I can say.
Conspiracy again! Nothing but conspiracy! The cardinal has enlightened me on this subject, and I do not want to be involved in such things.
THE CARDINAL? HAVE YOU SEEN THE CARDINAL?
Yes. In fact, I am now a friend of the great cardinal. And I forbid you to take part in plots that compromise the safety of the state.
Ah! Then you are a cardinalist, sir. You sell yourself to the man who mistreats your wife and insults your queen!
HOLD YOUR TONGUE! YOU ARE JUST A FOOLISH WOMAN! DO NOT CONCERN YOURSELF WITH MATTERS YOU DO NOT UNDERSTAND!
Monsieur Bonancieux, I never loved you much, but now I hate you!
Oh no! Oh no! I made a promise to my poor mistress. Her Majesty trusted me and I've failed her!
You haven't failed yet, my love. I heard every word of your conversation, and can take the place of your husband on this journey to London.

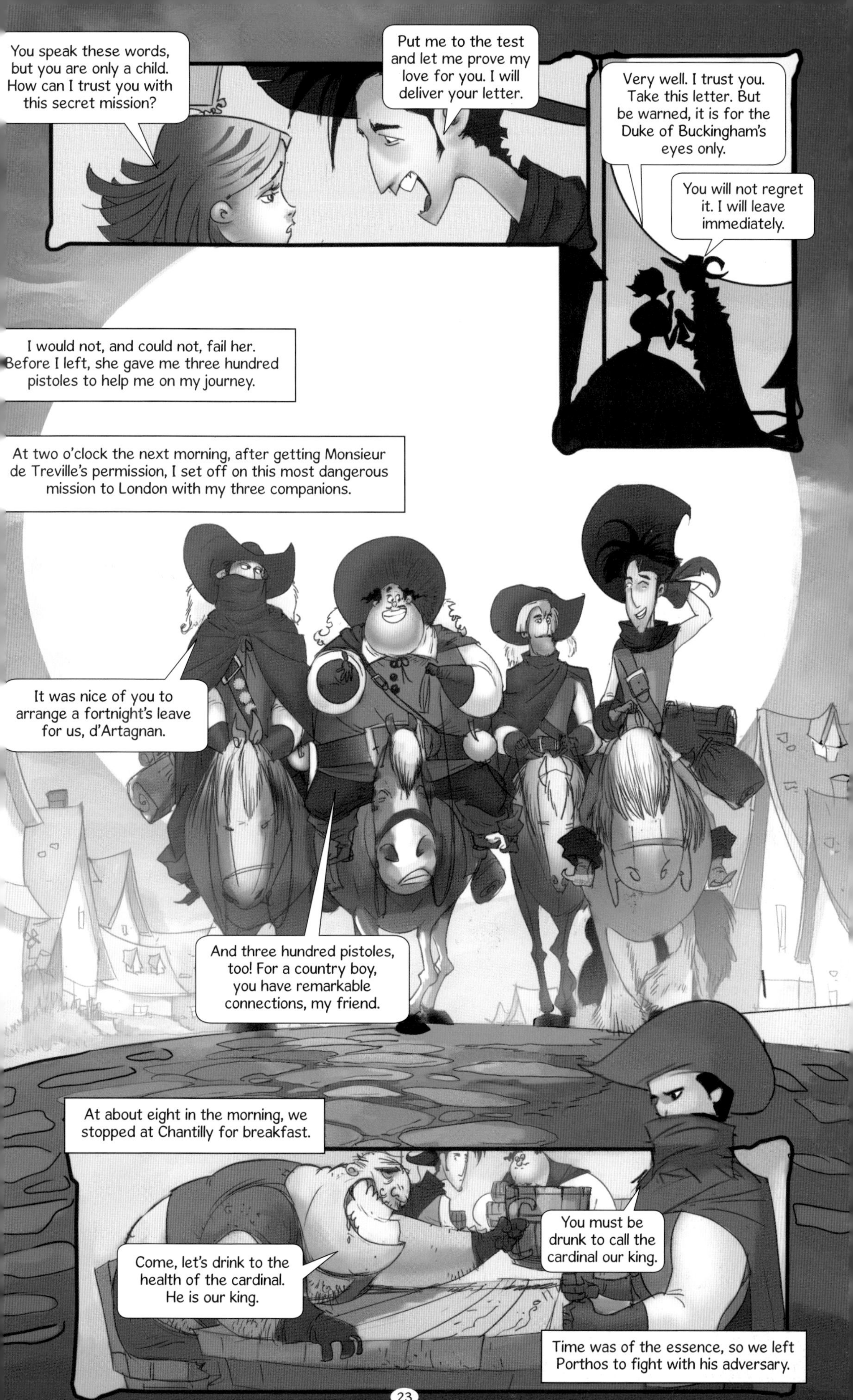
You speak these words, but you are only a child. How can I trust you with this secret mission?
Put me to the test and let me prove my love for you. I will deliver your letter.
Very well. I trust you. Take this letter. But be warned, it is for the Duke of Buckingham's eyes only.
You will not regret it. I will leave immediately.
I would not, and could not, fail her. Before I left, she gave me three hundred pistoles to help me on my journey.
At two o'clock the next morning, after getting Monsieur de Treville's permission, I set off on this most dangerous mission to London with my three companions.
It was nice of you to arrange a fortnight's leave for us, d'Artagnan.
And three hundred pistoles, too! For a country boy, you have remarkable connections, my friend.
At about eight in the morning, we stopped at Chantilly for breakfast.
Come, let's drink to the health of the cardinal. He is our king.
You must be drunk to call the cardinal our king.
Time was of the essence, so we left Porthos to fight with his adversary.

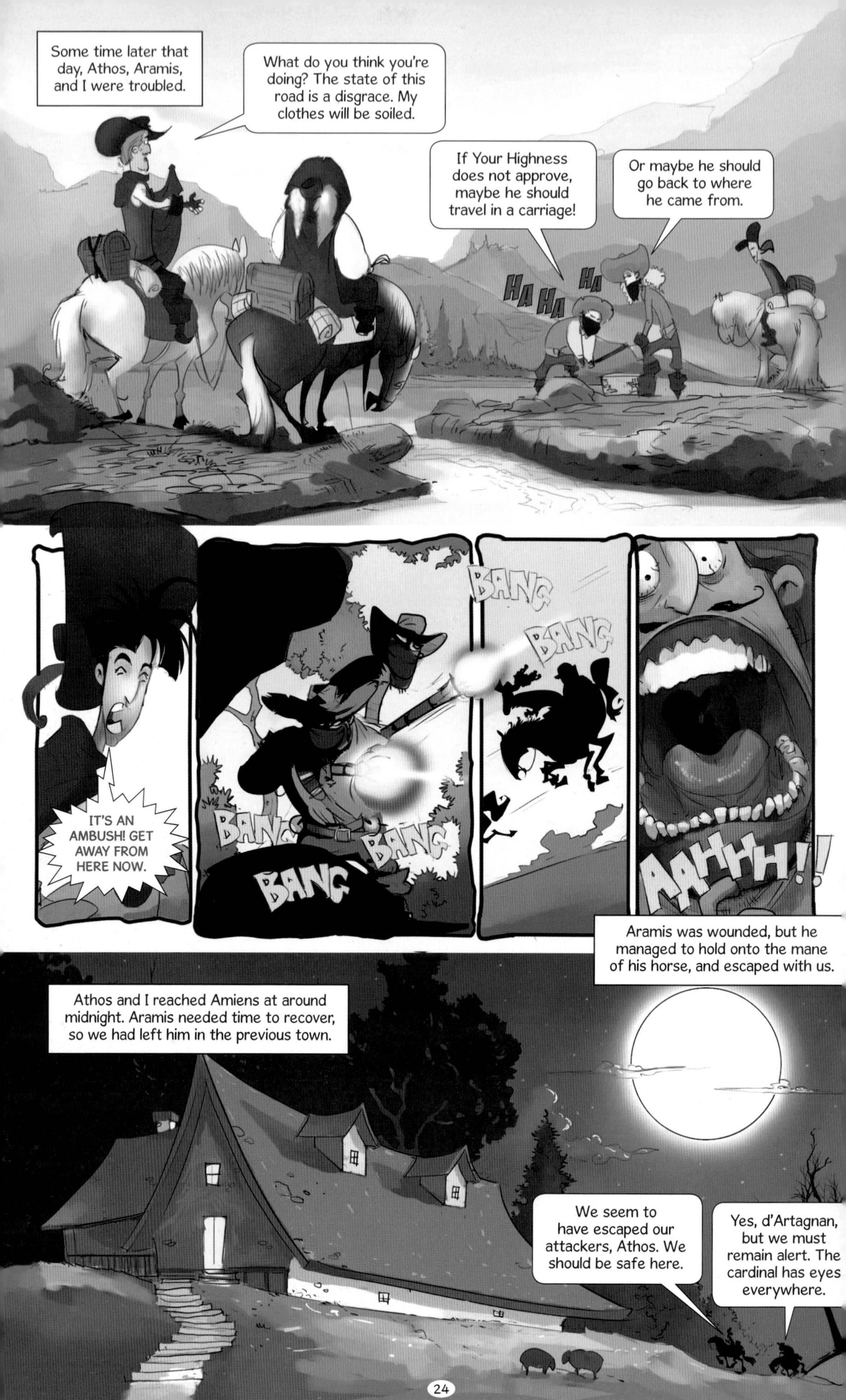

Some time later that day, Athos, Aramis, and I were troubled.
What do you think you're doing? The state of this road is a disgrace. My clothes will be soiled.
If Your Highness does not approve, maybe he should travel in a carriage!
Or maybe he should go back to where he came from.
HA HA HA
IT'S AN AMBUSH! GET AWAY FROM HERE NOW.
BANG
BANG
BANG
BANG
BANG
AAHHH!!
Aramis was wounded, but he managed to hold onto the mane of his horse, and escaped with us.
Athos and I reached Amiens at around midnight. Aramis needed time to recover, so we had left him in the previous town.
We seem to have escaped our attackers, Athos. We should be safe here.
Yes, d'Artagnan, but we must remain alert. The cardinal has eyes everywhere.

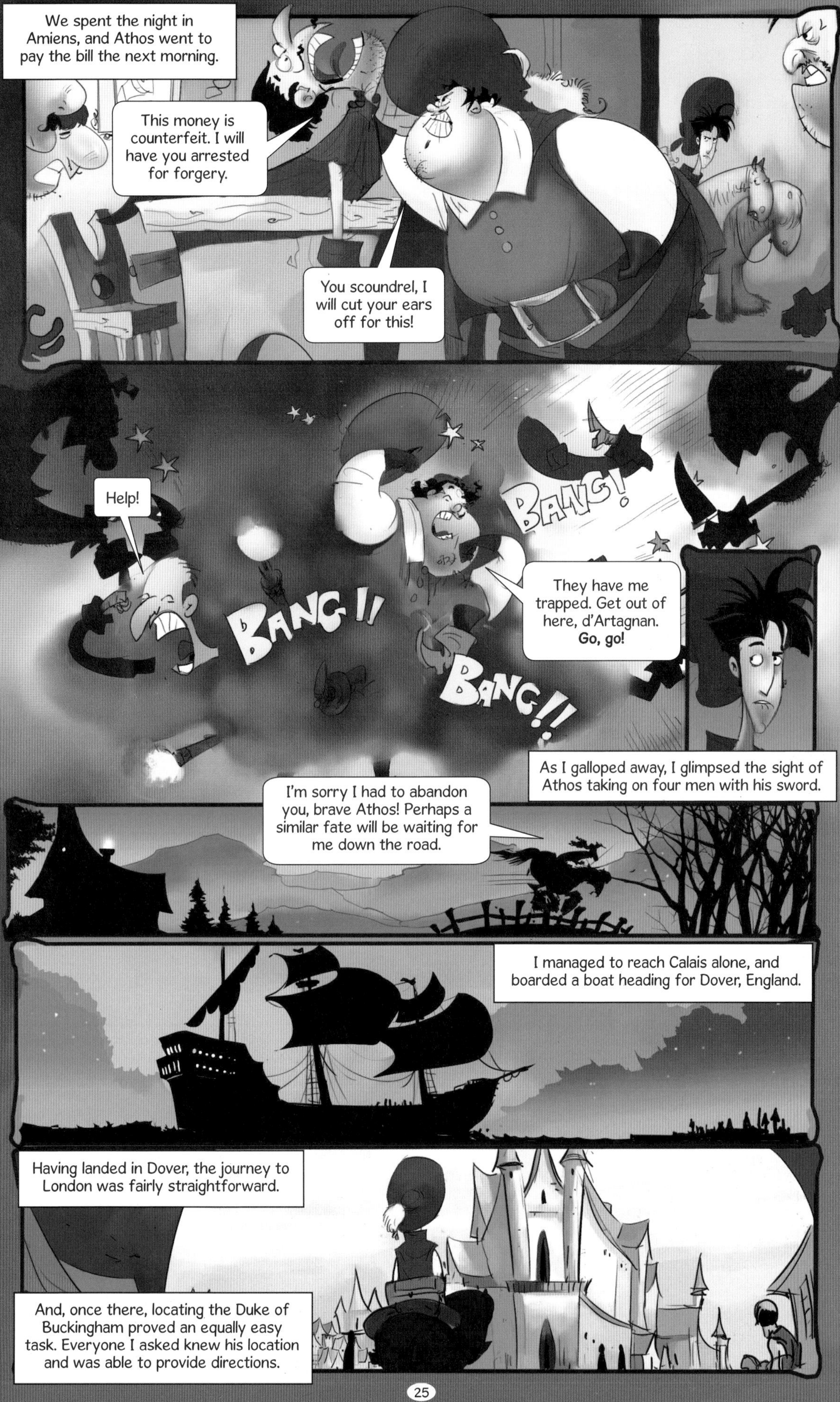

We spent the night in Amiens, and Athos went to pay the bill the next morning.
This money is counterfeit. I will have you arrested for forgery.
You scoundrel, I will cut your ears off for this!
Help!
BANG!
BANG!!
They have me trapped. Get out of here, d'Artagnan. **Go, go!**
BANG!!
As I galloped away, I glimpsed the sight of Athos taking on four men with his sword.
I'm sorry I had to abandon you, brave Athos! Perhaps a similar fate will be waiting for me down the road.
I managed to reach Calais alone, and boarded a boat heading for Dover, England.
Having landed in Dover, the journey to London was fairly straightforward.
And, once there, locating the Duke of Buckingham proved an equally easy task. Everyone I asked knew his location and was able to provide directions.

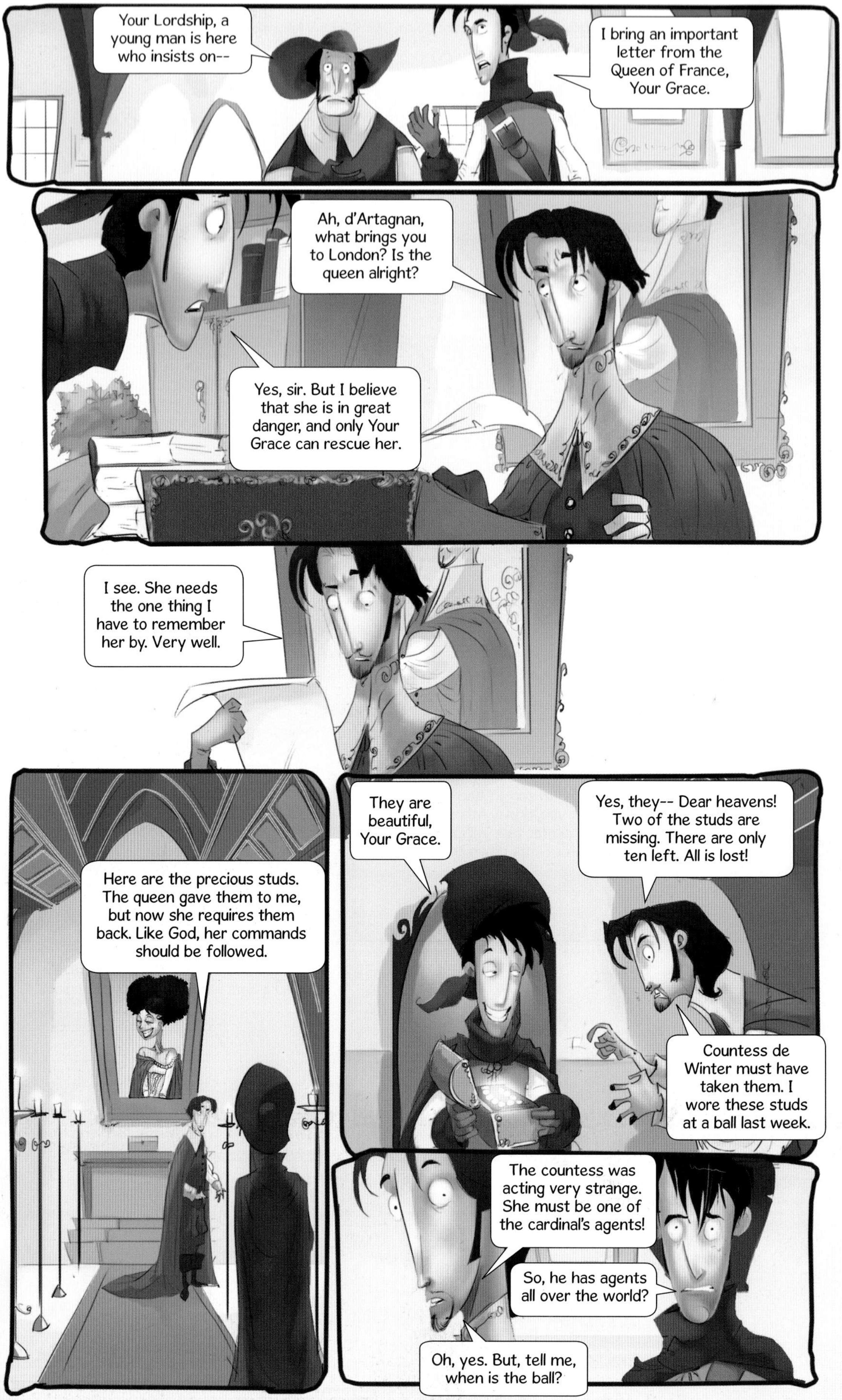
Your Lordship, a young man is here who insists on--
I bring an important letter from the Queen of France, Your Grace.
Ah, d'Artagnan, what brings you to London? Is the queen alright?
Yes, sir. But I believe that she is in great danger, and only Your Grace can rescue her.
I see. She needs the one thing I have to remember her by. Very well.
Here are the precious studs. The queen gave them to me, but now she requires them back. Like God, her commands should be followed.
They are beautiful, Your Grace.
Yes, they-- Dear heavens! Two of the studs are missing. There are only ten left. All is lost!
Countess de Winter must have taken them. I wore these studs at a ball last week.
The countess was acting very strange. She must be one of the cardinal's agents!
So, he has agents all over the world?
Oh, yes. But, tell me, when is the ball?

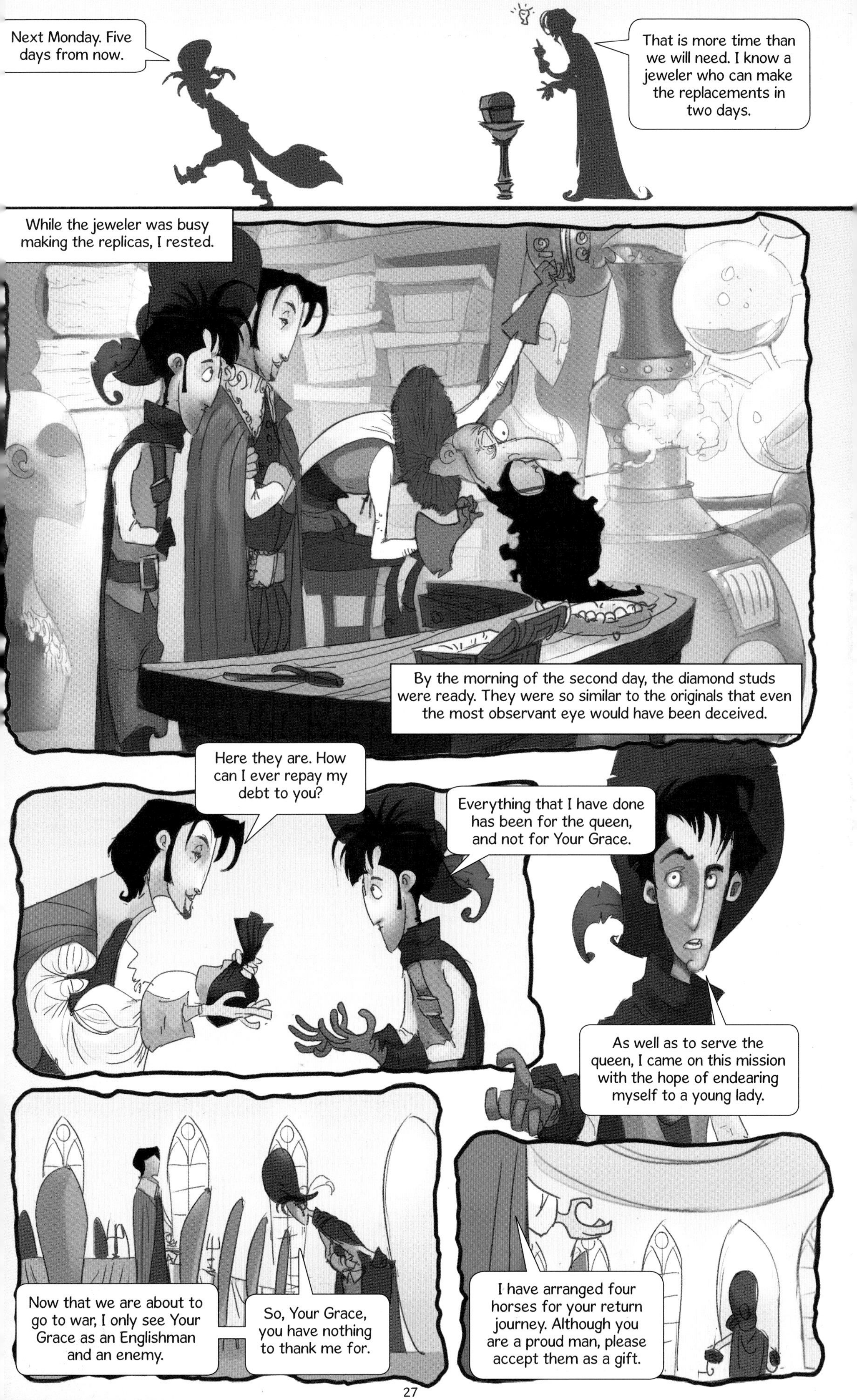

Next Monday. Five days from now.
That is more time than we will need. I know a jeweler who can make the replacements in two days.
While the jeweler was busy making the replicas, I rested.
By the morning of the second day, the diamond studs were ready. They were so similar to the originals that even the most observant eye would have been deceived.
Here they are. How can I ever repay my debt to you?
Everything that I have done has been for the queen, and not for Your Grace.
As well as to serve the queen, I came on this mission with the hope of endearing myself to a young lady.
Now that we are about to go to war, I only see Your Grace as an Englishman and an enemy.
So, Your Grace, you have nothing to thank me for.
I have arranged four horses for your return journey. Although you are a proud man, please accept them as a gift.

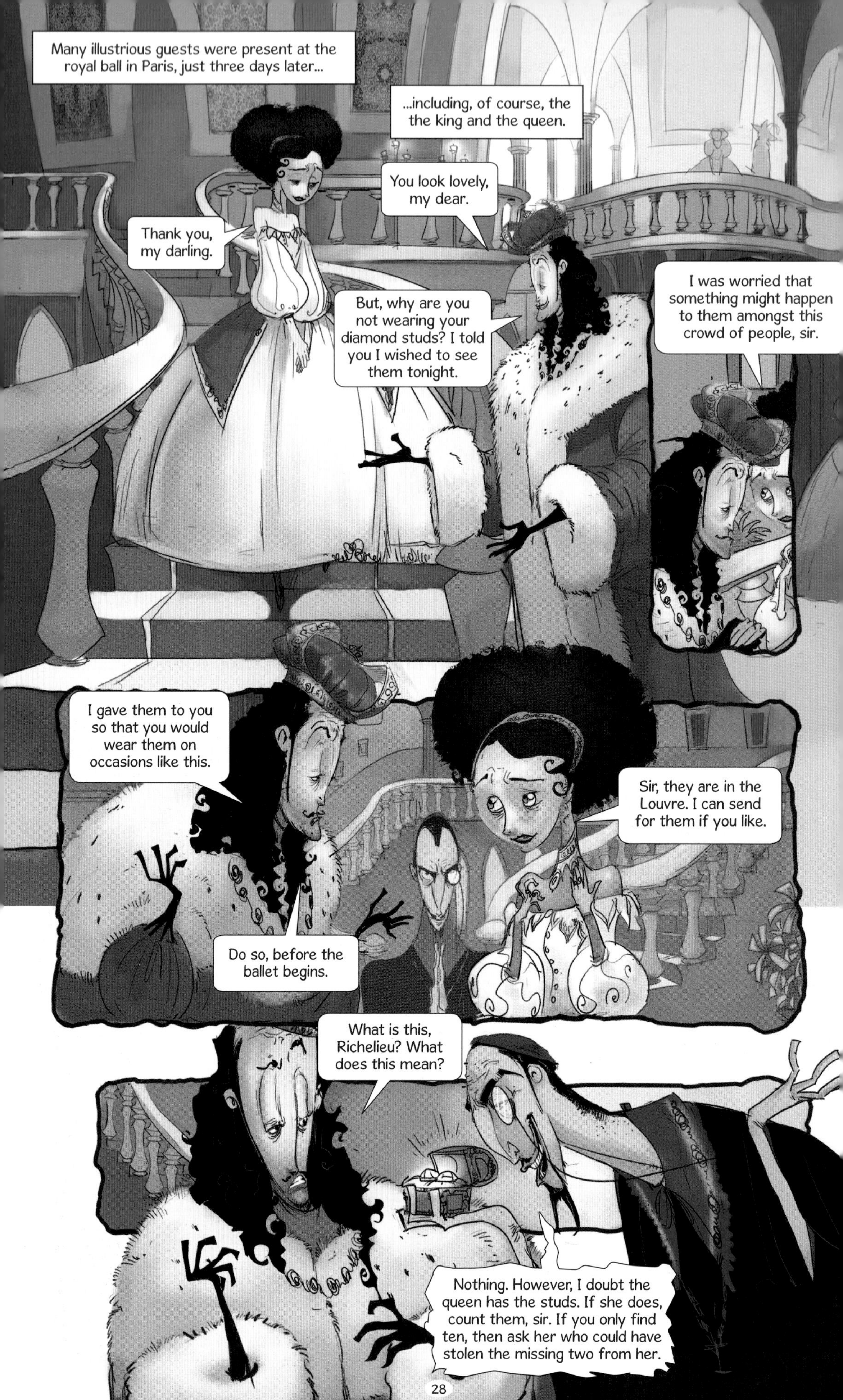
Many illustrious guests were present at the royal ball in Paris, just three days later...
...including, of course, the the king and the queen.
You look lovely, my dear.
Thank you, my darling.
But, why are you not wearing your diamond studs? I told you I wished to see them tonight.
I was worried that something might happen to them amongst this crowd of people, sir.
I gave them to you so that you would wear them on occasions like this.
Sir, they are in the Louvre. I can send for them if you like.
Do so, before the ballet begins.
What is this, Richelieu? What does this mean?
Nothing. However, I doubt the queen has the studs. If she does, count them, sir. If you only find ten, then ask her who could have stolen the missing two from her.

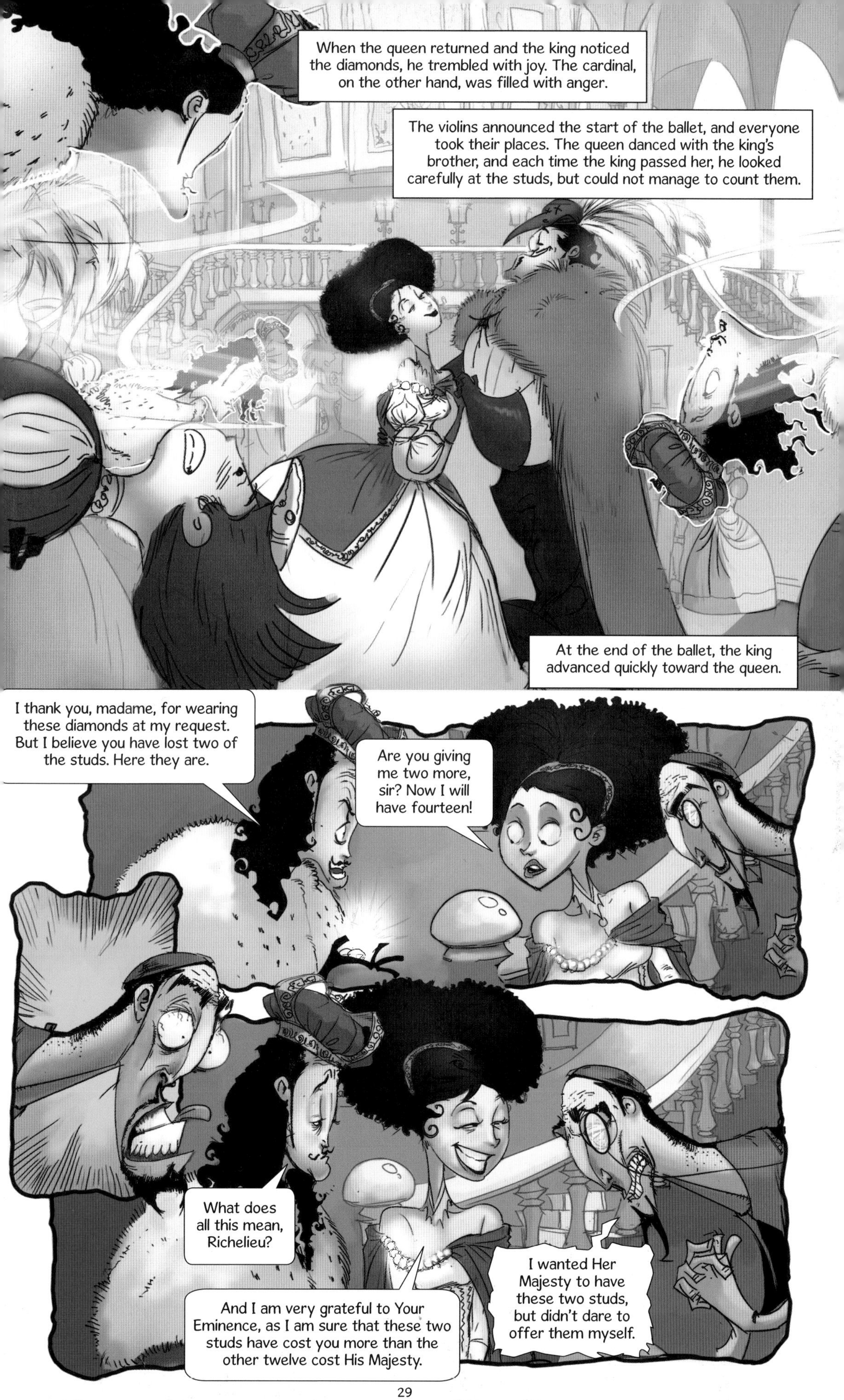
When the queen returned and the king noticed the diamonds, he trembled with joy. The cardinal, on the other hand, was filled with anger.
The violins announced the start of the ballet, and everyone took their places. The queen danced with the king's brother, and each time the king passed her, he looked carefully at the studs, but could not manage to count them.
At the end of the ballet, the king advanced quickly toward the queen.
I thank you, madame, for wearing these diamonds at my request. But I believe you have lost two of the studs. Here they are.
Are you giving me two more, sir? Now I will have fourteen!
What does all this mean, Richelieu?
I wanted Her Majesty to have these two studs, but didn't dare to offer them myself.
And I am very grateful to Your Eminence, as I am sure that these two studs have cost you more than the other twelve cost His Majesty.

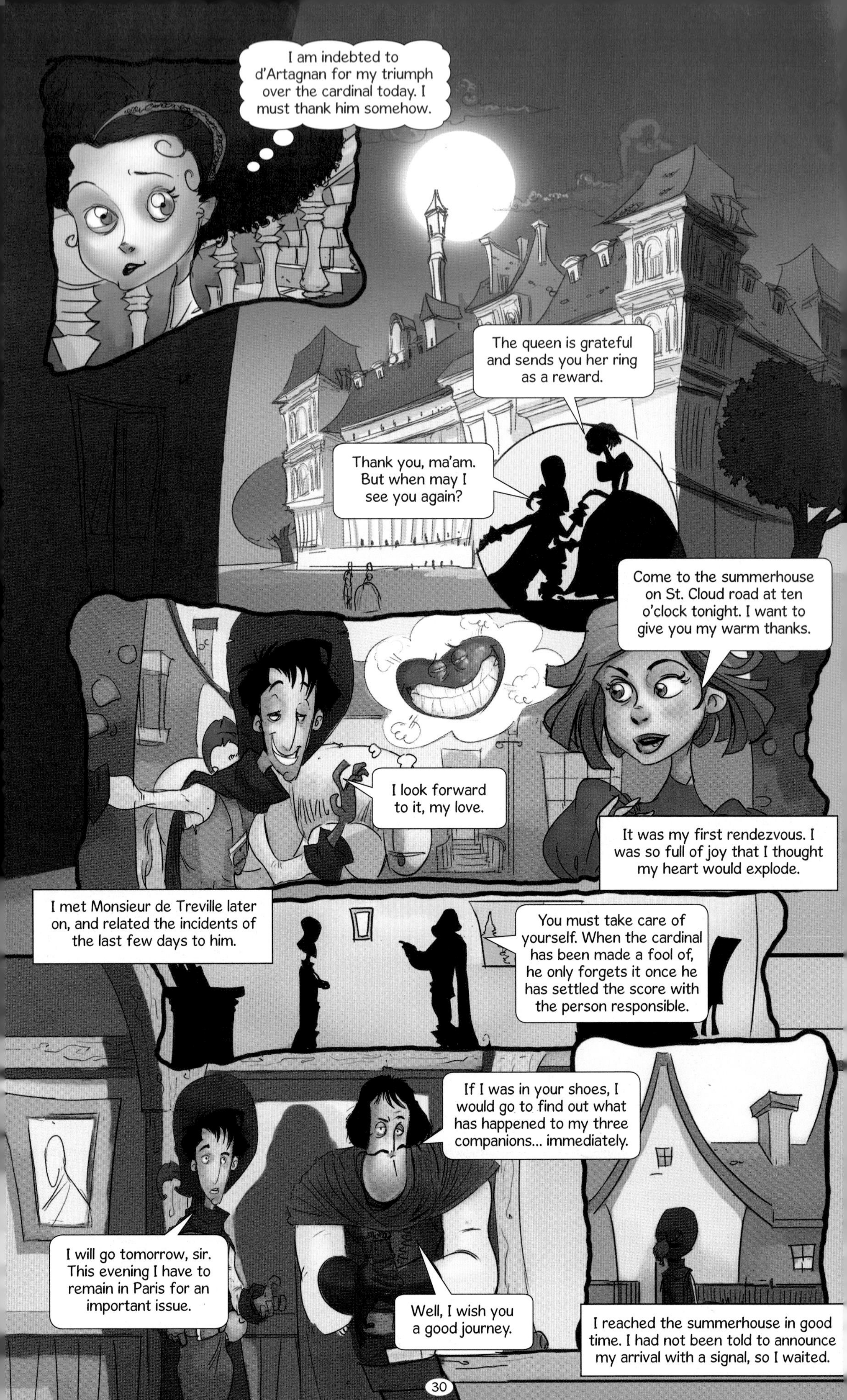
I am indebted to d'Artagnan for my triumph over the cardinal today. I must thank him somehow.
The queen is grateful and sends you her ring as a reward.
Thank you, ma'am. But when may I see you again?
Come to the summerhouse on St. Cloud road at ten o'clock tonight. I want to give you my warm thanks.
I look forward to it, my love.
It was my first rendezvous. I was so full of joy that I thought my heart would explode.
I met Monsieur de Treville later on, and related the incidents of the last few days to him.
You must take care of yourself. When the cardinal has been made a fool of, he only forgets it once he has settled the score with the person responsible.
If I was in your shoes, I would go to find out what has happened to my three companions... immediately.
I will go tomorrow, sir. This evening I have to remain in Paris for an important issue.
Well, I wish you a good journey.
I reached the summerhouse in good time. I had not been told to announce my arrival with a signal, so I waited.

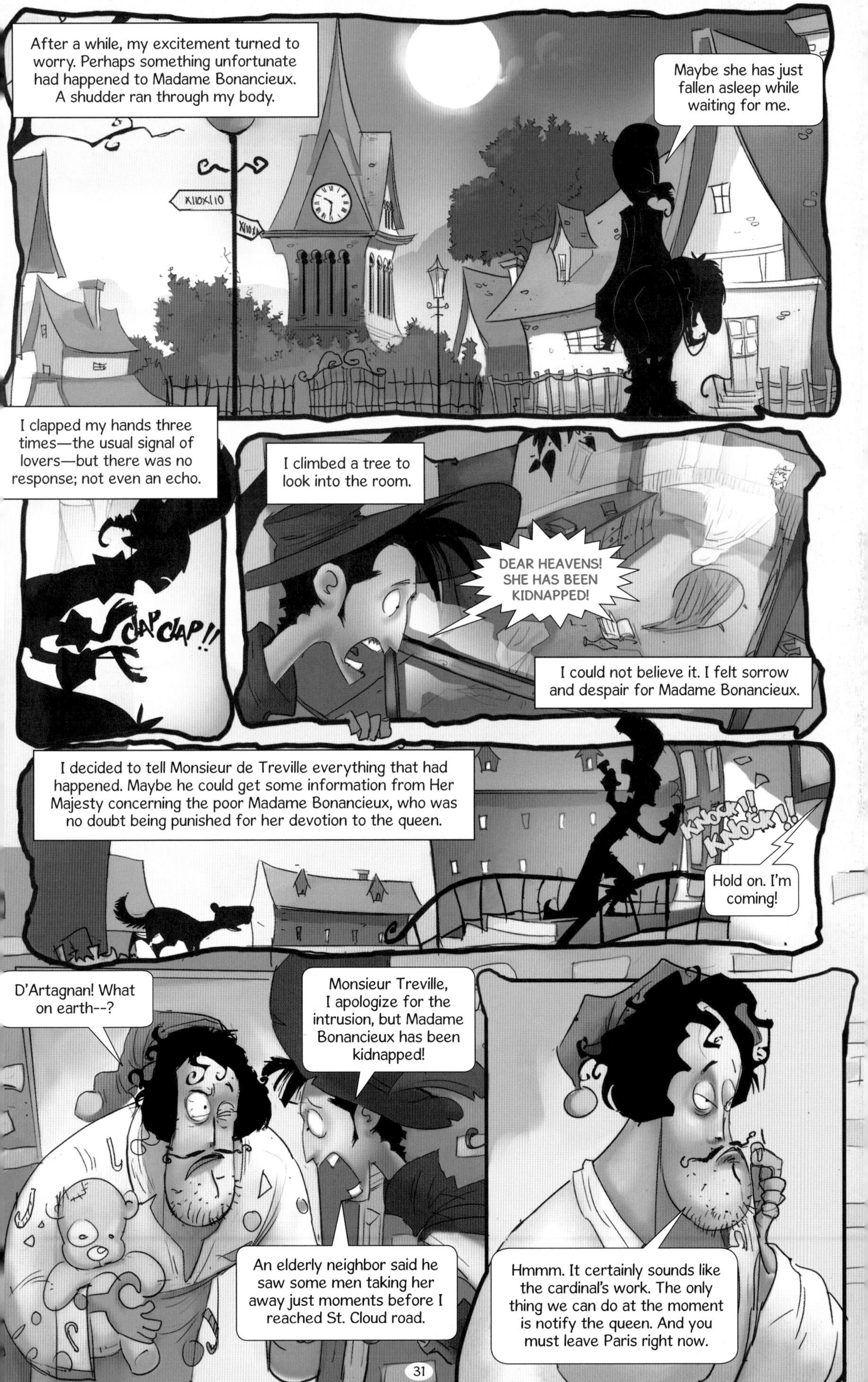

After a while, my excitement turned to worry. Perhaps something unfortunate had happened to Madame Bonancieux. A shudder ran through my body.
Maybe she has just fallen asleep while waiting for me.
I clapped my hands three times—the usual signal of lovers—but there was no response; not even an echo.
CLAP CLAP!!
I climbed a tree to look into the room.
DEAR HEAVENS! SHE HAS BEEN KIDNAPPED!
I could not believe it. I felt sorrow and despair for Madame Bonancieux.
I decided to tell Monsieur de Treville everything that had happened. Maybe he could get some information from Her Majesty concerning the poor Madame Bonancieux, who was no doubt being punished for her devotion to the queen.
KNOCK!! KNOCK!!
Hold on. I'm coming!
D'Artagnan! What on earth--?
Monsieur Treville, I apologize for the intrusion, but Madame Bonancieux has been kidnapped!
An elderly neighbor said he saw some men taking her away just moments before I reached St. Cloud road.
Hmmm. It certainly sounds like the cardinal's work. The only thing we can do at the moment is notify the queen. And you must leave Paris right now.

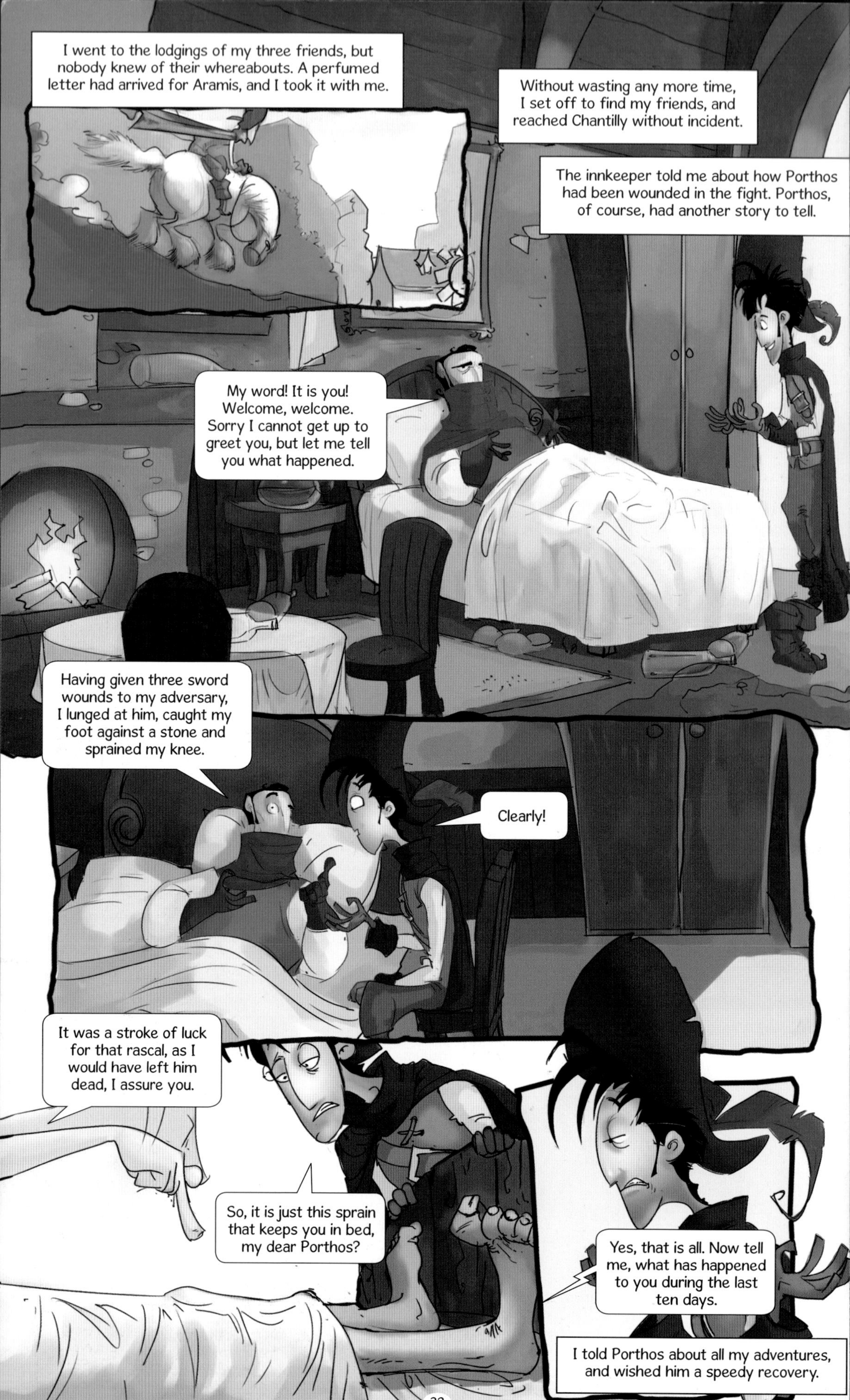

I went to the lodgings of my three friends, but nobody knew of their whereabouts. A perfumed letter had arrived for Aramis, and I took it with me.
Without wasting any more time, I set off to find my friends, and reached Chantilly without incident.
The innkeeper told me about how Porthos had been wounded in the fight. Porthos, of course, had another story to tell.
My word! It is you! Welcome, welcome. Sorry I cannot get up to greet you, but let me tell you what happened.
Having given three sword wounds to my adversary, I lunged at him, caught my foot against a stone and sprained my knee.
Clearly!
It was a stroke of luck for that rascal, as I would have left him dead, I assure you.
So, it is just this sprain that keeps you in bed, my dear Porthos?
Yes, that is all. Now tell me, what has happened to you during the last ten days.
I told Porthos about all my adventures, and wished him a speedy recovery.

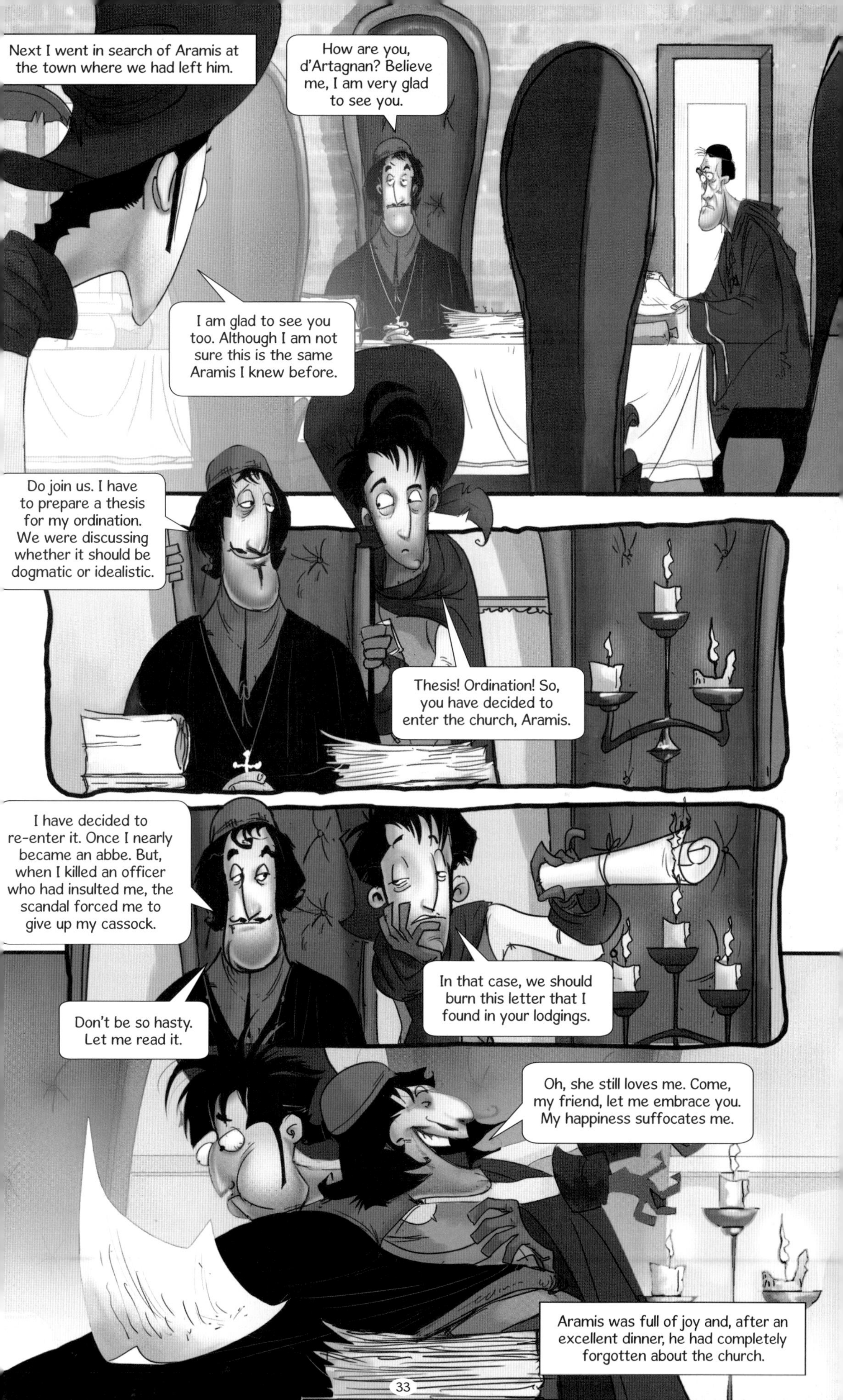
Next I went in search of Aramis at the town where we had left him.
How are you, d'Artagnan? Believe me, I am very glad to see you.
I am glad to see you too. Although I am not sure this is the same Aramis I knew before.
Do join us. I have to prepare a thesis for my ordination. We were discussing whether it should be dogmatic or idealistic.
Thesis! Ordination! So, you have decided to enter the church, Aramis.
I have decided to re-enter it. Once I nearly became an abbe. But, when I killed an officer who had insulted me, the scandal forced me to give up my cassock.
In that case, we should burn this letter that I found in your lodgings.
Don't be so hasty. Let me read it.
Oh, she still loves me. Come, my friend, let me embrace you. My happiness suffocates me.
Aramis was full of joy and, after an excellent dinner, he had completely forgotten about the church.

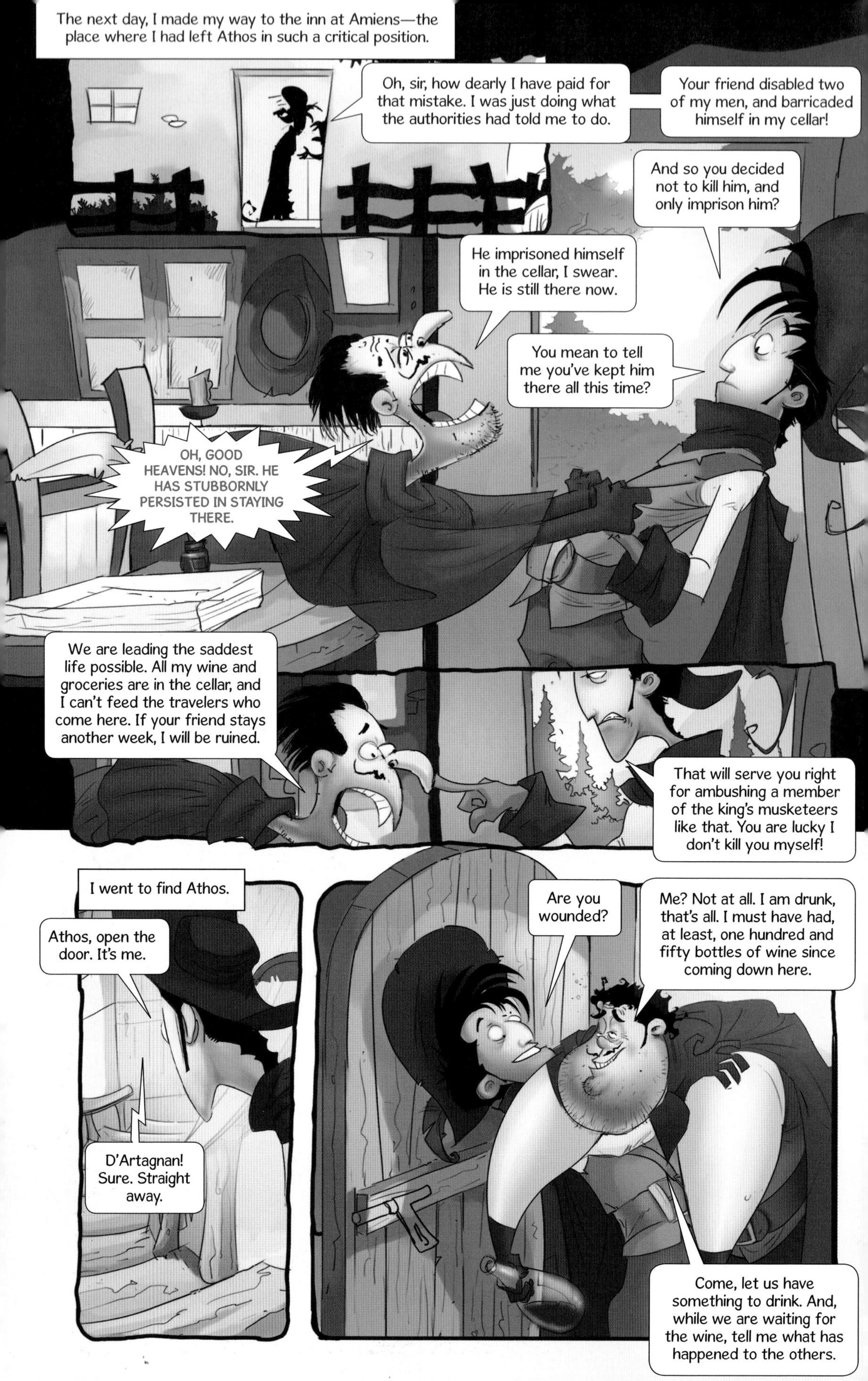
The next day, I made my way to the inn at Amiens—the place where I had left Athos in such a critical position.
Oh, sir, how dearly I have paid for that mistake. I was just doing what the authorities had told me to do.
Your friend disabled two of my men, and barricaded himself in my cellar!
And so you decided not to kill him, and only imprison him?
He imprisoned himself in the cellar, I swear. He is still there now.
You mean to tell me you've kept him there all this time?
OH, GOOD HEAVENS! NO, SIR. HE HAS STUBBORNLY PERSISTED IN STAYING THERE.
We are leading the saddest life possible. All my wine and groceries are in the cellar, and I can't feed the travelers who come here. If your friend stays another week, I will be ruined.
That will serve you right for ambushing a member of the king's musketeers like that. You are lucky I don't kill you myself!
I went to find Athos.
Athos, open the door. It's me.
D'Artagnan! Sure. Straight away.
Are you wounded?
Me? Not at all. I am drunk, that's all. I must have had, at least, one hundred and fifty bottles of wine since coming down here.
Come, let us have something to drink. And, while we are waiting for the wine, tell me what has happened to the others.

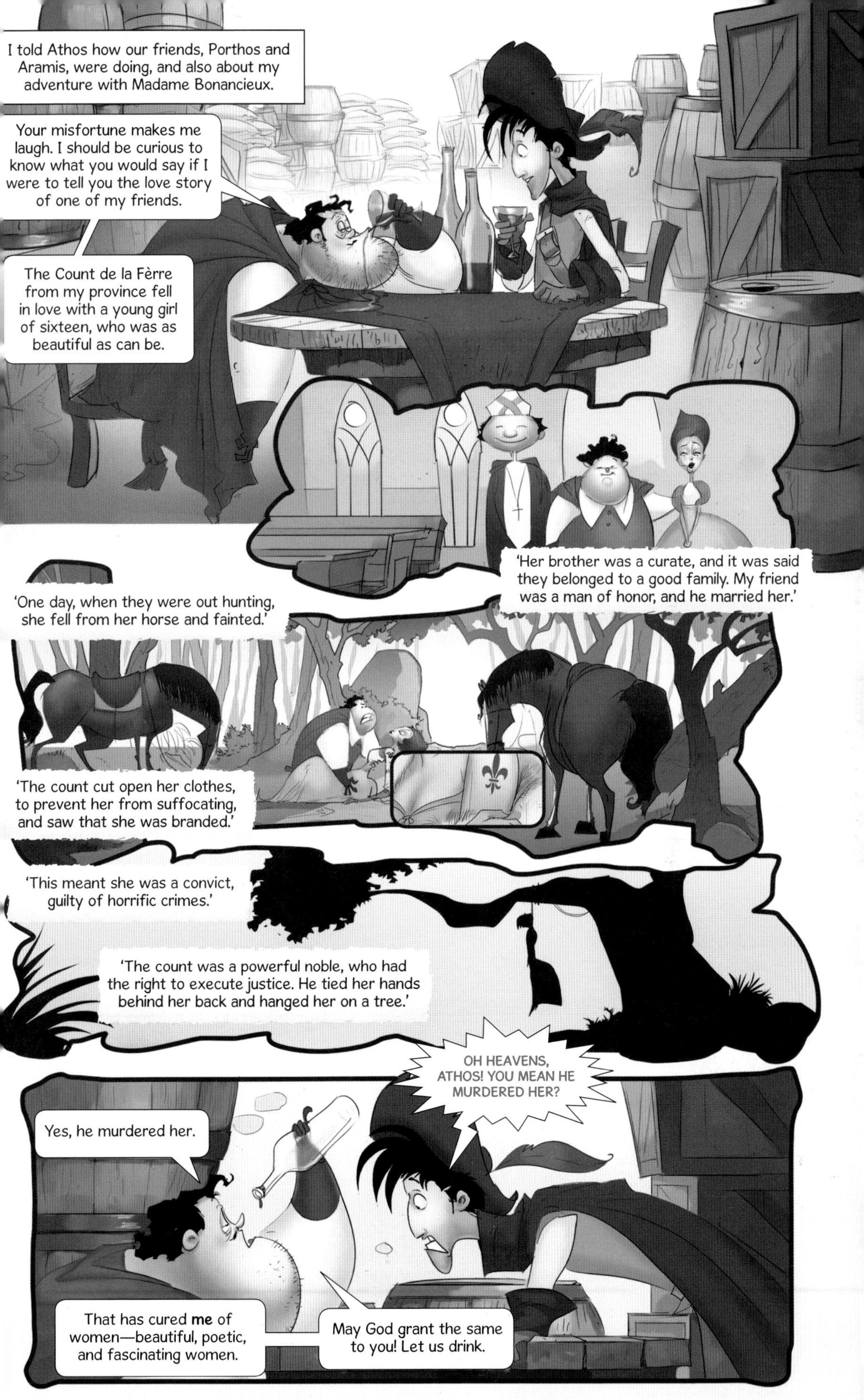
I told Athos how our friends, Porthos and Aramis, were doing, and also about my adventure with Madame Bonancieux.
Your misfortune makes me laugh. I should be curious to know what you would say if I were to tell you the love story of one of my friends.
The Count de la Fèrre from my province fell in love with a young girl of sixteen, who was as beautiful as can be.
'Her brother was a curate, and it was said they belonged to a good family. My friend was a man of honor, and he married her.'
'One day, when they were out hunting, she fell from her horse and fainted.'
'The count cut open her clothes, to prevent her from suffocating, and saw that she was branded.'
'This meant she was a convict, guilty of horrific crimes.'
'The count was a powerful noble, who had the right to execute justice. He tied her hands behind her back and hanged her on a tree.'
OH HEAVENS, ATHOS! YOU MEAN HE MURDERED HER?
Yes, he murdered her.
That has cured **me** of women—beautiful, poetic, and fascinating women.
May God grant the same to you! Let us drink.

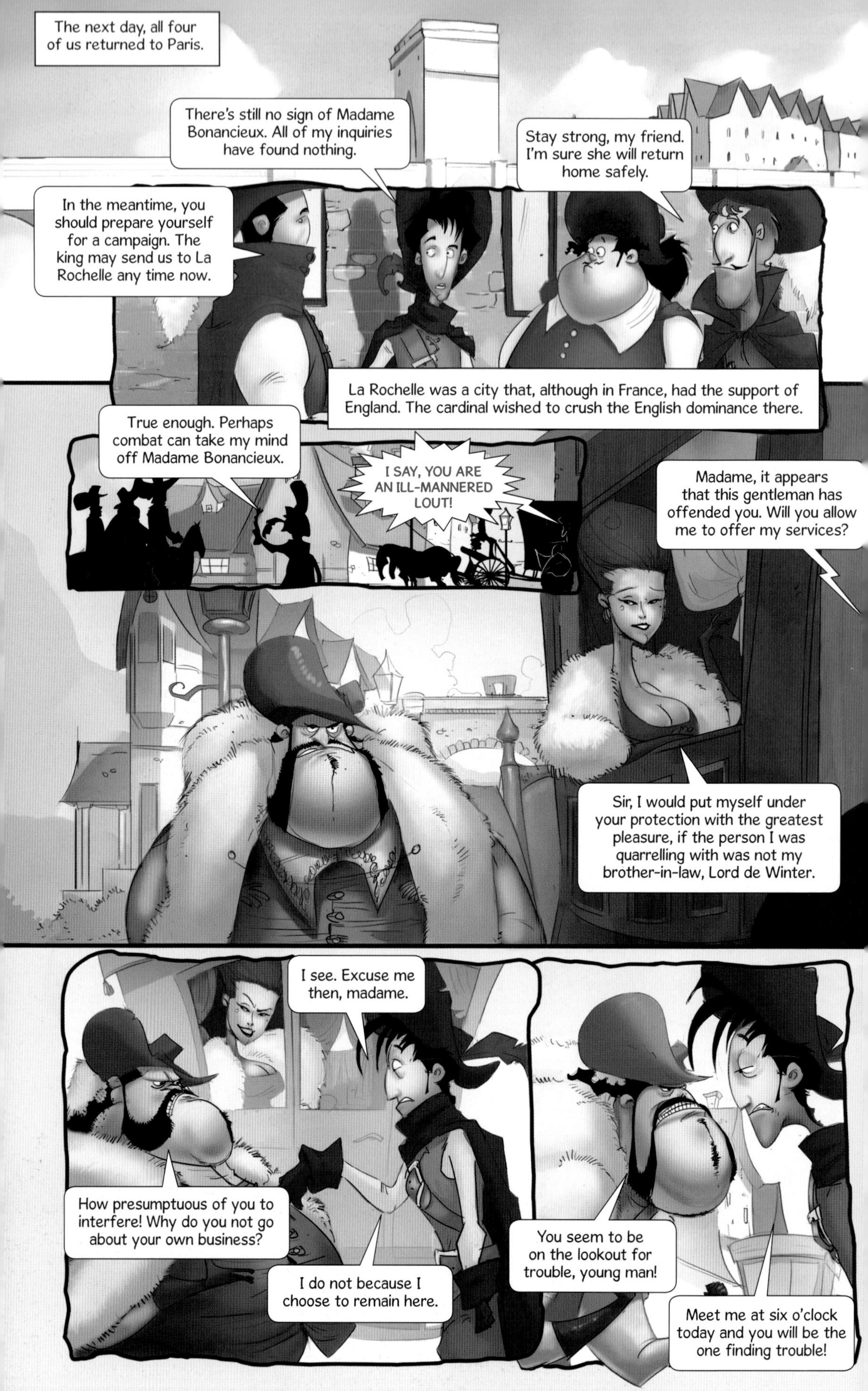

The next day, all four of us returned to Paris.
There's still no sign of Madame Bonancieux. All of my inquiries have found nothing.
Stay strong, my friend. I'm sure she will return home safely.
In the meantime, you should prepare yourself for a campaign. The king may send us to La Rochelle any time now.
La Rochelle was a city that, although in France, had the support of England. The cardinal wished to crush the English dominance there.
True enough. Perhaps combat can take my mind off Madame Bonancieux.
I SAY, YOU ARE AN ILL-MANNERED LOUT!
Madame, it appears that this gentleman has offended you. Will you allow me to offer my services?
Sir, I would put myself under your protection with the greatest pleasure, if the person I was quarrelling with was not my brother-in-law, Lord de Winter.
I see. Excuse me then, madame.
How presumptuous of you to interfere! Why do you not go about your own business?
I do not because I choose to remain here.
You seem to be on the lookout for trouble, young man!
Meet me at six o'clock today and you will be the one finding trouble!

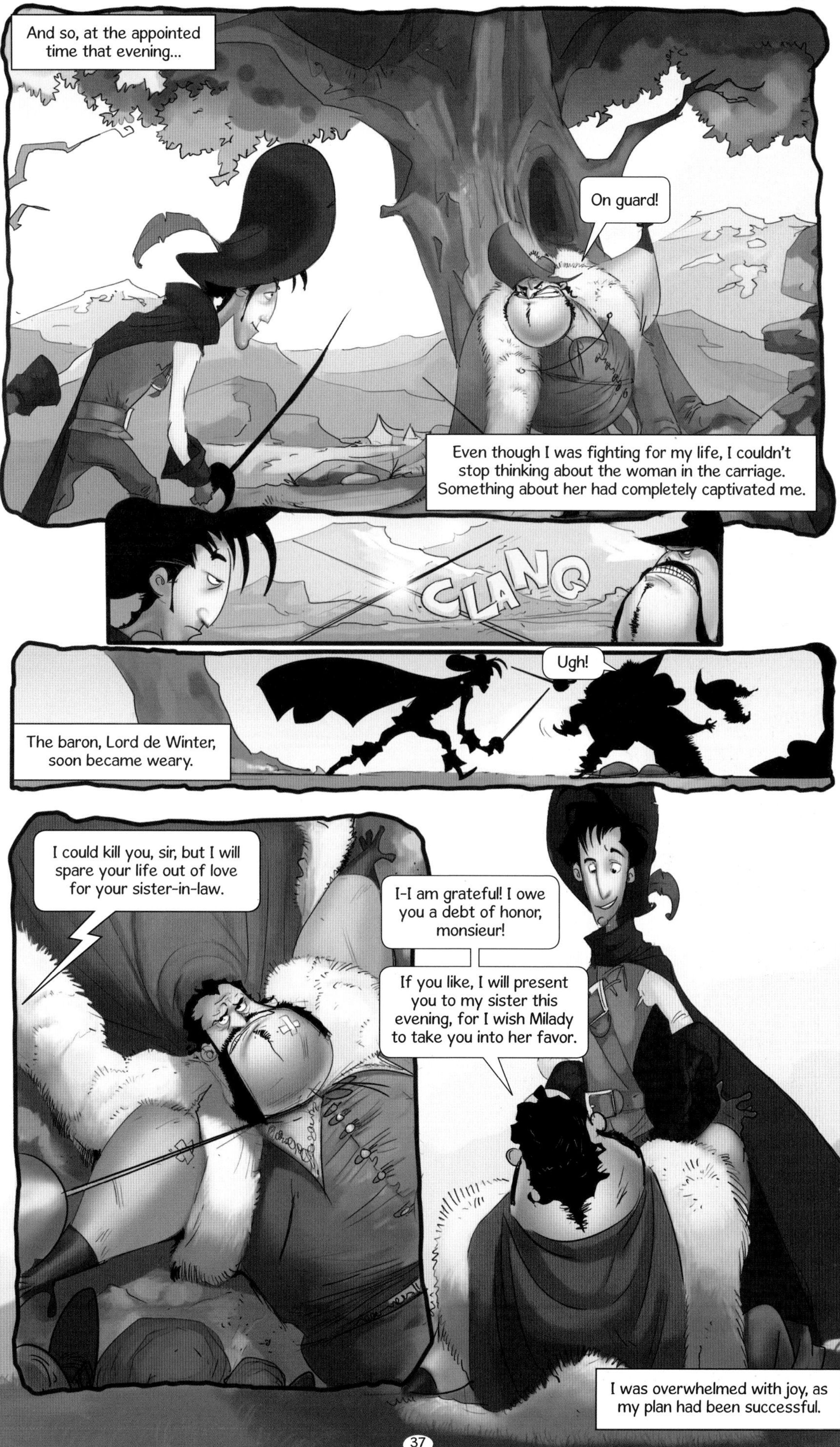
And so, at the appointed time that evening...
On guard!
Even though I was fighting for my life, I couldn't stop thinking about the woman in the carriage. Something about her had completely captivated me.
CLANG
Ugh!
The baron, Lord de Winter, soon became weary.
I could kill you, sir, but I will spare your life out of love for your sister-in-law.
I-I am grateful! I owe you a debt of honor, monsieur!
If you like, I will present you to my sister this evening, for I wish Milady to take you into her favor.
I was overwhelmed with joy, as my plan had been successful.

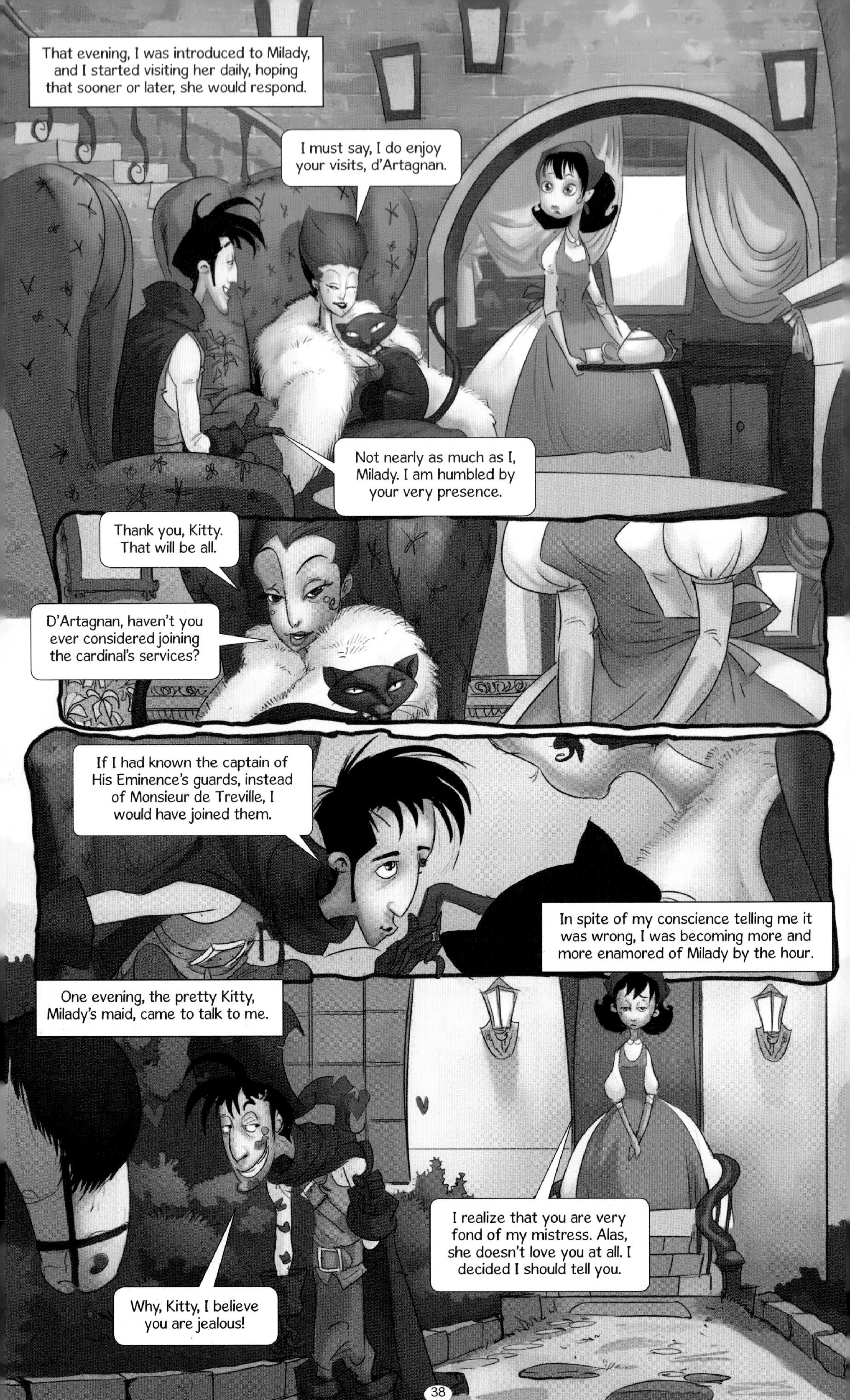

That evening, I was introduced to Milady, and I started visiting her daily, hoping that sooner or later, she would respond.
I must say, I do enjoy your visits, d'Artagnan.
Not nearly as much as I, Milady. I am humbled by your very presence.
Thank you, Kitty. That will be all.
D'Artagnan, haven't you ever considered joining the cardinal's services?
If I had known the captain of His Eminence's guards, instead of Monsieur de Treville, I would have joined them.
In spite of my conscience telling me it was wrong, I was becoming more and more enamored of Milady by the hour.
One evening, the pretty Kitty, Milady's maid, came to talk to me.
I realize that you are very fond of my mistress. Alas, she doesn't love you at all. I decided I should tell you.
Why, Kitty, I believe you are jealous!

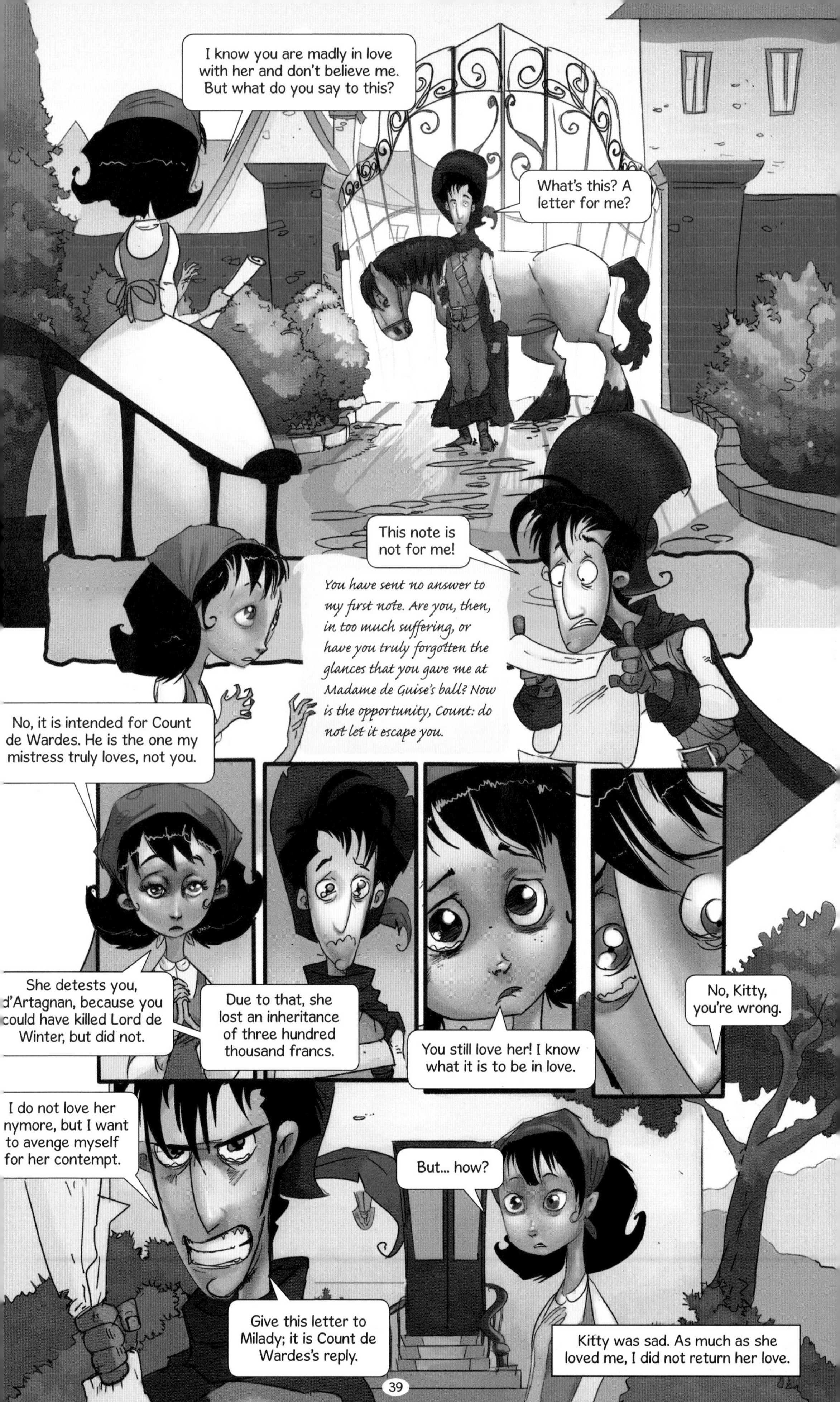

I know you are madly in love with her and don't believe me. But what do you say to this?
What's this? A letter for me?
This note is not for me!
You have sent no answer to my first note. Are you, then, in too much suffering, or have you truly forgotten the glances that you gave me at Madame de Guise's ball? Now is the opportunity, Count: do not let it escape you.
No, it is intended for Count de Wardes. He is the one my mistress truly loves, not you.
She detests you, d'Artagnan, because you could have killed Lord de Winter, but did not.
Due to that, she lost an inheritance of three hundred thousand francs.
You still love her! I know what it is to be in love.
No, Kitty, you're wrong.
I do not love her nymore, but I want to avenge myself for her contempt.
But... how?
Give this letter to Milady; it is Count de Wardes's reply.
Kitty was sad. As much as she loved me, I did not return her love.

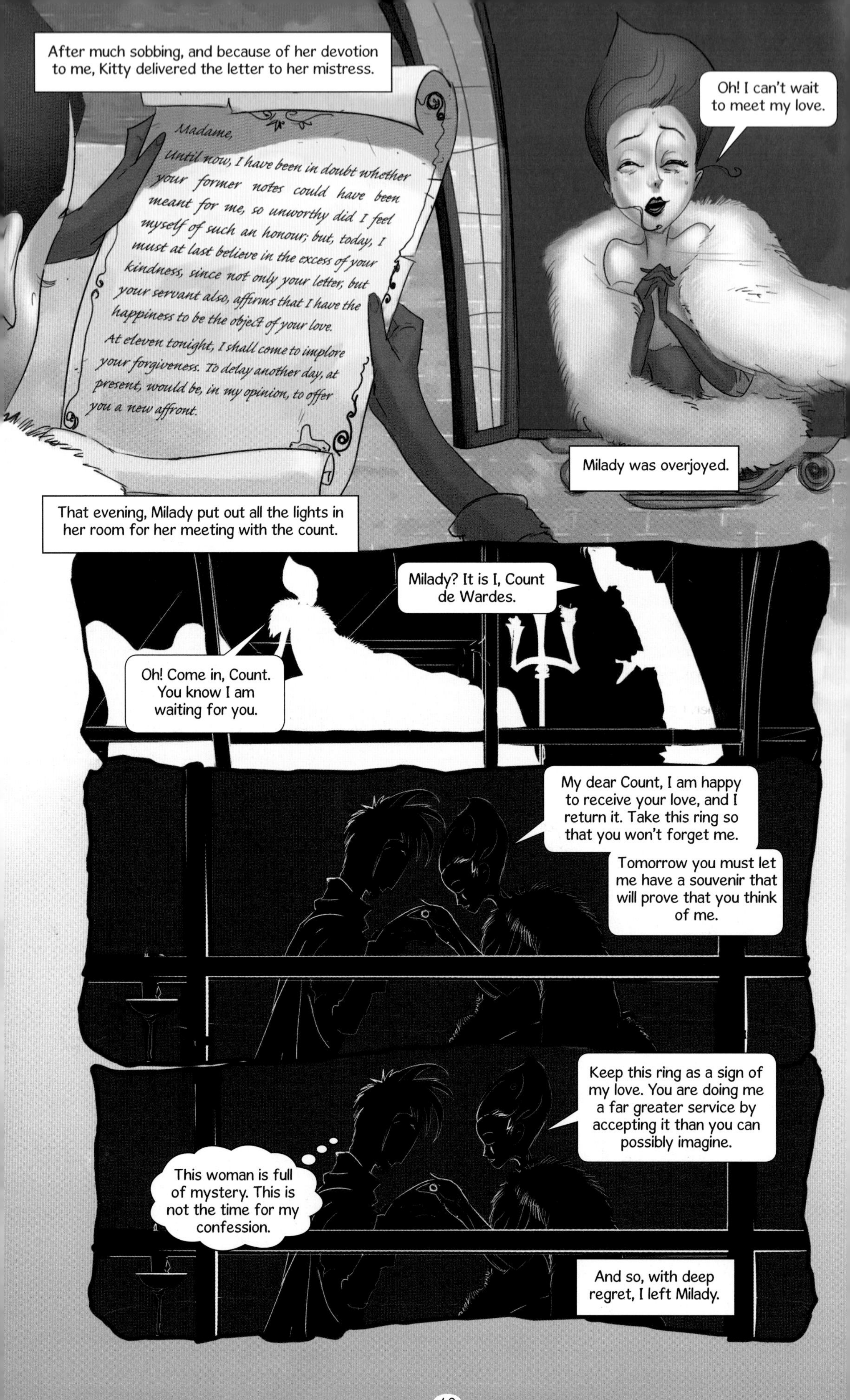
After much sobbing, and because of her devotion to me, Kitty delivered the letter to her mistress.
Madame,
Until now, I have been in doubt whether your former notes could have been meant for me, so unworthy did I feel myself of such an honour; but, today, I must at last believe in the excess of your kindness, since not only your letter, but your servant also, affirms that I have the happiness to be the object of your love.
At eleven tonight, I shall come to implore your forgiveness. To delay another day, at present, would be, in my opinion, to offer you a new affront.
Oh! I can't wait to meet my love.
Milady was overjoyed.
That evening, Milady put out all the lights in her room for her meeting with the count.
Milady? It is I, Count de Wardes.
Oh! Come in, Count. You know I am waiting for you.
My dear Count, I am happy to receive your love, and I return it. Take this ring so that you won't forget me.
Tomorrow you must let me have a souvenir that will prove that you think of me.
Keep this ring as a sign of my love. You are doing me a far greater service by accepting it than you can possibly imagine.
This woman is full of mystery. This is not the time for my confession.
And so, with deep regret, I left Milady.

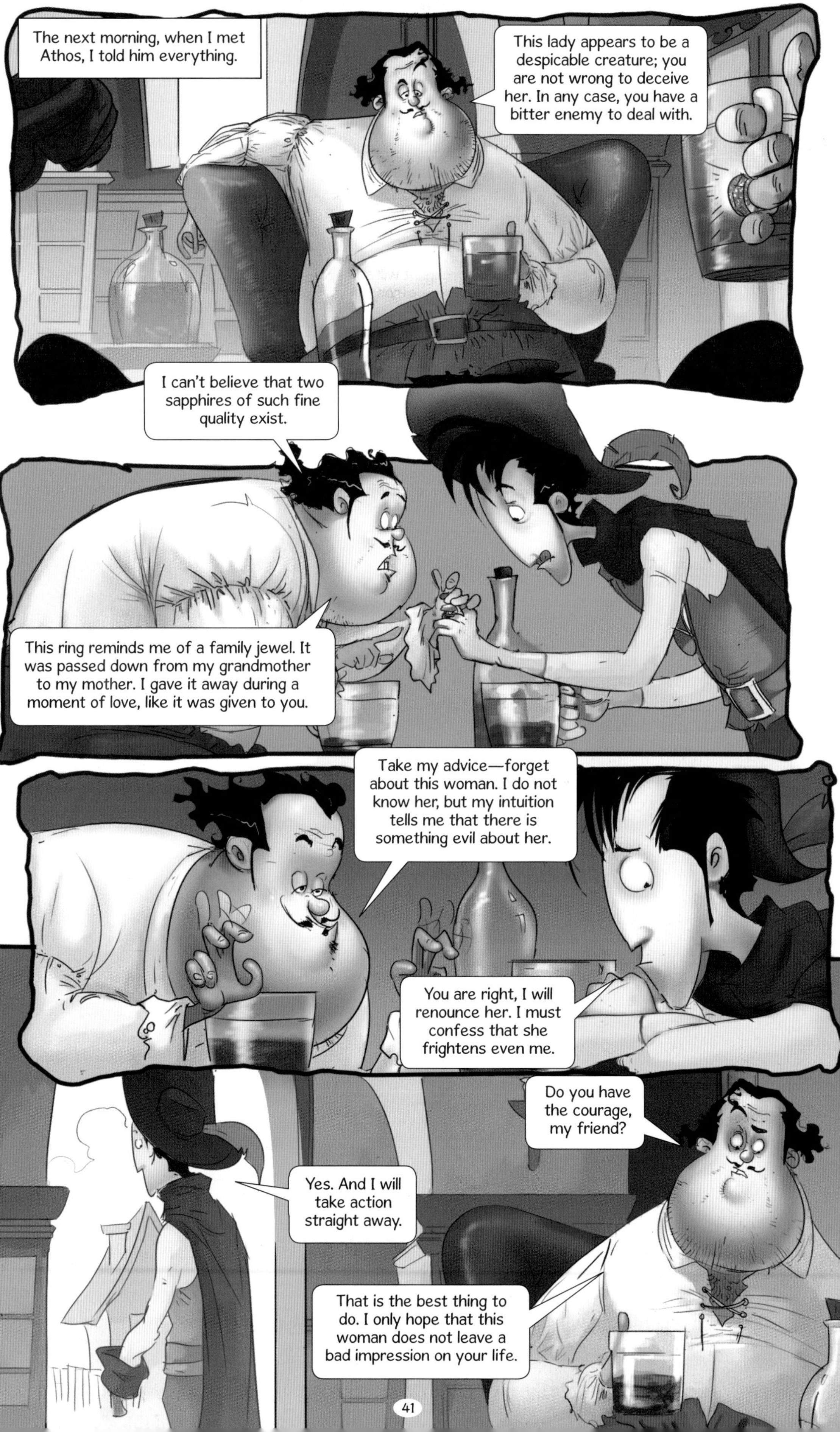
The next morning, when I met Athos, I told him everything.
This lady appears to be a despicable creature; you are not wrong to deceive her. In any case, you have a bitter enemy to deal with.
I can't believe that two sapphires of such fine quality exist.
This ring reminds me of a family jewel. It was passed down from my grandmother to my mother. I gave it away during a moment of love, like it was given to you.
Take my advice—forget about this woman. I do not know her, but my intuition tells me that there is something evil about her.
You are right, I will renounce her. I must confess that she frightens even me.
Do you have the courage, my friend?
Yes. And I will take action straight away.
That is the best thing to do. I only hope that this woman does not leave a bad impression on your life.

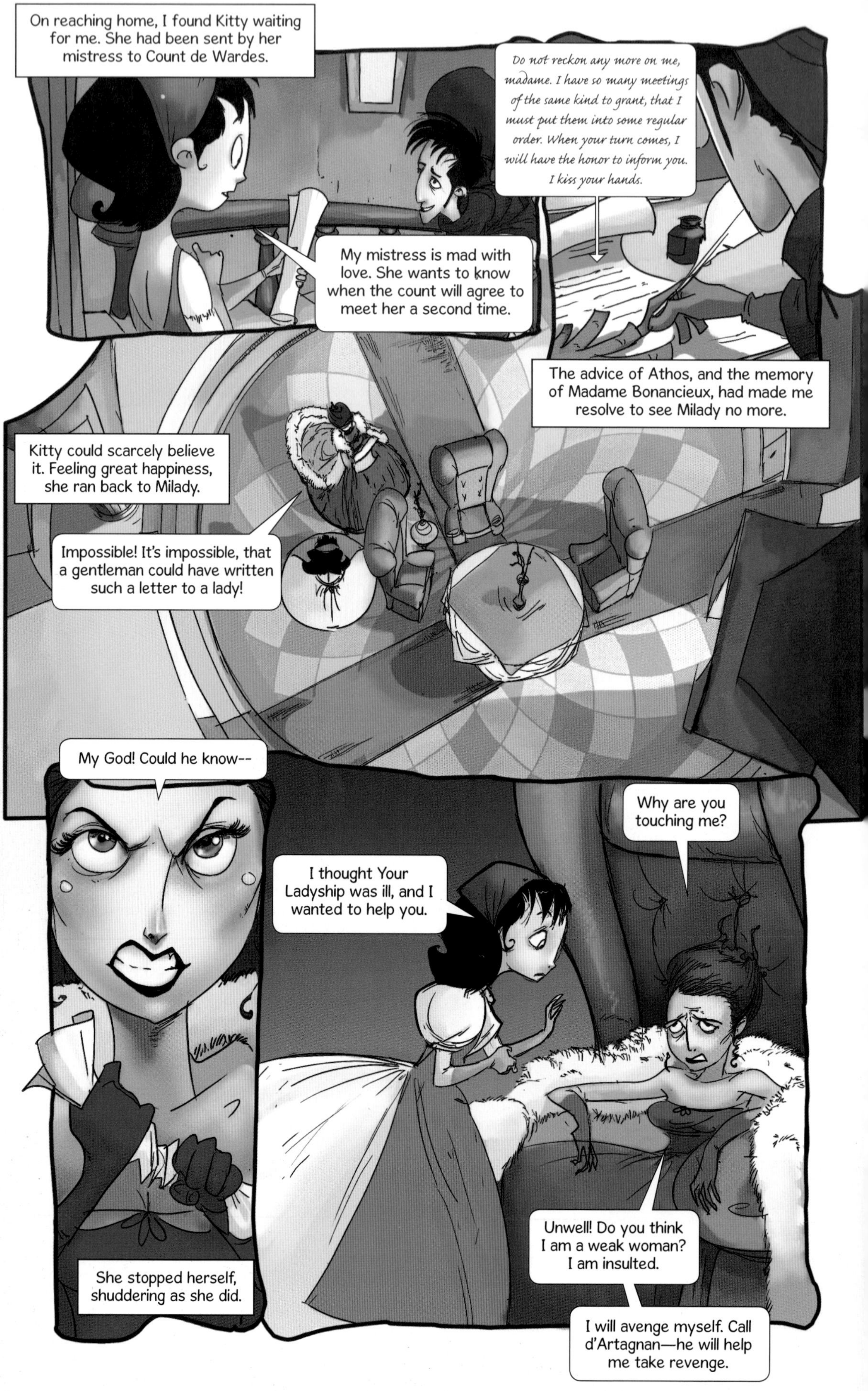
On reaching home, I found Kitty waiting for me. She had been sent by her mistress to Count de Wardes.
My mistress is mad with love. She wants to know when the count will agree to meet her a second time.
Do not reckon any more on me, madame. I have so many meetings of the same kind to grant, that I must put them into some regular order. When your turn comes, I will have the honor to inform you. I kiss your hands.
The advice of Athos, and the memory of Madame Bonancieux, had made me resolve to see Milady no more.
Kitty could scarcely believe it. Feeling great happiness, she ran back to Milady.
Impossible! It's impossible, that a gentleman could have written such a letter to a lady!
My God! Could he know--
She stopped herself, shuddering as she did.
I thought Your Ladyship was ill, and I wanted to help you.
Why are you touching me?
Unwell! Do you think I am a weak woman? I am insulted.
I will avenge myself. Call d'Artagnan—he will help me take revenge.

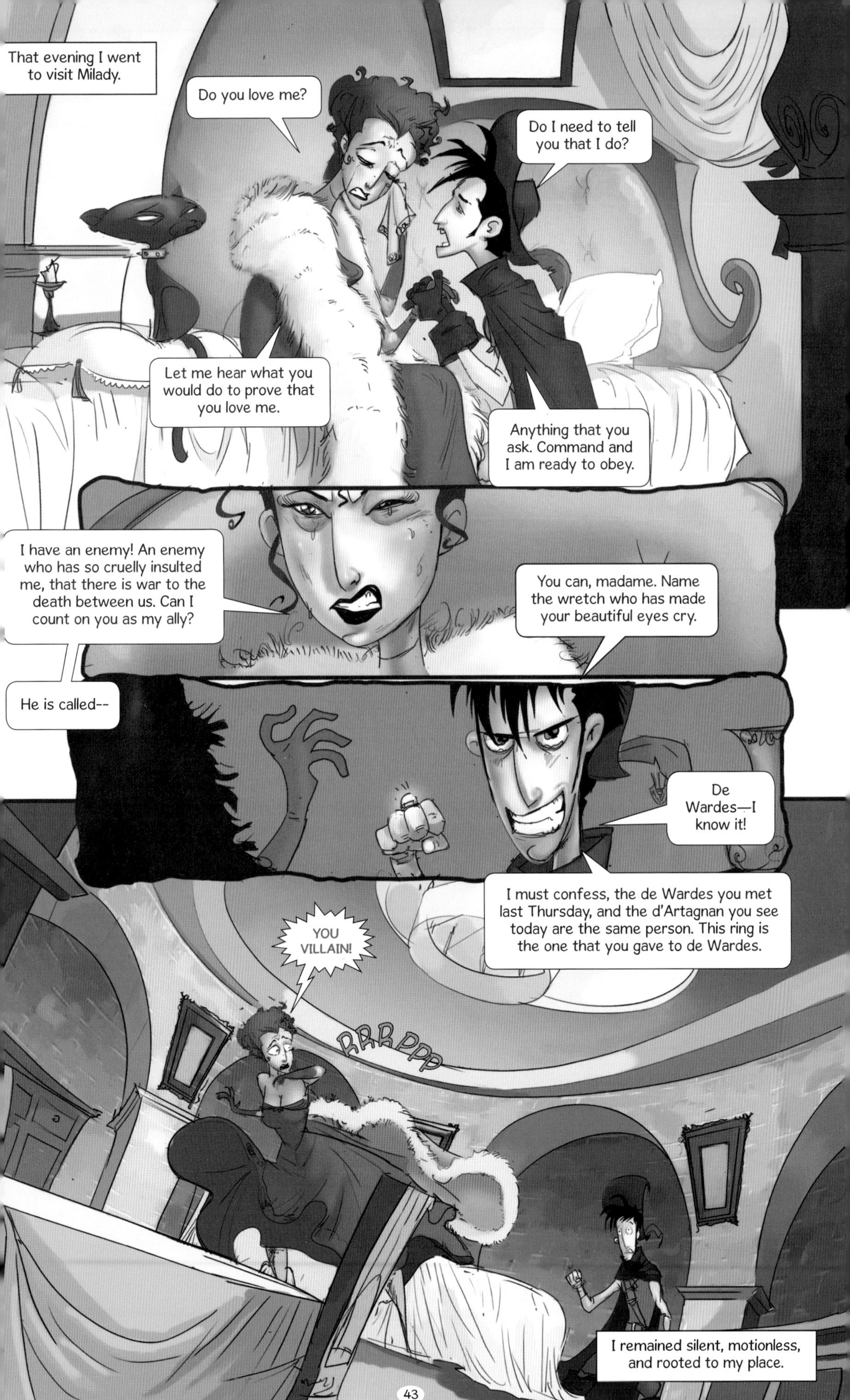
That evening I went to visit Milady.
Do you love me?
Do I need to tell you that I do?
Let me hear what you would do to prove that you love me.
Anything that you ask. Command and I am ready to obey.
I have an enemy! An enemy who has so cruelly insulted me, that there is war to the death between us. Can I count on you as my ally?
You can, madame. Name the wretch who has made your beautiful eyes cry.
He is called--
De Wardes—I know it!
I must confess, the de Wardes you met last Thursday, and the d'Artagnan you see today are the same person. This ring is the one that you gave to de Wardes.
YOU VILLAIN!
RRRRPPP
I remained silent, motionless, and rooted to my place.

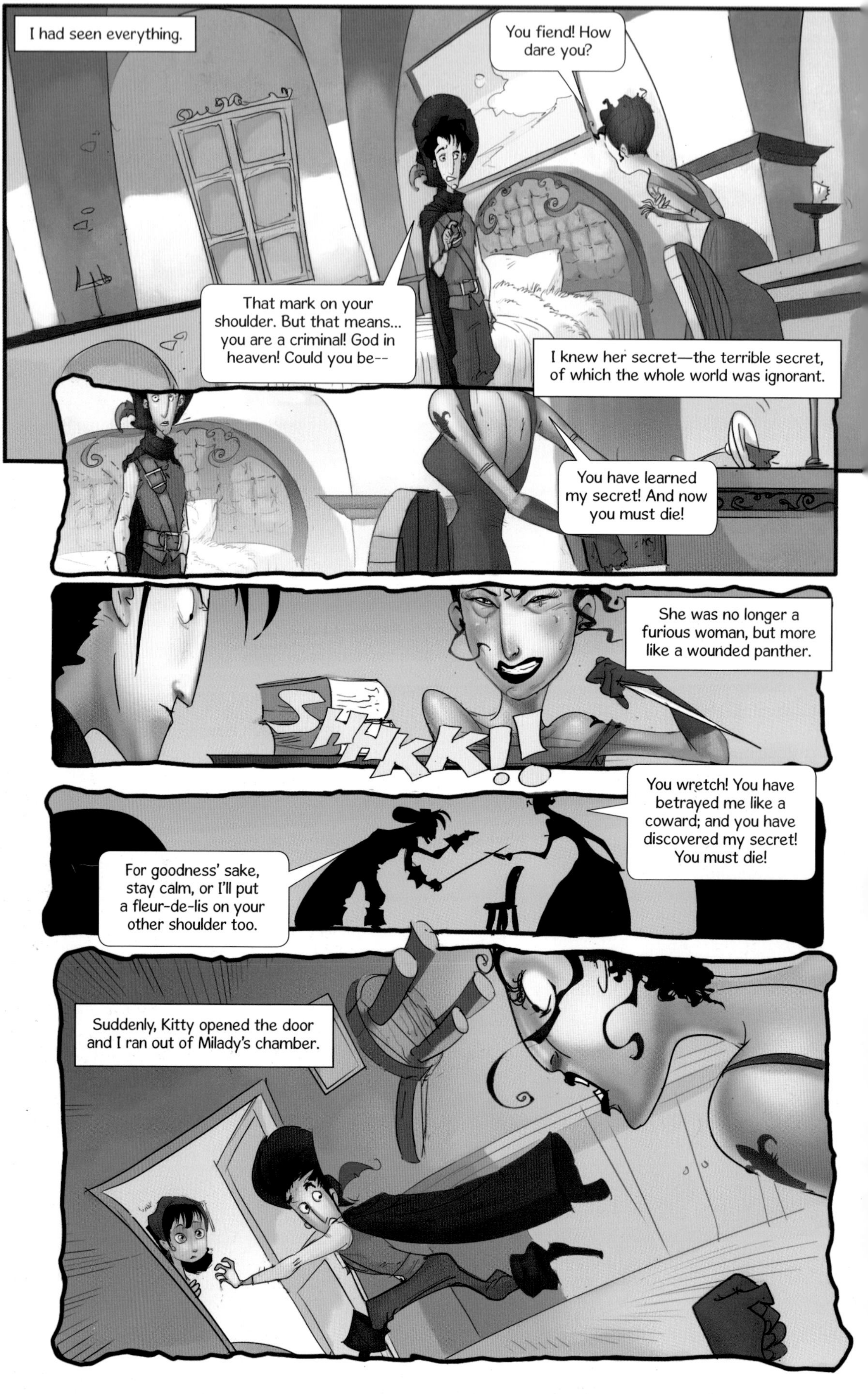
I had seen everything.
You fiend! How dare you?
That mark on your shoulder. But that means... you are a criminal! God in heaven! Could you be--
I knew her secret—the terrible secret, of which the whole world was ignorant.
You have learned my secret! And now you must die!
She was no longer a furious woman, but more like a wounded panther.
SHKK!!
You wretch! You have betrayed me like a coward; and you have discovered my secret! You must die!
For goodness' sake, stay calm, or I'll put a fleur-de-lis on your other shoulder too.
Suddenly, Kitty opened the door and I ran out of Milady's chamber.

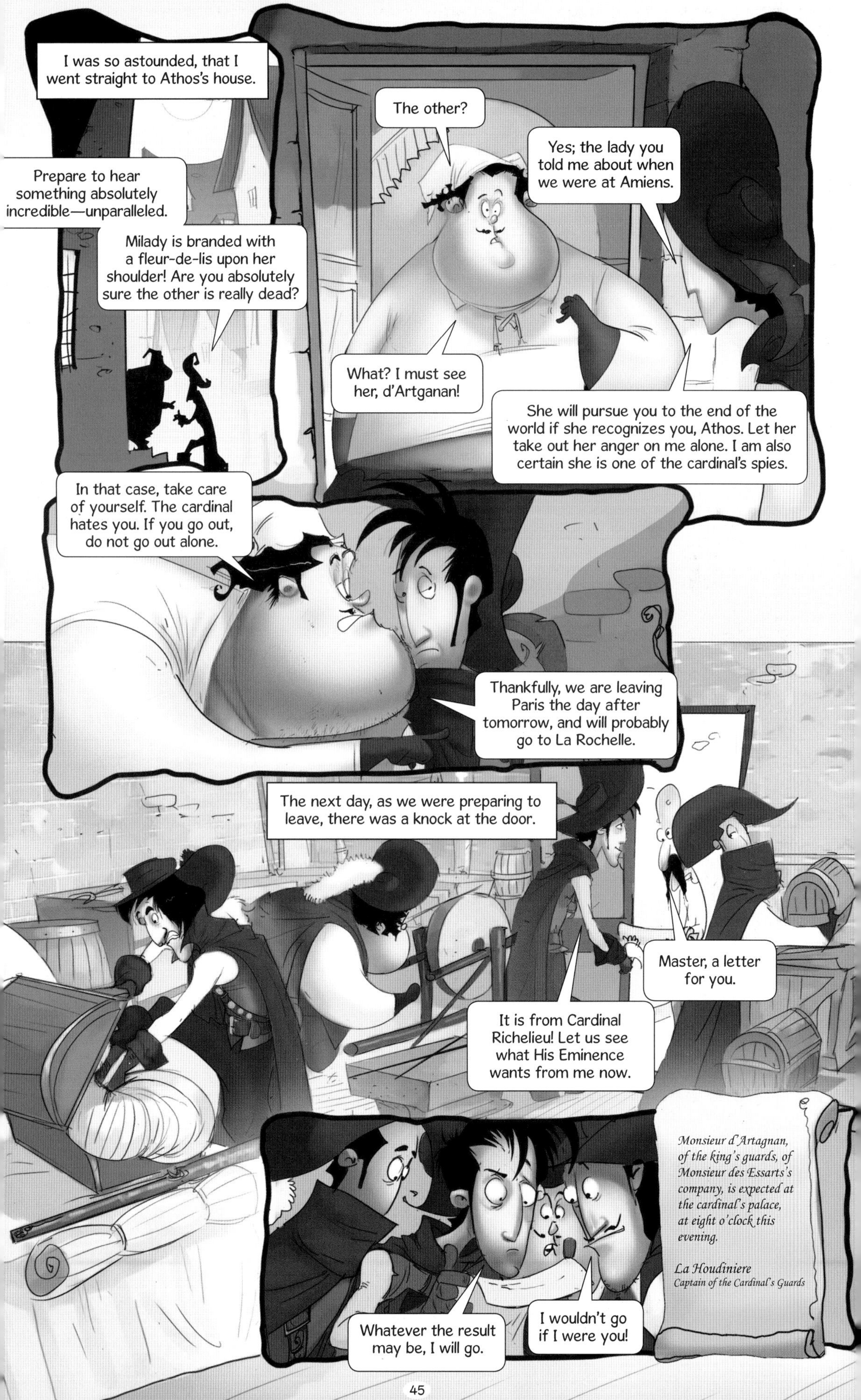
I was so astounded, that I went straight to Athos's house.
Prepare to hear something absolutely incredible—unparalleled.
Milady is branded with a fleur-de-lis upon her shoulder! Are you absolutely sure the other is really dead?
The other?
Yes; the lady you told me about when we were at Amiens.
What? I must see her, d'Artganan!
She will pursue you to the end of the world if she recognizes you, Athos. Let her take out her anger on me alone. I am also certain she is one of the cardinal's spies.
In that case, take care of yourself. The cardinal hates you. If you go out, do not go out alone.
Thankfully, we are leaving Paris the day after tomorrow, and will probably go to La Rochelle.
The next day, as we were preparing to leave, there was a knock at the door.
Master, a letter for you.
It is from Cardinal Richelieu! Let us see what His Eminence wants from me now.
Monsieur d'Artagnan, of the king's guards, of Monsieur des Essarts's company, is expected at the cardinal's palace, at eight o'clock this evening.
La Houdiniere
Captain of the Cardinal's Guards
Whatever the result may be, I will go.
I wouldn't go if I were you!

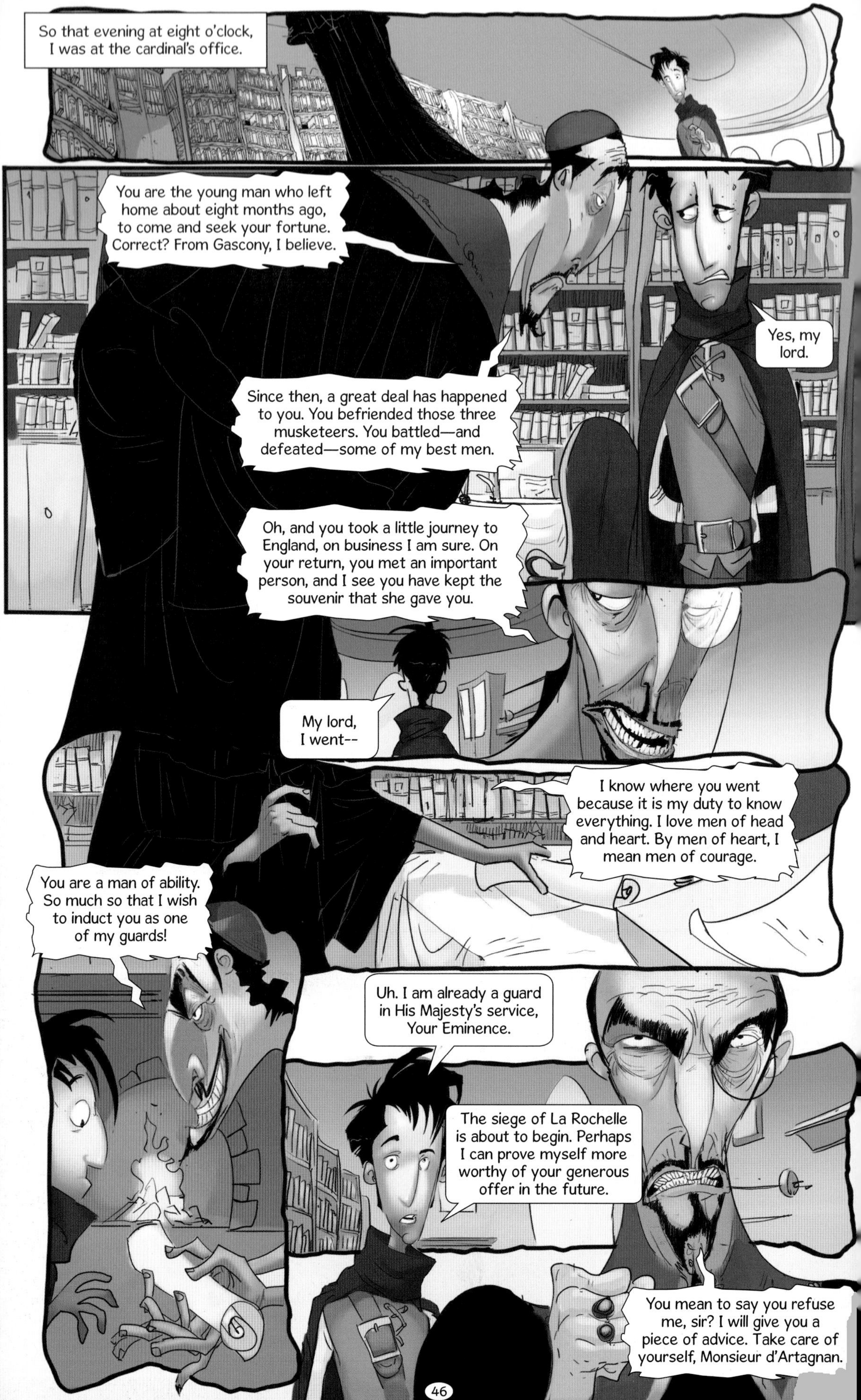
So that evening at eight o'clock, I was at the cardinal's office.
You are the young man who left home about eight months ago, to come and seek your fortune. Correct? From Gascony, I believe.
Yes, my lord.
Since then, a great deal has happened to you. You befriended those three musketeers. You battled—and defeated—some of my best men.
Oh, and you took a little journey to England, on business I am sure. On your return, you met an important person, and I see you have kept the souvenir that she gave you.
My lord, I went--
I know where you went because it is my duty to know everything. I love men of head and heart. By men of heart, I mean men of courage.
You are a man of ability. So much so that I wish to induct you as one of my guards!
Uh. I am already a guard in His Majesty's service, Your Eminence.
The siege of La Rochelle is about to begin. Perhaps I can prove myself more worthy of your generous offer in the future.
You mean to say you refuse me, sir? I will give you a piece of advice. Take care of yourself, Monsieur d'Artagnan.

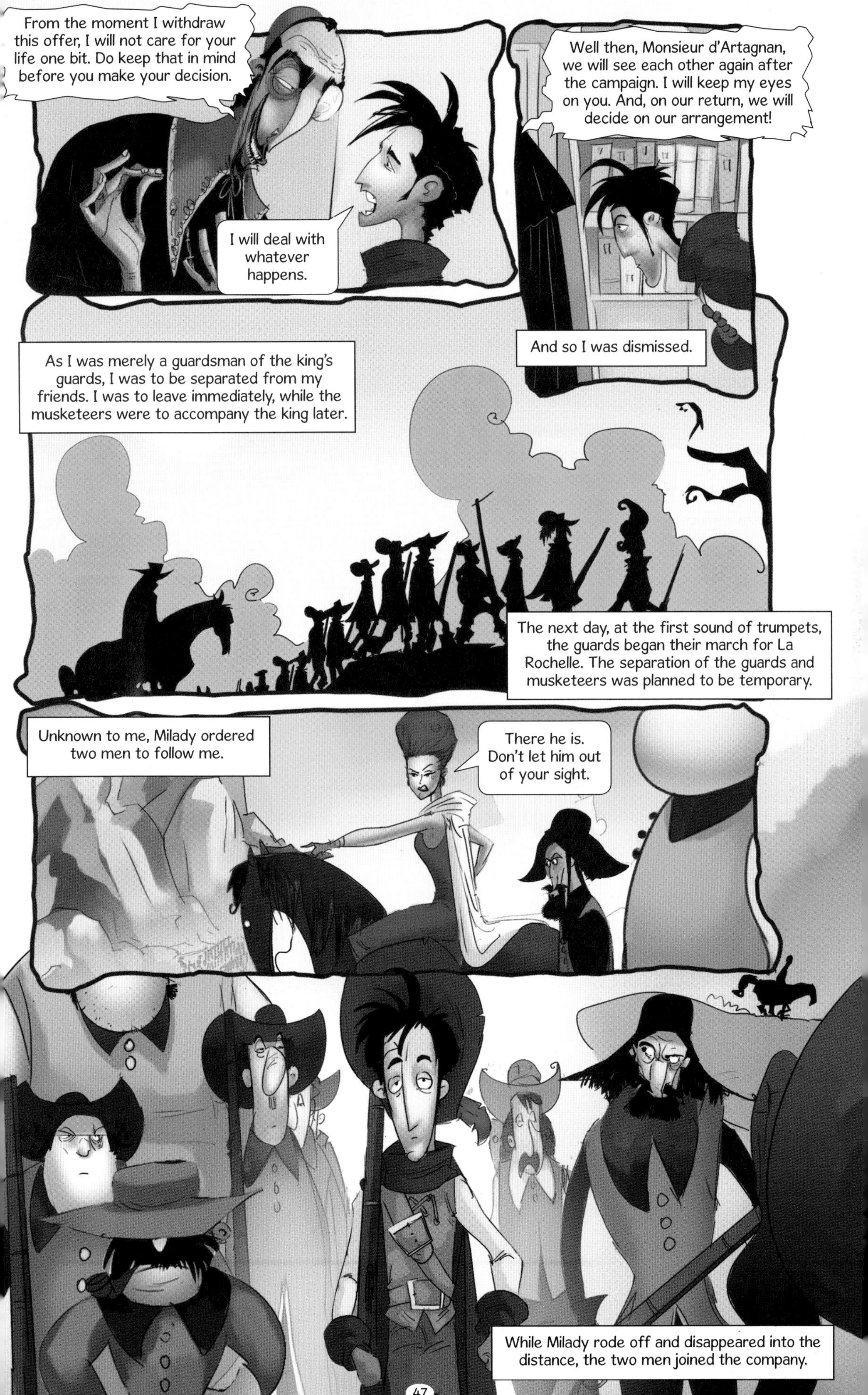
From the moment I withdraw this offer, I will not care for your life one bit. Do keep that in mind before you make your decision.
I will deal with whatever happens.
Well then, Monsieur d'Artagnan, we will see each other again after the campaign. I will keep my eyes on you. And, on our return, we will decide on our arrangement!
And so I was dismissed.
As I was merely a guardsman of the king's guards, I was to be separated from my friends. I was to leave immediately, while the musketeers were to accompany the king later.
The next day, at the first sound of trumpets, the guards began their march for La Rochelle. The separation of the guards and musketeers was planned to be temporary.
Unknown to me, Milady ordered two men to follow me.
There he is. Don't let him out of your sight.
While Milady rode off and disappeared into the distance, the two men joined the company.

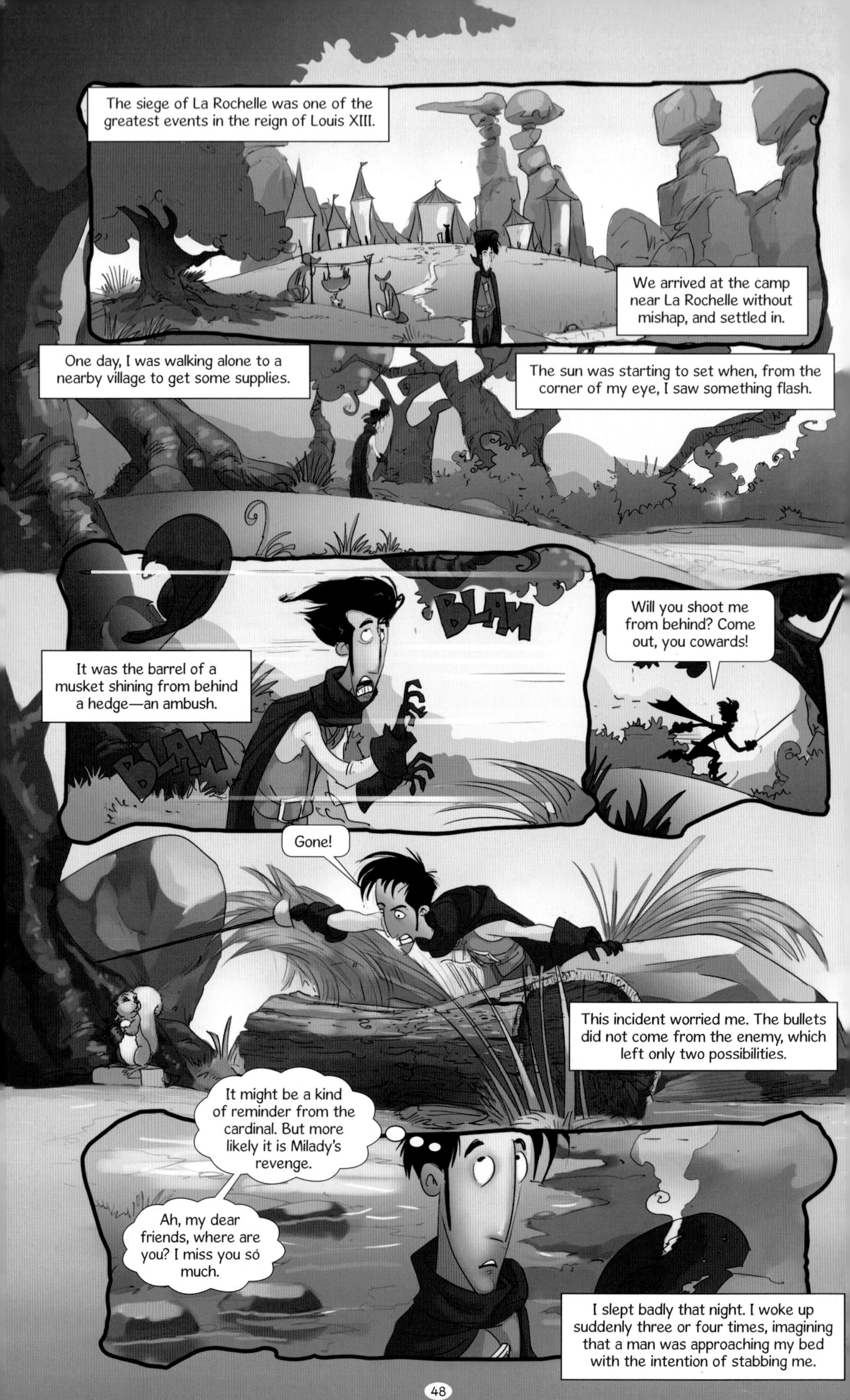

The siege of La Rochelle was one of the greatest events in the reign of Louis XIII.
We arrived at the camp near La Rochelle without mishap, and settled in.
One day, I was walking alone to a nearby village to get some supplies.
The sun was starting to set when, from the corner of my eye, I saw something flash.
BLAM
It was the barrel of a musket shining from behind a hedge—an ambush.
BLAM
Will you shoot me from behind? Come out, you cowards!
Gone!
This incident worried me. The bullets did not come from the enemy, which left only two possibilities.
It might be a kind of reminder from the cardinal. But more likely it is Milady's revenge.
Ah, my dear friends, where are you? I miss you so much.
I slept badly that night. I woke up suddenly three or four times, imagining that a man was approaching my bed with the intention of stabbing me.

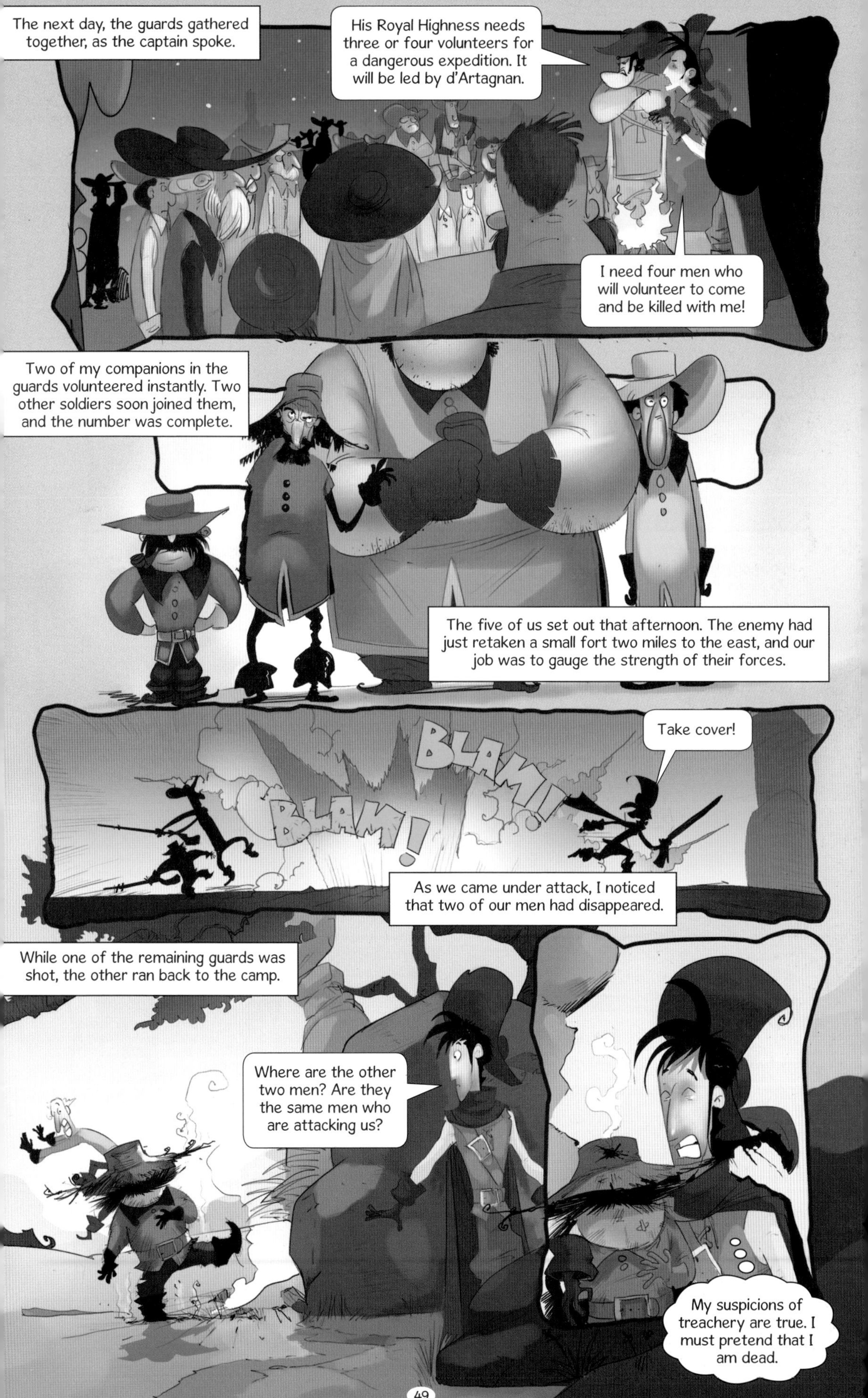

The next day, the guards gathered together, as the captain spoke.
His Royal Highness needs three or four volunteers for a dangerous expedition. It will be led by d'Artagnan.
I need four men who will volunteer to come and be killed with me!
Two of my companions in the guards volunteered instantly. Two other soldiers soon joined them, and the number was complete.
The five of us set out that afternoon. The enemy had just retaken a small fort two miles to the east, and our job was to gauge the strength of their forces.
BLAM!!
BLAM!
Take cover!
As we came under attack, I noticed that two of our men had disappeared.
While one of the remaining guards was shot, the other ran back to the camp.
Where are the other two men? Are they the same men who are attacking us?
My suspicions of treachery are true. I must pretend that I am dead.

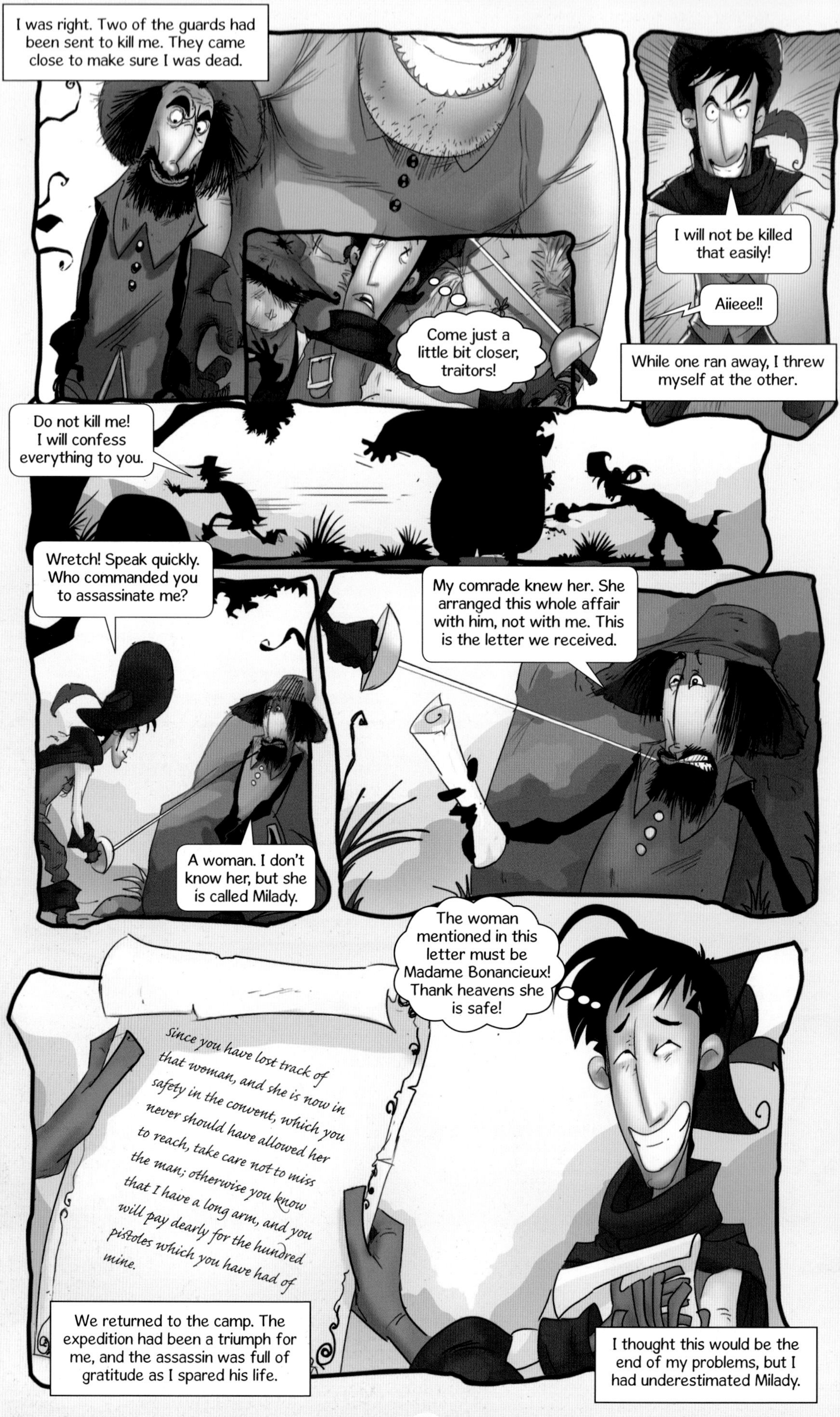
I was right. Two of the guards had been sent to kill me. They came close to make sure I was dead.
Come just a little bit closer, traitors!
I will not be killed that easily!
Aiieee!!
While one ran away, I threw myself at the other.
Do not kill me! I will confess everything to you.
Wretch! Speak quickly. Who commanded you to assassinate me?
A woman. I don't know her, but she is called Milady.
My comrade knew her. She arranged this whole affair with him, not with me. This is the letter we received.
Since you have lost track of that woman, and she is now in safety in the convent, which you never should have allowed her to reach, take care not to miss the man; otherwise you know that I have a long arm, and you will pay dearly for the hundred pistoles which you have had of mine.
The woman mentioned in this letter must be Madame Bonancieux! Thank heavens she is safe!
We returned to the camp. The expedition had been a triumph for me, and the assassin was full of gratitude as I spared his life.
I thought this would be the end of my problems, but I had underestimated Milady.

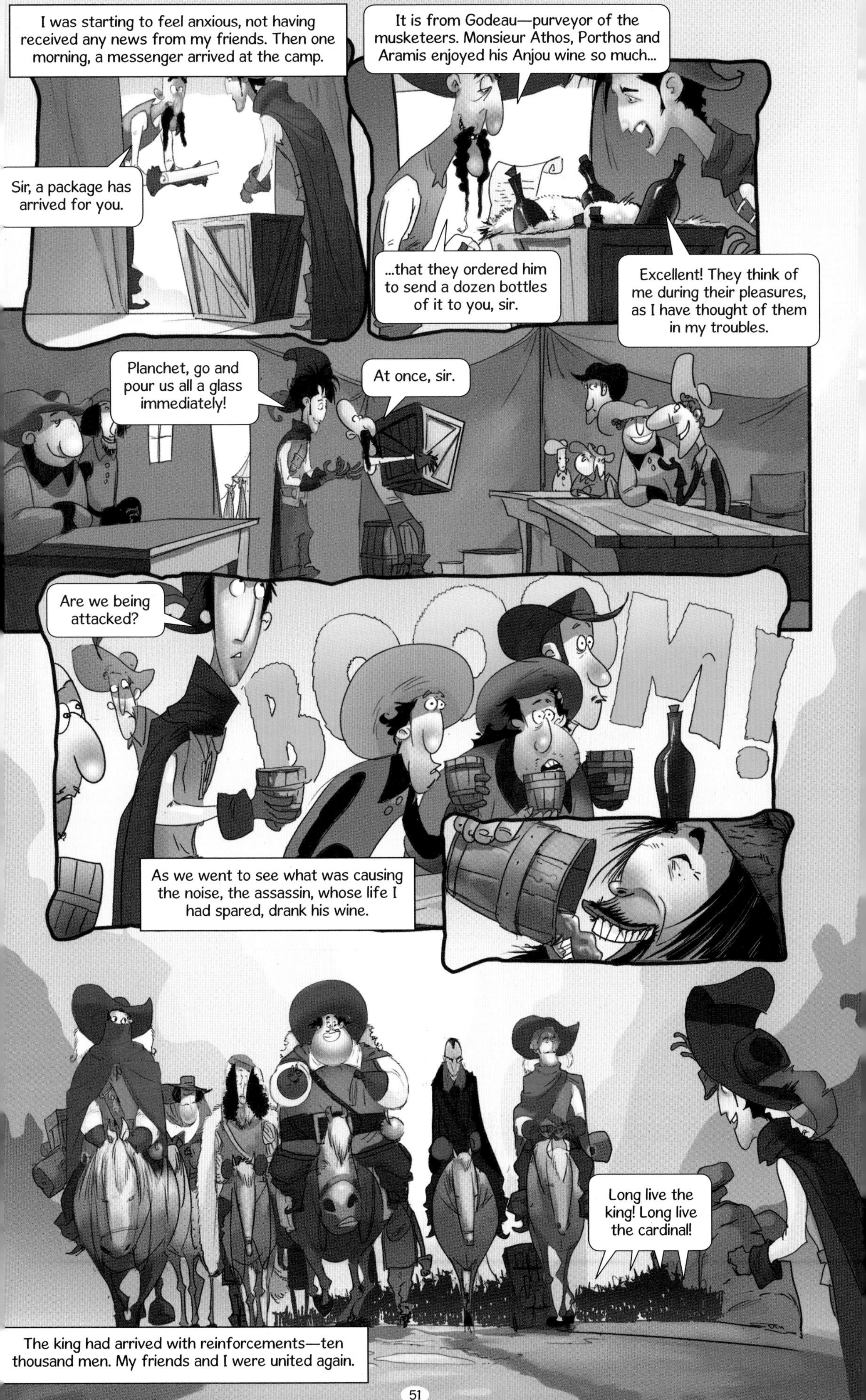

I was starting to feel anxious, not having received any news from my friends. Then one morning, a messenger arrived at the camp.
Sir, a package has arrived for you.
It is from Godeau—purveyor of the musketeers. Monsieur Athos, Porthos and Aramis enjoyed his Anjou wine so much...
...that they ordered him to send a dozen bottles of it to you, sir.
Excellent! They think of me during their pleasures, as I have thought of them in my troubles.
Planchet, go and pour us all a glass immediately!
At once, sir.
Are we being attacked?
BOOM!
As we went to see what was causing the noise, the assassin, whose life I had spared, drank his wine.
Long live the king! Long live the cardinal!
The king had arrived with reinforcements—ten thousand men. My friends and I were united again.

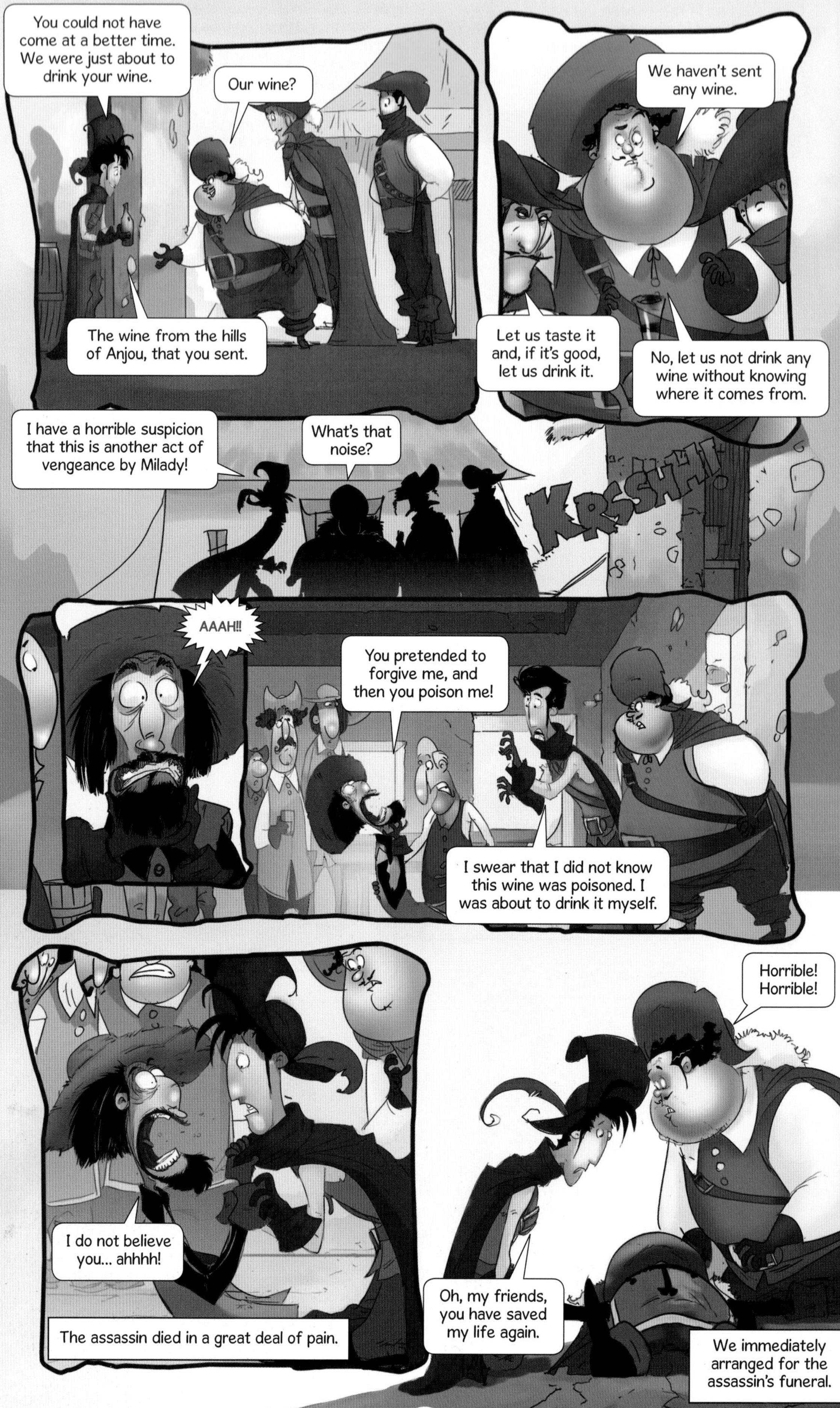

You could not have come at a better time. We were just about to drink your wine.
Our wine?
The wine from the hills of Anjou, that you sent.
We haven't sent any wine.
Let us taste it and, if it's good, let us drink it.
No, let us not drink any wine without knowing where it comes from.
I have a horrible suspicion that this is another act of vengeance by Milady!
What's that noise?
KRSSHH!
AAAH!!
You pretended to forgive me, and then you poison me!
I swear that I did not know this wine was poisoned. I was about to drink it myself.
I do not believe you... ahhhh!
The assassin died in a great deal of pain.
Horrible! Horrible!
Oh, my friends, you have saved my life again.
We immediately arranged for the assassin's funeral.

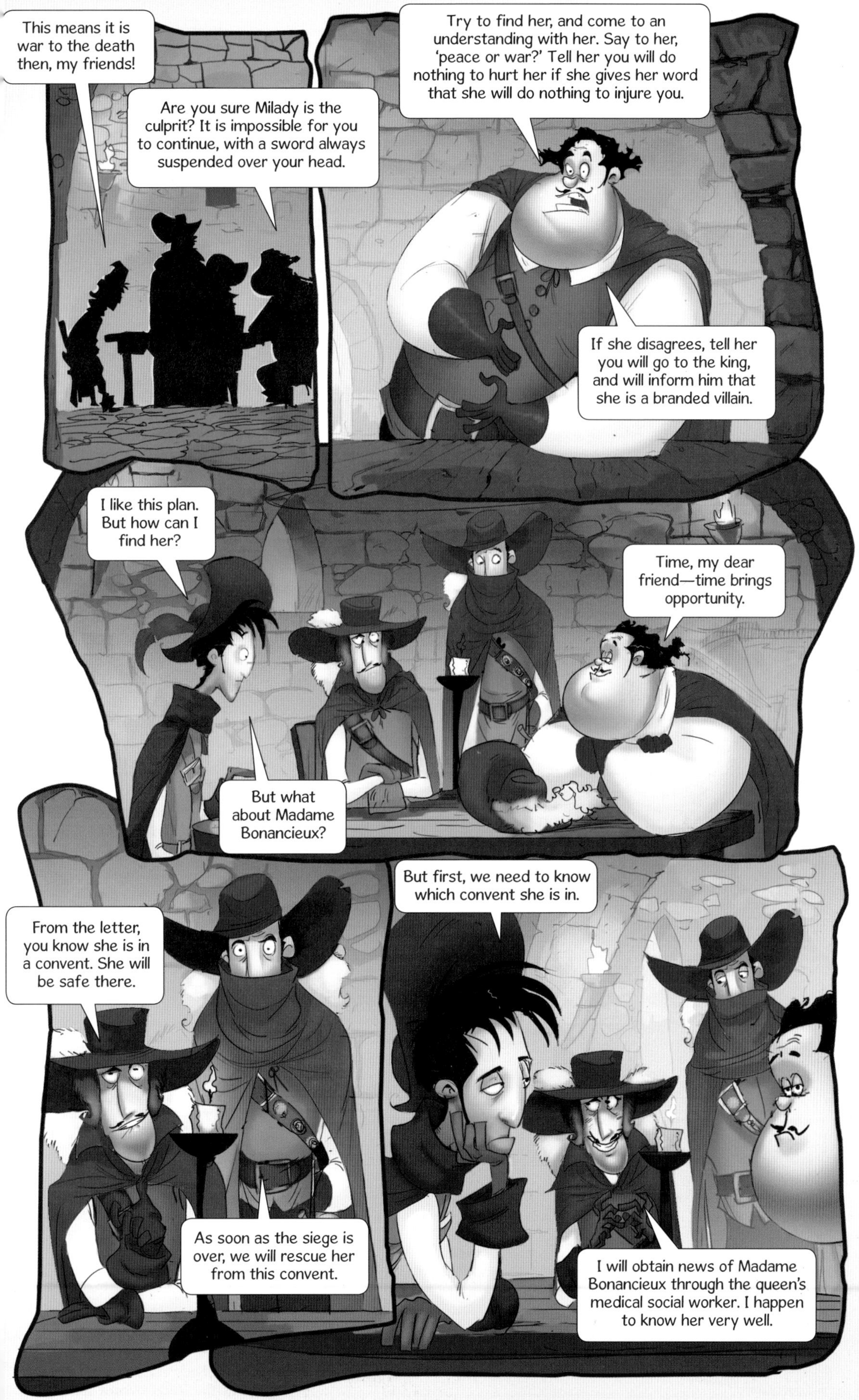

This means it is war to the death then, my friends!
Are you sure Milady is the culprit? It is impossible for you to continue, with a sword always suspended over your head.
Try to find her, and come to an understanding with her. Say to her, 'peace or war?' Tell her you will do nothing to hurt her if she gives her word that she will do nothing to injure you.
If she disagrees, tell her you will go to the king, and will inform him that she is a branded villain.
I like this plan. But how can I find her?
Time, my dear friend—time brings opportunity.
But what about Madame Bonancieux?
From the letter, you know she is in a convent. She will be safe there.
As soon as the siege is over, we will rescue her from this convent.
But first, we need to know which convent she is in.
I will obtain news of Madame Bonancieux through the queen's medical social worker. I happen to know her very well.

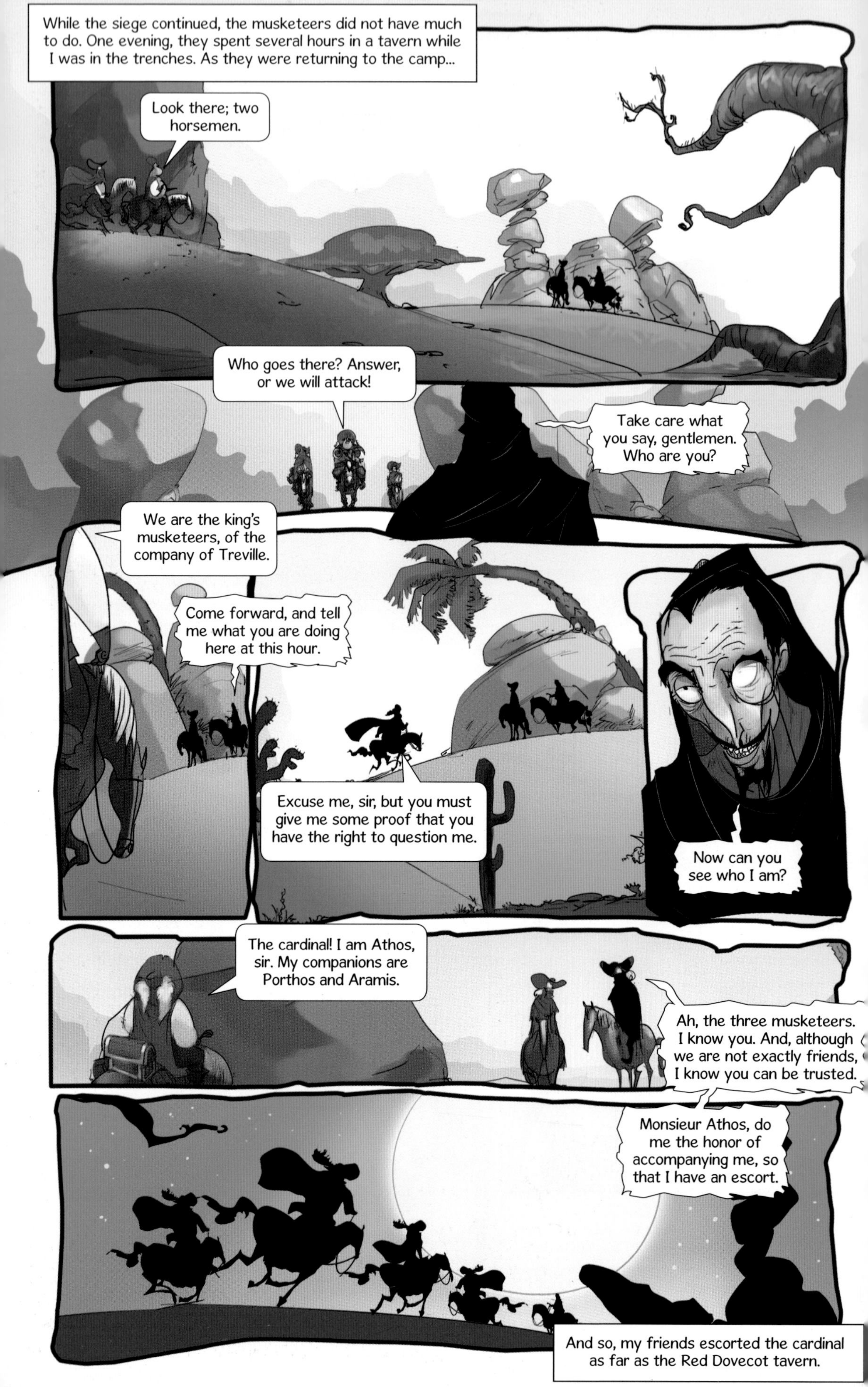

While the siege continued, the musketeers did not have much to do. One evening, they spent several hours in a tavern while I was in the trenches. As they were returning to the camp...
Look there; two horsemen.
Who goes there? Answer, or we will attack!
Take care what you say, gentlemen. Who are you?
We are the king's musketeers, of the company of Treville.
Come forward, and tell me what you are doing here at this hour.
Excuse me, sir, but you must give me some proof that you have the right to question me.
Now can you see who I am?
The cardinal! I am Athos, sir. My companions are Porthos and Aramis.
Ah, the three musketeers. I know you. And, although we are not exactly friends, I know you can be trusted.
Monsieur Athos, do me the honor of accompanying me, so that I have an escort.
And so, my friends escorted the cardinal as far as the Red Dovecot tavern.

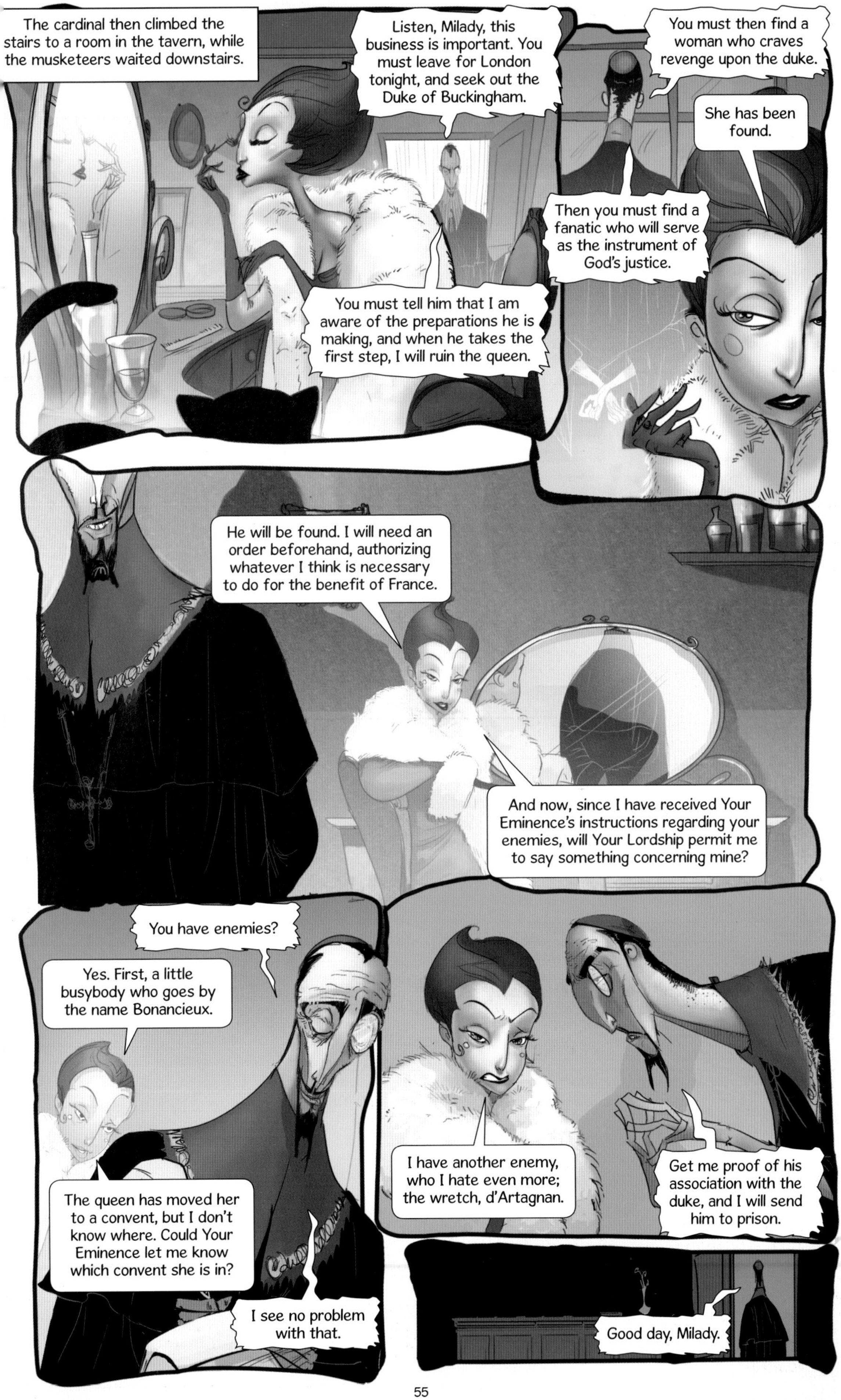

The cardinal then climbed the stairs to a room in the tavern, while the musketeers waited downstairs.
Listen, Milady, this business is important. You must leave for London tonight, and seek out the Duke of Buckingham.
You must tell him that I am aware of the preparations he is making, and when he takes the first step, I will ruin the queen.
You must then find a woman who craves revenge upon the duke.
She has been found.
Then you must find a fanatic who will serve as the instrument of God's justice.
He will be found. I will need an order beforehand, authorizing whatever I think is necessary to do for the benefit of France.
And now, since I have received Your Eminence's instructions regarding your enemies, will Your Lordship permit me to say something concerning mine?
You have enemies?
Yes. First, a little busybody who goes by the name Bonancieux.
The queen has moved her to a convent, but I don't know where. Could Your Eminence let me know which convent she is in?
I see no problem with that.
I have another enemy, who I hate even more; the wretch, d'Artagnan.
Get me proof of his association with the duke, and I will send him to prison.
Good day, Milady.

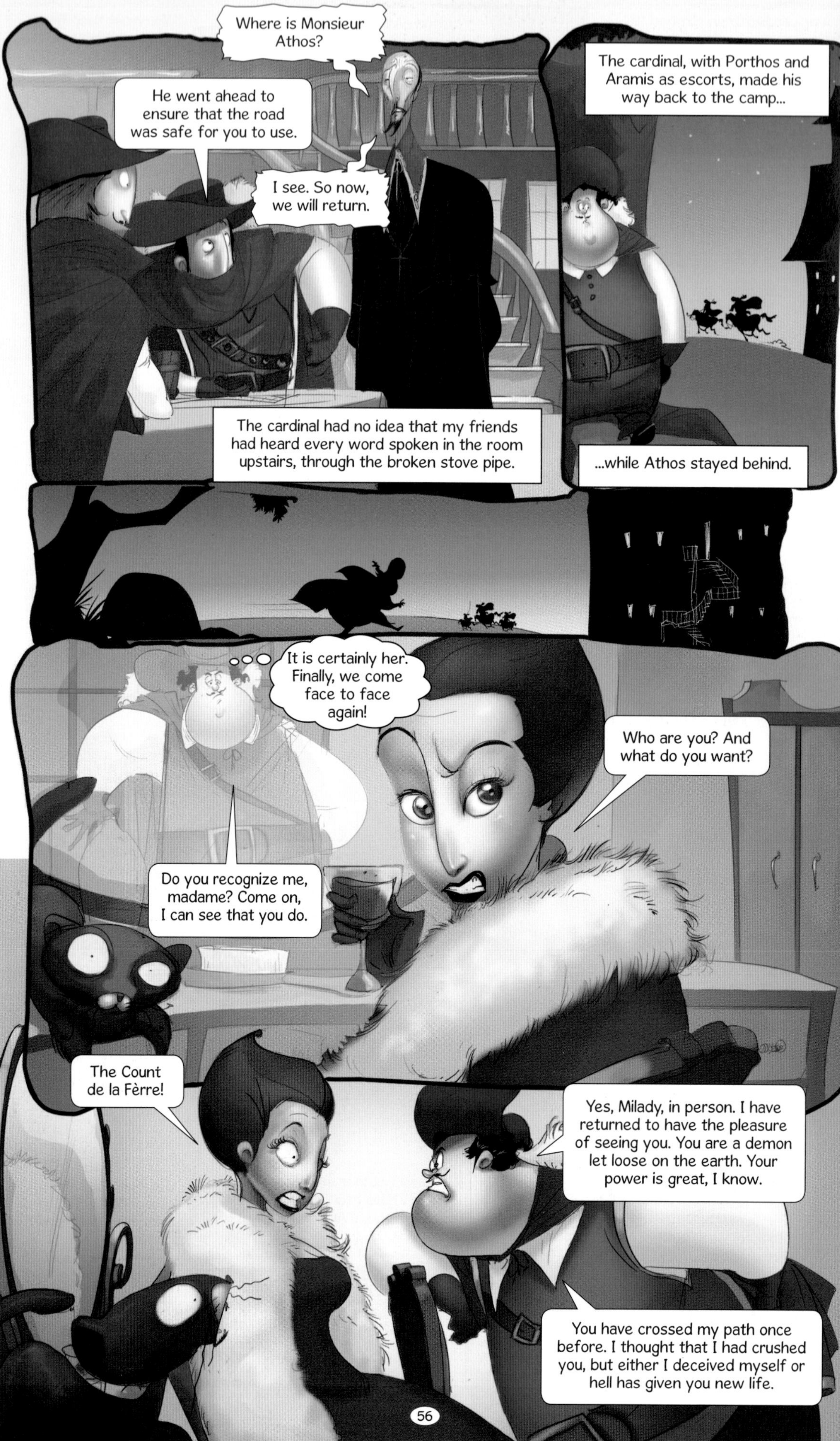
Where is Monsieur Athos?
He went ahead to ensure that the road was safe for you to use.
I see. So now, we will return.
The cardinal had no idea that my friends had heard every word spoken in the room upstairs, through the broken stove pipe.
The cardinal, with Porthos and Aramis as escorts, made his way back to the camp...
...while Athos stayed behind.
It is certainly her. Finally, we come face to face again!
Who are you? And what do you want?
Do you recognize me, madame? Come on, I can see that you do.
The Count de la Fèrre!
Yes, Milady, in person. I have returned to have the pleasure of seeing you. You are a demon let loose on the earth. Your power is great, I know.
You have crossed my path once before. I thought that I had crushed you, but either I deceived myself or hell has given you new life.

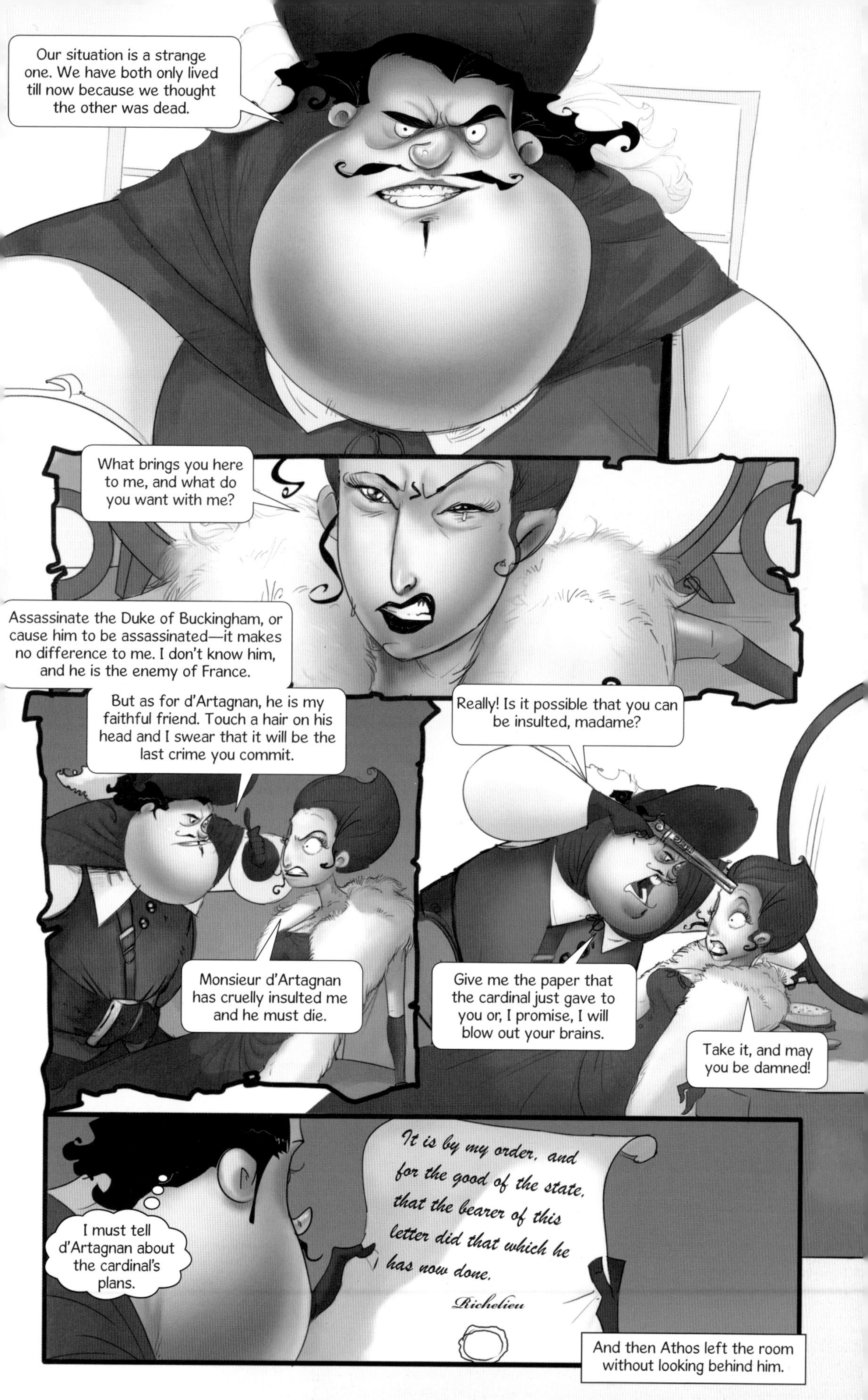
Our situation is a strange one. We have both only lived till now because we thought the other was dead.
What brings you here to me, and what do you want with me?
Assassinate the Duke of Buckingham, or cause him to be assassinated—it makes no difference to me. I don't know him, and he is the enemy of France.
But as for d'Artagnan, he is my faithful friend. Touch a hair on his head and I swear that it will be the last crime you commit.
Monsieur d'Artagnan has cruelly insulted me and he must die.
Really! Is it possible that you can be insulted, madame?
Give me the paper that the cardinal just gave to you or, I promise, I will blow out your brains.
Take it, and may you be damned!
I must tell d'Artagnan about the cardinal's plans.
It is by my order, and for the good of the state, that the bearer of this letter did that which he has now done.
Richelieu
And then Athos left the room without looking behind him.

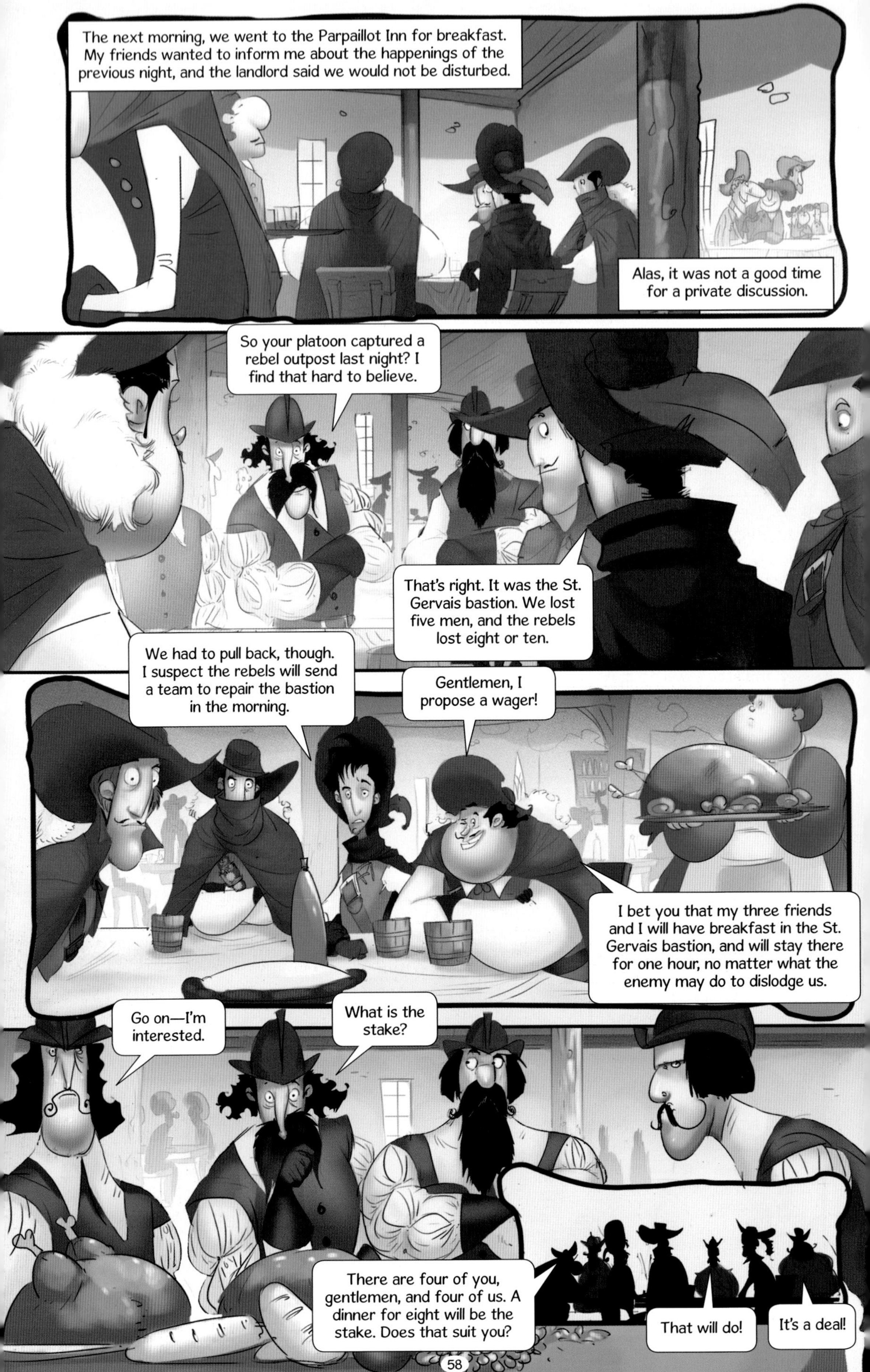

The next morning, we went to the Parpaillot Inn for breakfast. My friends wanted to inform me about the happenings of the previous night, and the landlord said we would not be disturbed.
Alas, it was not a good time for a private discussion.
So your platoon captured a rebel outpost last night? I find that hard to believe.
That's right. It was the St. Gervais bastion. We lost five men, and the rebels lost eight or ten.
We had to pull back, though. I suspect the rebels will send a team to repair the bastion in the morning.
Gentlemen, I propose a wager!
I bet you that my three friends and I will have breakfast in the St. Gervais bastion, and will stay there for one hour, no matter what the enemy may do to dislodge us.
Go on—I'm interested.
What is the stake?
There are four of you, gentlemen, and four of us. A dinner for eight will be the stake. Does that suit you?
That will do!
It's a deal!

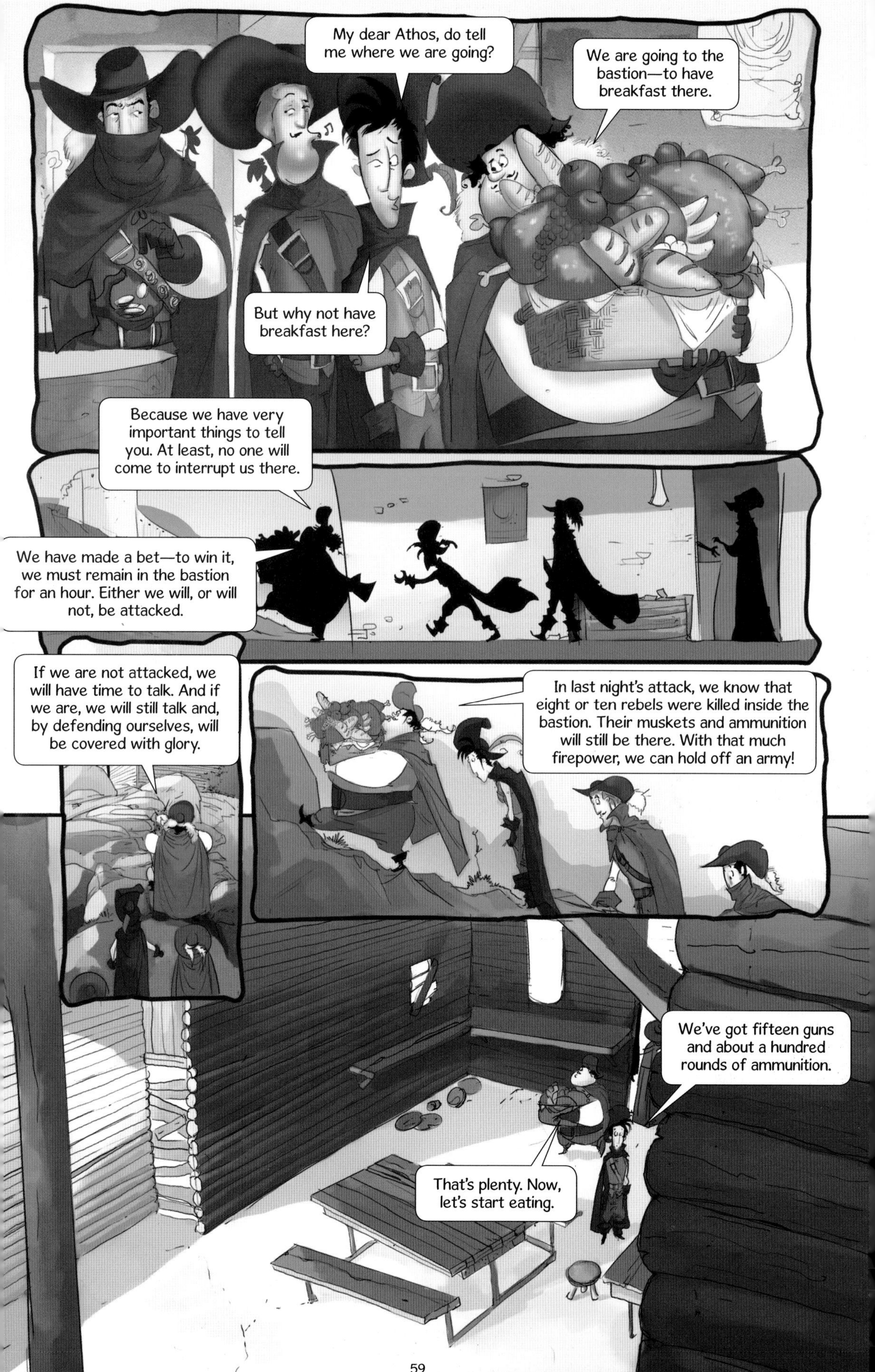
My dear Athos, do tell me where we are going?
We are going to the bastion—to have breakfast there.
But why not have breakfast here?
Because we have very important things to tell you. At least, no one will come to interrupt us there.
We have made a bet—to win it, we must remain in the bastion for an hour. Either we will, or will not, be attacked.
If we are not attacked, we will have time to talk. And if we are, we will still talk and, by defending ourselves, will be covered with glory.
In last night's attack, we know that eight or ten rebels were killed inside the bastion. Their muskets and ammunition will still be there. With that much firepower, we can hold off an army!
We've got fifteen guns and about a hundred rounds of ammunition.
That's plenty. Now, let's start eating.

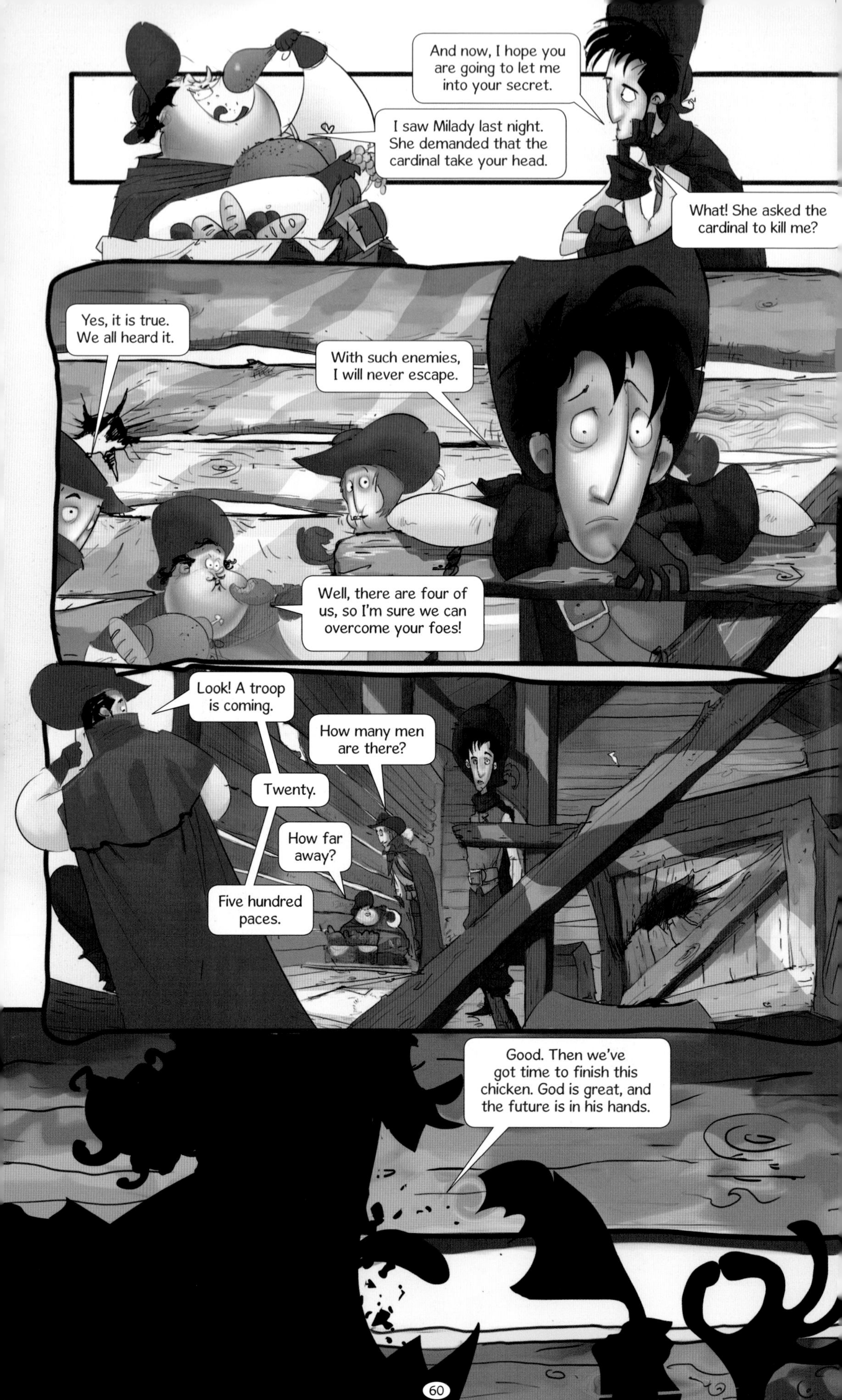
And now, I hope you are going to let me into your secret.
I saw Milady last night. She demanded that the cardinal take your head.
What! She asked the cardinal to kill me?
Yes, it is true. We all heard it.
With such enemies, I will never escape.
Well, there are four of us, so I'm sure we can overcome your foes!
Look! A troop is coming.
How many men are there?
Twenty.
How far away?
Five hundred paces.
Good. Then we've got time to finish this chicken. God is great, and the future is in his hands.

Where are you going?

Just to make a quick speech.

Gentlemen, my friends and I were just enjoying breakfast and, as you know, there is nothing worse than being interrupted in the middle of a meal.

So, if you would kindly wait until we've finished, that would be appreciated.

Unless, of course, you would consider switching sides and joining us in a toast to the King of France.

BANG
BANG

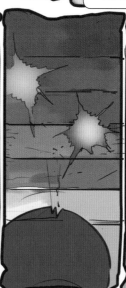

I'll take that as a no then!

BLAM!
BLAM!

So, did you learn anything else about Milady's plans?

BLAM!

Just that she's going to England to assassinate the Duke of Buckingham, or arrange for him to be assassinated.

BLAM!
BLAM!

Assassination? That's outrageous!

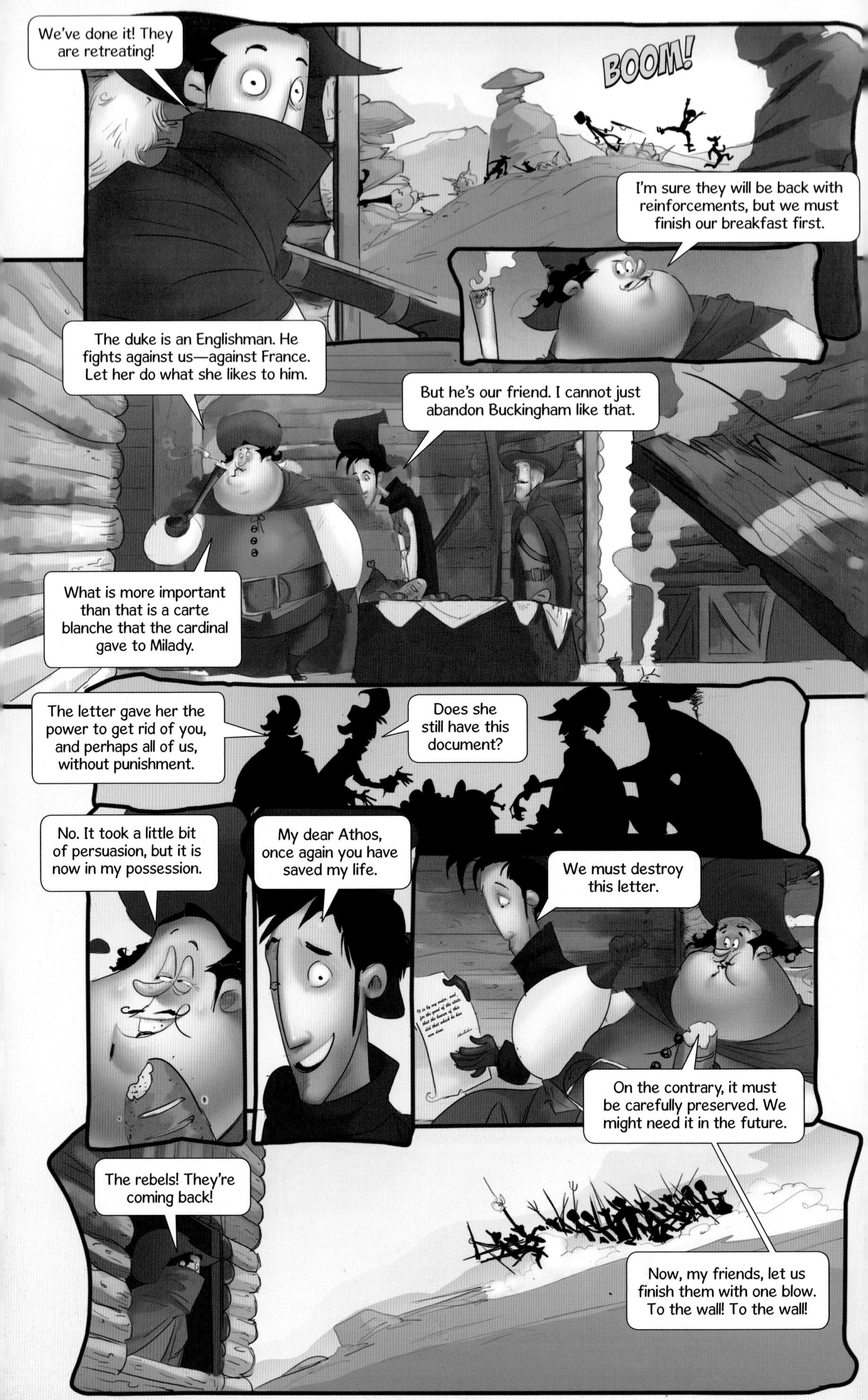
We've done it! They are retreating!
BOOM!
I'm sure they will be back with reinforcements, but we must finish our breakfast first.
The duke is an Englishman. He fights against us—against France. Let her do what she likes to him.
But he's our friend. I cannot just abandon Buckingham like that.
What is more important than that is a carte blanche that the cardinal gave to Milady.
The letter gave her the power to get rid of you, and perhaps all of us, without punishment.
Does she still have this document?
No. It took a little bit of persuasion, but it is now in my possession.
My dear Athos, once again you have saved my life.
We must destroy this letter.
On the contrary, it must be carefully preserved. We might need it in the future.
The rebels! They're coming back!
Now, my friends, let us finish them with one blow. To the wall! To the wall!

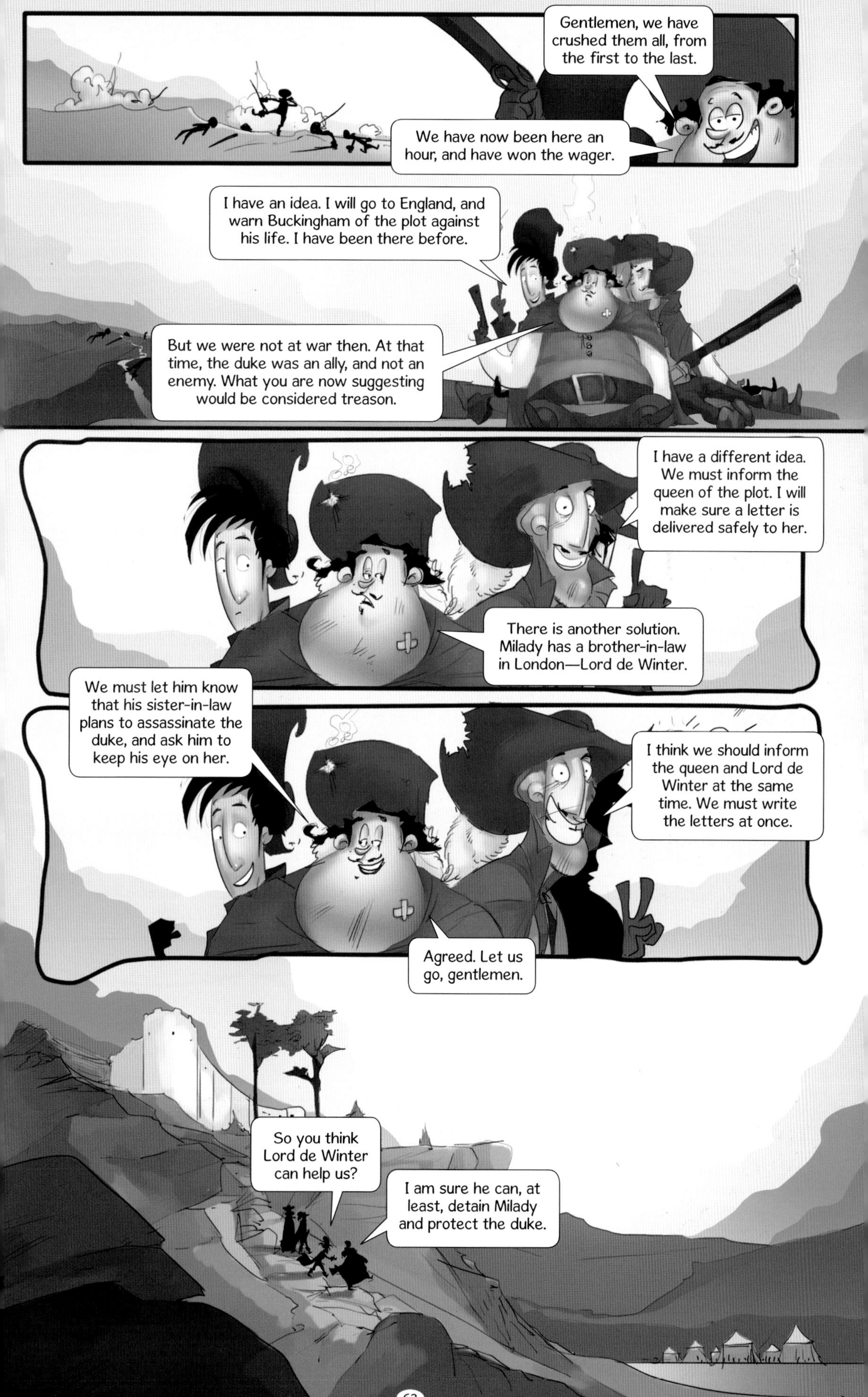
Gentlemen, we have crushed them all, from the first to the last.
We have now been here an hour, and have won the wager.
I have an idea. I will go to England, and warn Buckingham of the plot against his life. I have been there before.
But we were not at war then. At that time, the duke was an ally, and not an enemy. What you are now suggesting would be considered treason.
I have a different idea. We must inform the queen of the plot. I will make sure a letter is delivered safely to her.
There is another solution. Milady has a brother-in-law in London—Lord de Winter.
We must let him know that his sister-in-law plans to assassinate the duke, and ask him to keep his eye on her.
I think we should inform the queen and Lord de Winter at the same time. We must write the letters at once.
Agreed. Let us go, gentlemen.
So you think Lord de Winter can help us?
I am sure he can, at least, detain Milady and protect the duke.

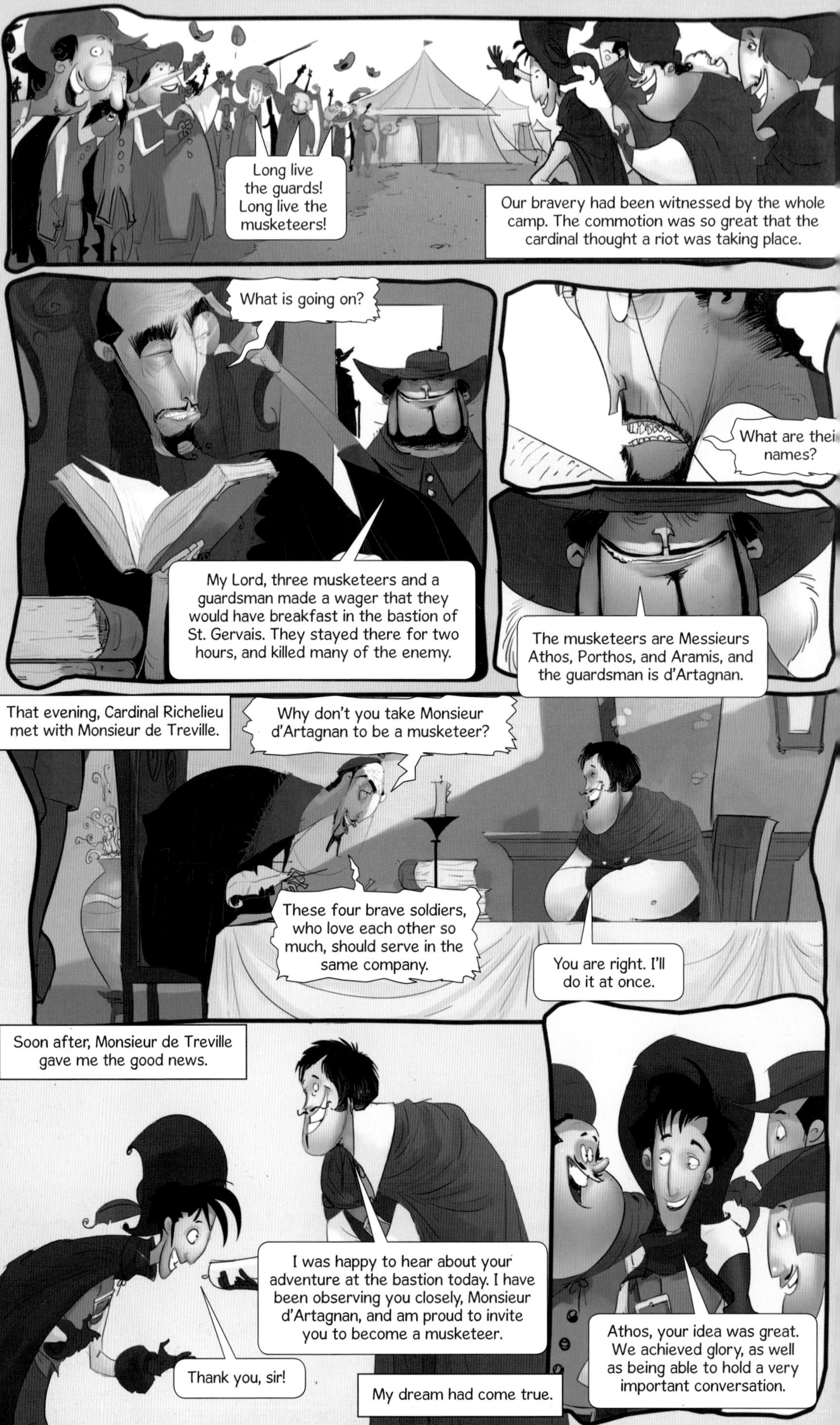
Long live the guards! Long live the musketeers!
Our bravery had been witnessed by the whole camp. The commotion was so great that the cardinal thought a riot was taking place.
What is going on?
My Lord, three musketeers and a guardsman made a wager that they would have breakfast in the bastion of St. Gervais. They stayed there for two hours, and killed many of the enemy.
What are thei names?
The musketeers are Messieurs Athos, Porthos, and Aramis, and the guardsman is d'Artagnan.
That evening, Cardinal Richelieu met with Monsieur de Treville.
Why don't you take Monsieur d'Artagnan to be a musketeer?
These four brave soldiers, who love each other so much, should serve in the same company.
You are right. I'll do it at once.
Soon after, Monsieur de Treville gave me the good news.
I was happy to hear about your adventure at the bastion today. I have been observing you closely, Monsieur d'Artagnan, and am proud to invite you to become a musketeer.
Thank you, sir!
My dream had come true.
Athos, your idea was great. We achieved glory, as well as being able to hold a very important conversation.

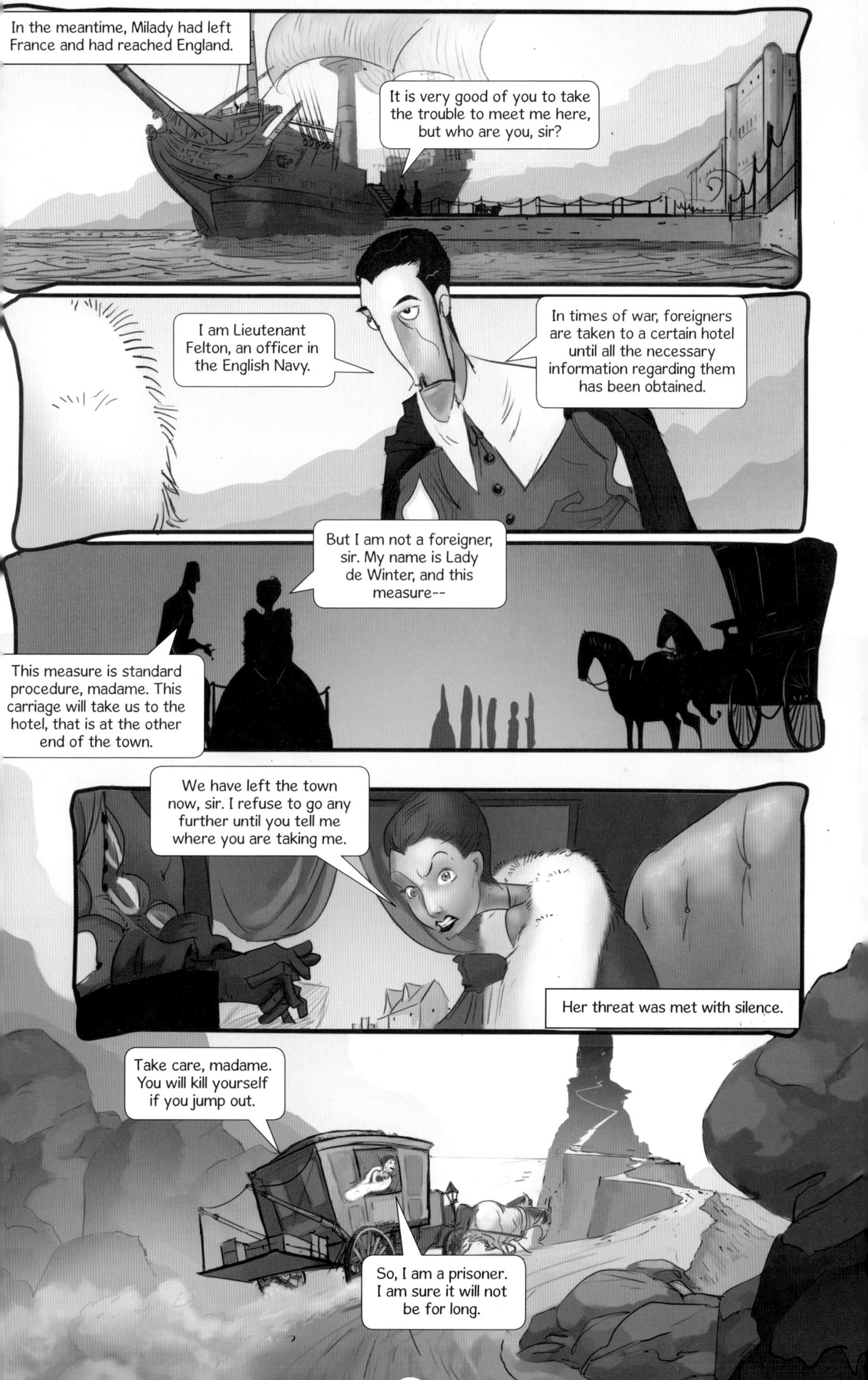

In the meantime, Milady had left France and had reached England.
It is very good of you to take the trouble to meet me here, but who are you, sir?
I am Lieutenant Felton, an officer in the English Navy.
In times of war, foreigners are taken to a certain hotel until all the necessary information regarding them has been obtained.
But I am not a foreigner, sir. My name is Lady de Winter, and this measure--
This measure is standard procedure, madame. This carriage will take us to the hotel, that is at the other end of the town.
We have left the town now, sir. I refuse to go any further until you tell me where you are taking me.
Her threat was met with silence.
Take care, madame. You will kill yourself if you jump out.
So, I am a prisoner. I am sure it will not be for long.

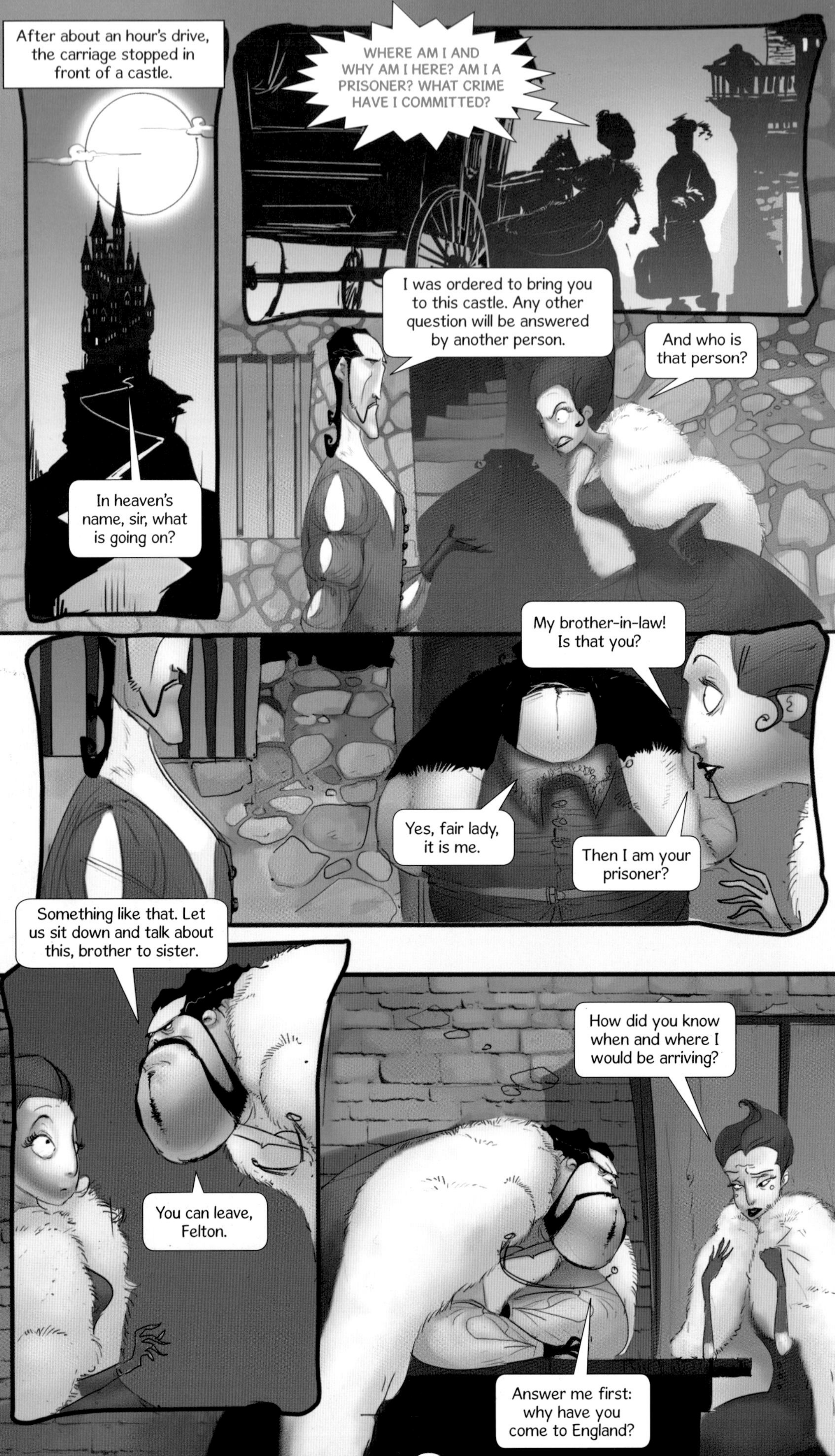

After about an hour's drive, the carriage stopped in front of a castle.
WHERE AM I AND WHY AM I HERE? AM I A PRISONER? WHAT CRIME HAVE I COMMITTED?
In heaven's name, sir, what is going on?
I was ordered to bring you to this castle. Any other question will be answered by another person.
And who is that person?
My brother-in-law! Is that you?
Yes, fair lady, it is me.
Then I am your prisoner?
Something like that. Let us sit down and talk about this, brother to sister.
You can leave, Felton.
How did you know when and where I would be arriving?
Answer me first: why have you come to England?

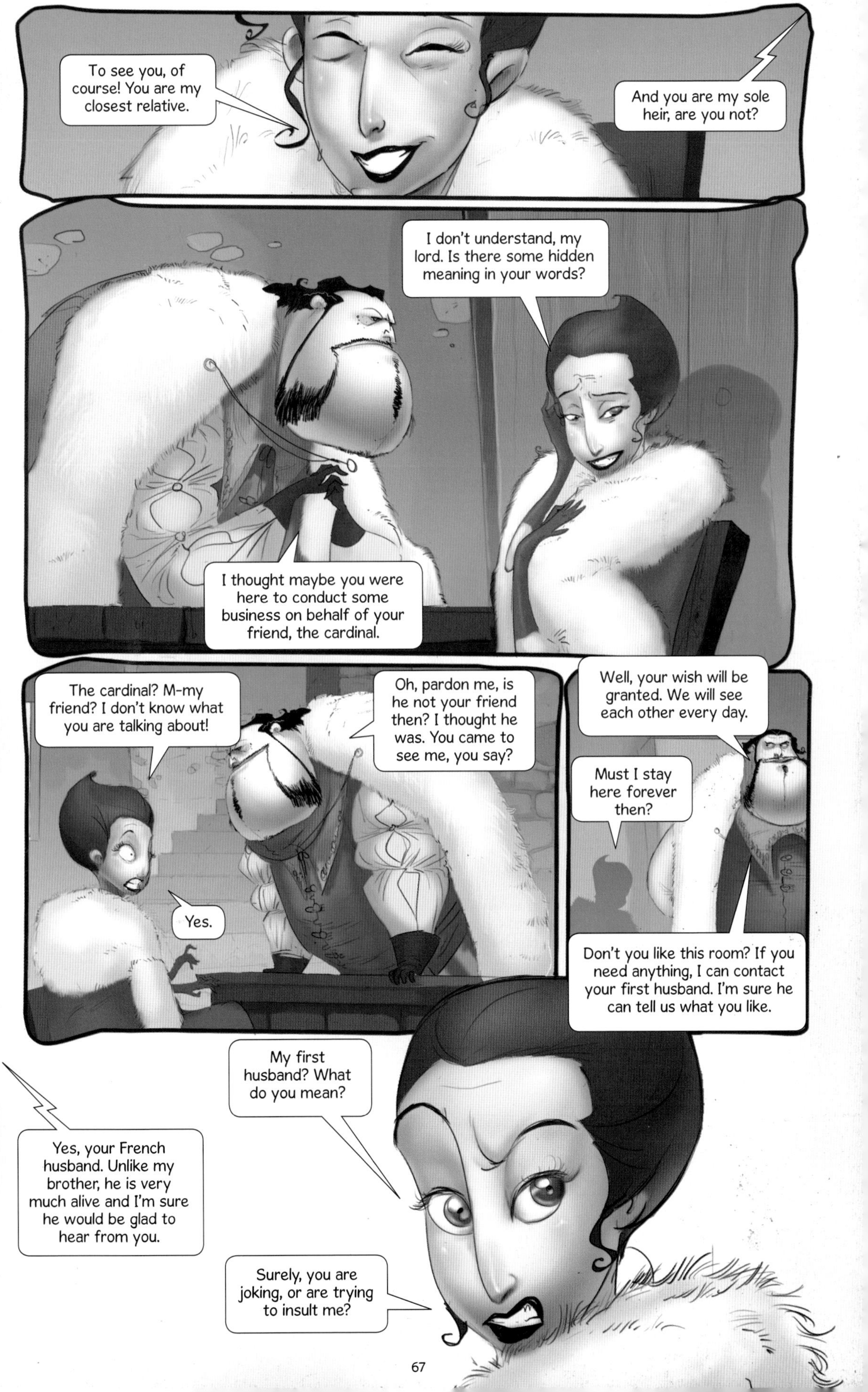
To see you, of course! You are my closest relative.
And you are my sole heir, are you not?
I don't understand, my lord. Is there some hidden meaning in your words?
I thought maybe you were here to conduct some business on behalf of your friend, the cardinal.
The cardinal? M-my friend? I don't know what you are talking about!
Oh, pardon me, is he not your friend then? I thought he was. You came to see me, you say?
Yes.
Well, your wish will be granted. We will see each other every day.
Must I stay here forever then?
Don't you like this room? If you need anything, I can contact your first husband. I'm sure he can tell us what you like.
My first husband? What do you mean?
Yes, your French husband. Unlike my brother, he is very much alive and I'm sure he would be glad to hear from you.
Surely, you are joking, or are trying to insult me?

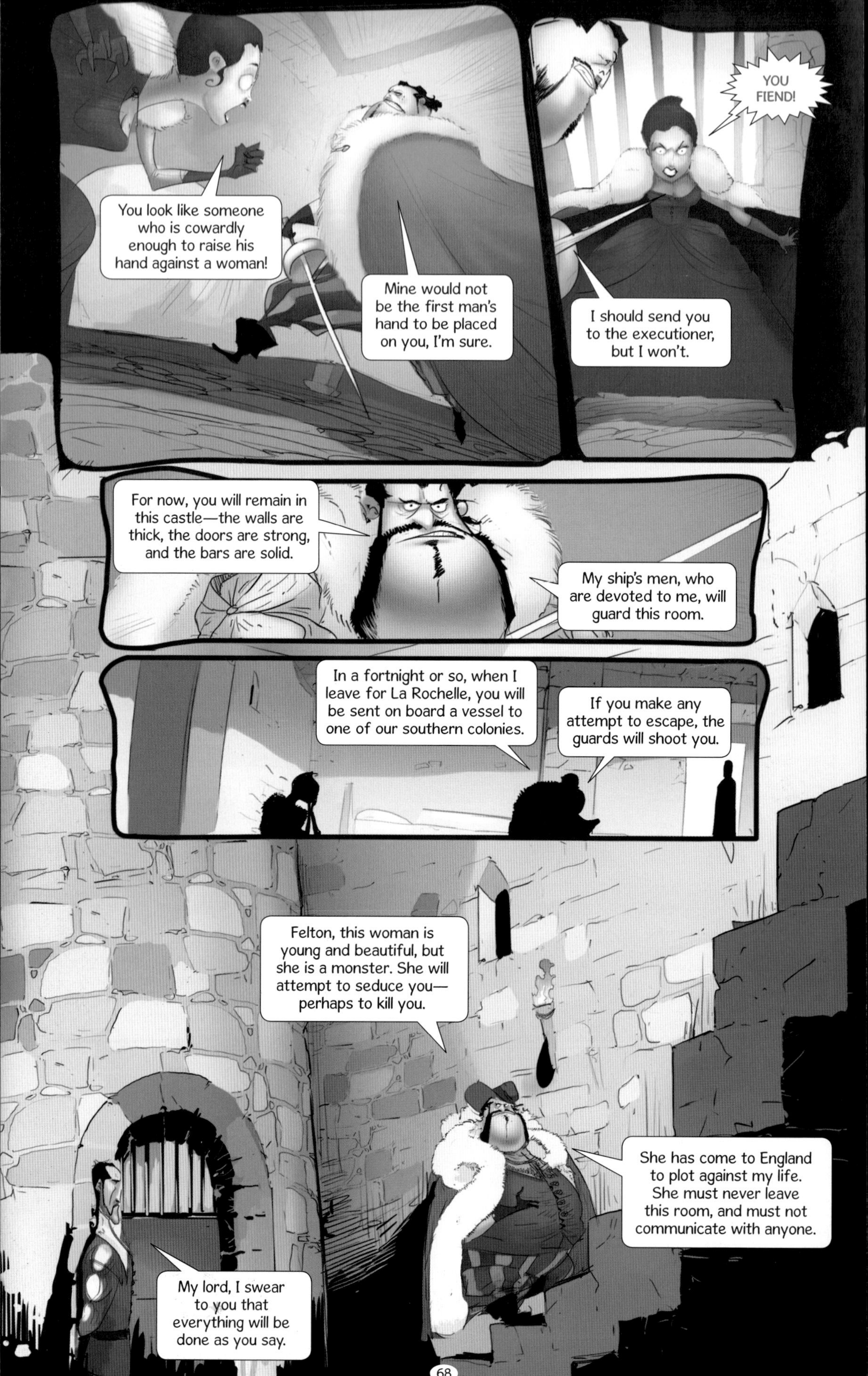
You look like someone who is cowardly enough to raise his hand against a woman!
Mine would not be the first man's hand to be placed on you, I'm sure.
YOU FIEND!
I should send you to the executioner, but I won't.
For now, you will remain in this castle—the walls are thick, the doors are strong, and the bars are solid.
My ship's men, who are devoted to me, will guard this room.
In a fortnight or so, when I leave for La Rochelle, you will be sent on board a vessel to one of our southern colonies.
If you make any attempt to escape, the guards will shoot you.
Felton, this woman is young and beautiful, but she is a monster. She will attempt to seduce you—perhaps to kill you.
She has come to England to plot against my life. She must never leave this room, and must not communicate with anyone.
My lord, I swear to you that everything will be done as you say.

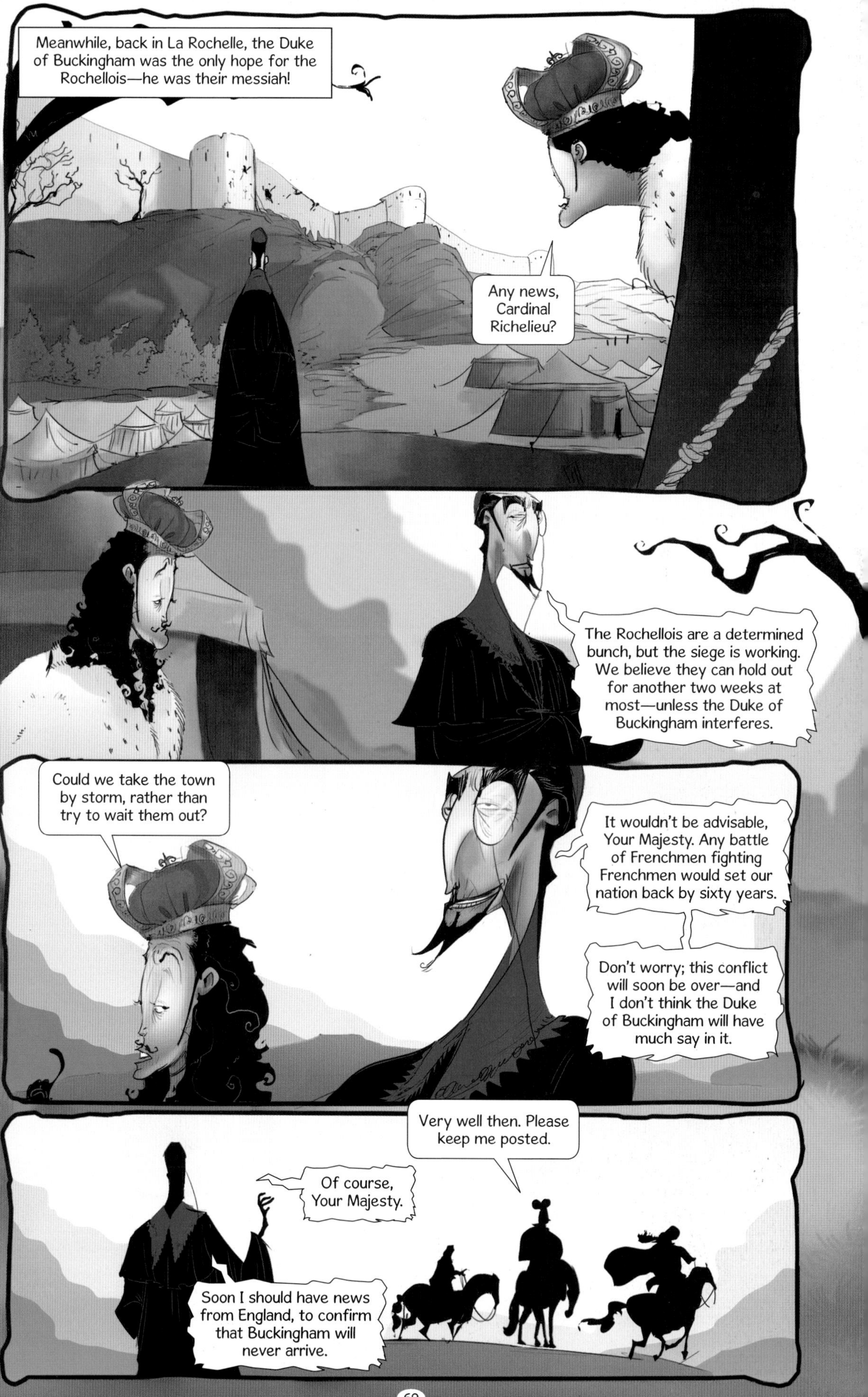
Meanwhile, back in La Rochelle, the Duke of Buckingham was the only hope for the Rochellois—he was their messiah!
Any news, Cardinal Richelieu?
The Rochellois are a determined bunch, but the siege is working. We believe they can hold out for another two weeks at most—unless the Duke of Buckingham interferes.
Could we take the town by storm, rather than try to wait them out?
It wouldn't be advisable, Your Majesty. Any battle of Frenchmen fighting Frenchmen would set our nation back by sixty years.
Don't worry; this conflict will soon be over—and I don't think the Duke of Buckingham will have much say in it.
Very well then. Please keep me posted.
Of course, Your Majesty.
Soon I should have news from England, to confirm that Buckingham will never arrive.

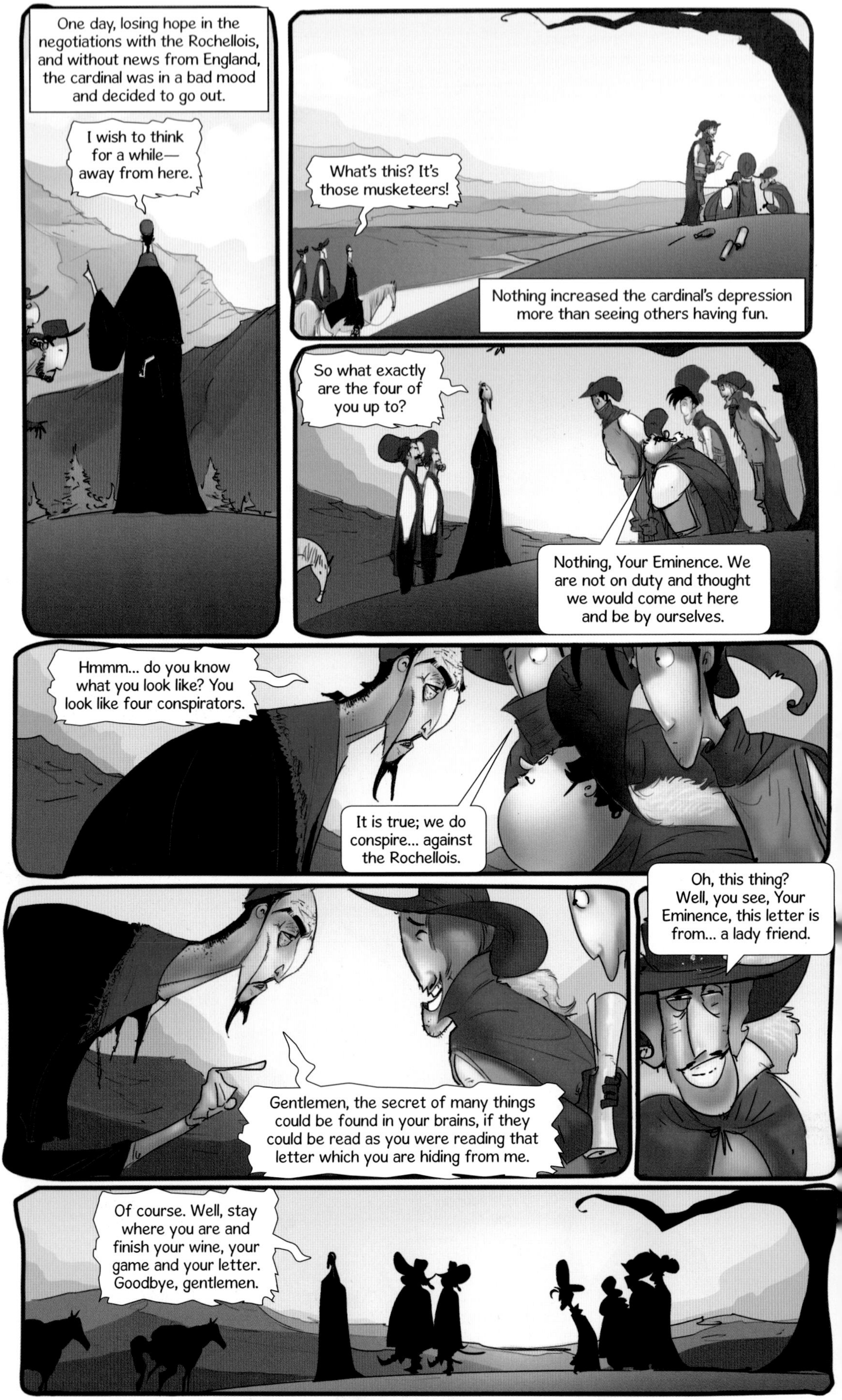

One day, losing hope in the negotiations with the Rochellois, and without news from England, the cardinal was in a bad mood and decided to go out.
I wish to think for a while— away from here.
What's this? It's those musketeers!
Nothing increased the cardinal's depression more than seeing others having fun.
So what exactly are the four of you up to?
Nothing, Your Eminence. We are not on duty and thought we would come out here and be by ourselves.
Hmmm... do you know what you look like? You look like four conspirators.
It is true; we do conspire... against the Rochellois.
Gentlemen, the secret of many things could be found in your brains, if they could be read as you were reading that letter which you are hiding from me.
Oh, this thing? Well, you see, Your Eminence, this letter is from... a lady friend.
Of course. Well, stay where you are and finish your wine, your game and your letter. Goodbye, gentlemen.

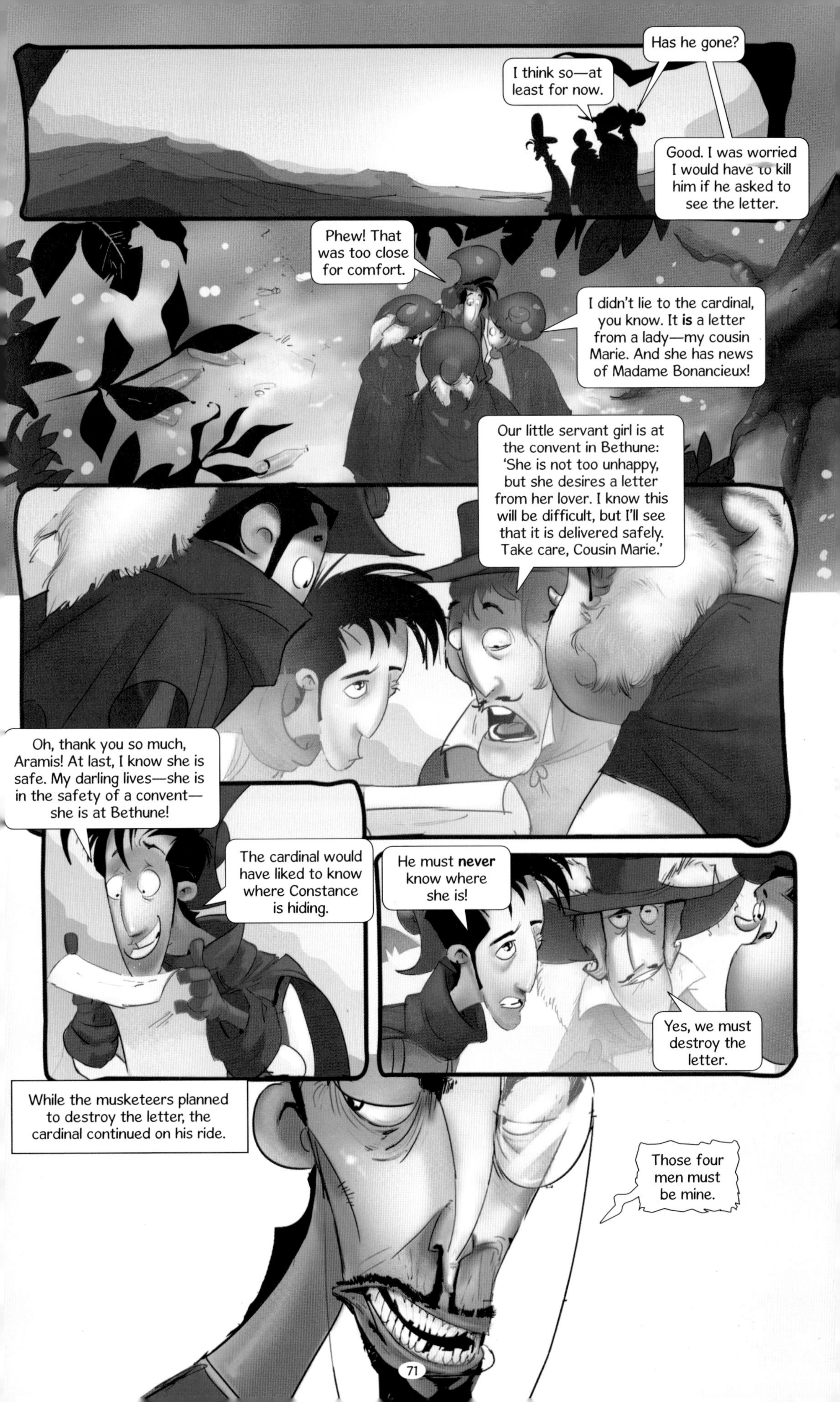
Has he gone?
I think so—at least for now.
Good. I was worried I would have to kill him if he asked to see the letter.
Phew! That was too close for comfort.
I didn't lie to the cardinal, you know. It **is** a letter from a lady—my cousin Marie. And she has news of Madame Bonancieux!
Our little servant girl is at the convent in Bethune: 'She is not too unhappy, but she desires a letter from her lover. I know this will be difficult, but I'll see that it is delivered safely. Take care, Cousin Marie.'
Oh, thank you so much, Aramis! At last, I know she is safe. My darling lives—she is in the safety of a convent—she is at Bethune!
The cardinal would have liked to know where Constance is hiding.
He must **never** know where she is!
Yes, we must destroy the letter.
While the musketeers planned to destroy the letter, the cardinal continued on his ride.
Those four men must be mine.

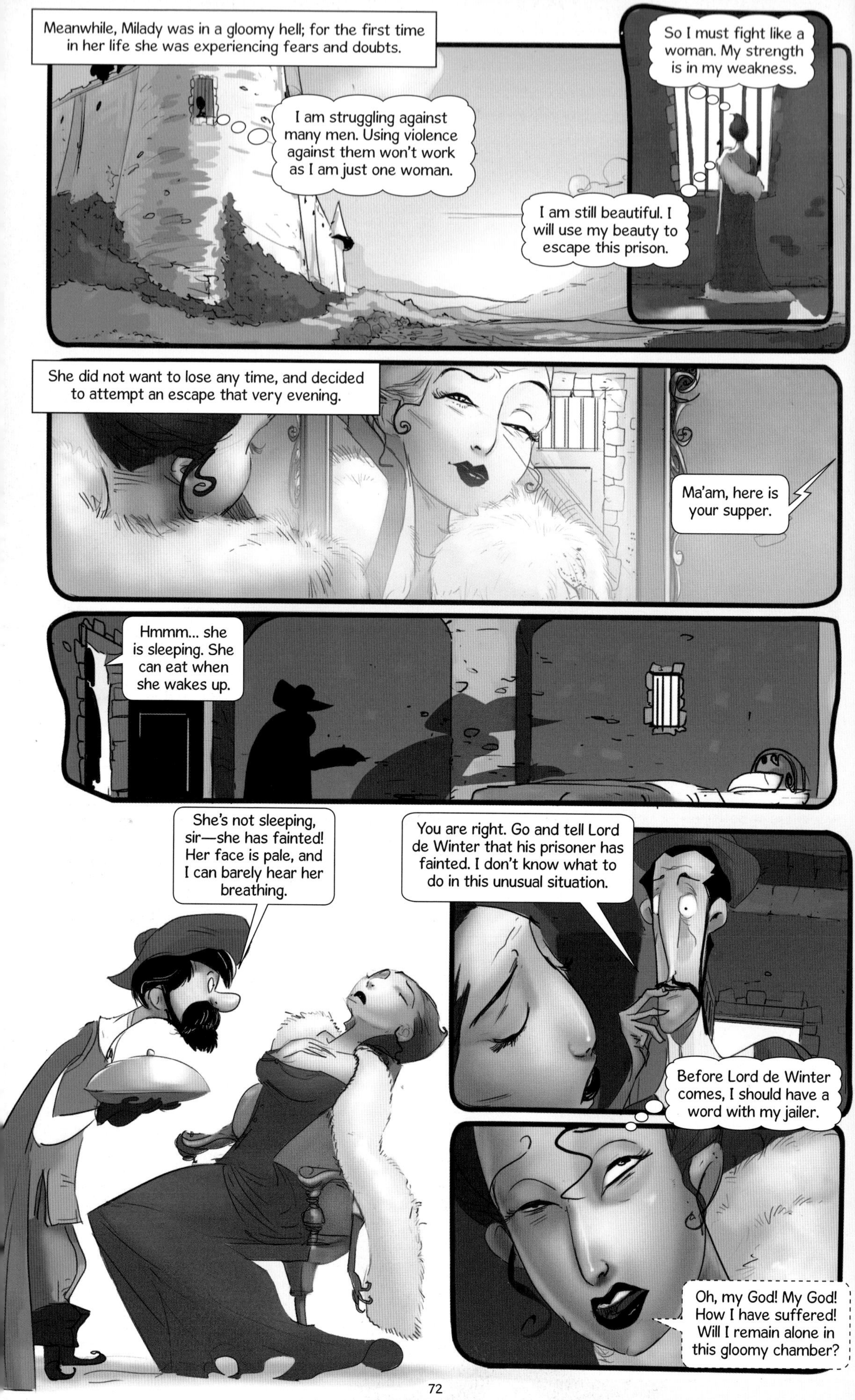
Meanwhile, Milady was in a gloomy hell; for the first time in her life she was experiencing fears and doubts.
I am struggling against many men. Using violence against them won't work as I am just one woman.
So I must fight like a woman. My strength is in my weakness.
I am still beautiful. I will use my beauty to escape this prison.
She did not want to lose any time, and decided to attempt an escape that very evening.
Ma'am, here is your supper.
Hmmm... she is sleeping. She can eat when she wakes up.
She's not sleeping, sir—she has fainted! Her face is pale, and I can barely hear her breathing.
You are right. Go and tell Lord de Winter that his prisoner has fainted. I don't know what to do in this unusual situation.
Before Lord de Winter comes, I should have a word with my jailer.
Oh, my God! My God! How I have suffered! Will I remain alone in this gloomy chamber?

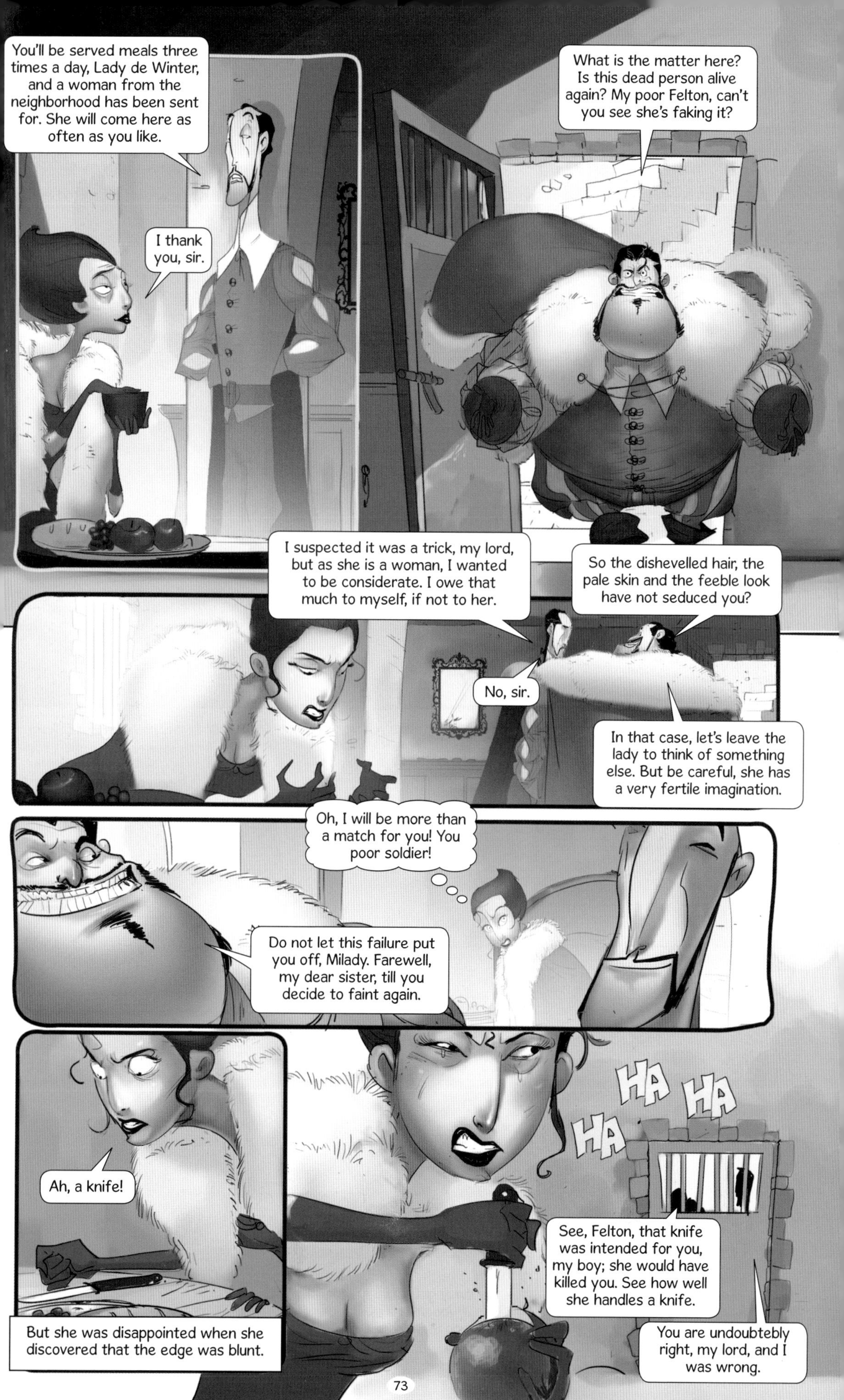

You'll be served meals three times a day, Lady de Winter, and a woman from the neighborhood has been sent for. She will come here as often as you like.
I thank you, sir.
What is the matter here? Is this dead person alive again? My poor Felton, can't you see she's faking it?
I suspected it was a trick, my lord, but as she is a woman, I wanted to be considerate. I owe that much to myself, if not to her.
So the dishevelled hair, the pale skin and the feeble look have not seduced you?
No, sir.
In that case, let's leave the lady to think of something else. But be careful, she has a very fertile imagination.
Oh, I will be more than a match for you! You poor soldier!
Do not let this failure put you off, Milady. Farewell, my dear sister, till you decide to faint again.
Ah, a knife!
But she was disappointed when she discovered that the edge was blunt.
HA HA HA
See, Felton, that knife was intended for you, my boy; she would have killed you. See how well she handles a knife.
You are undoubtebly right, my lord, and I was wrong.

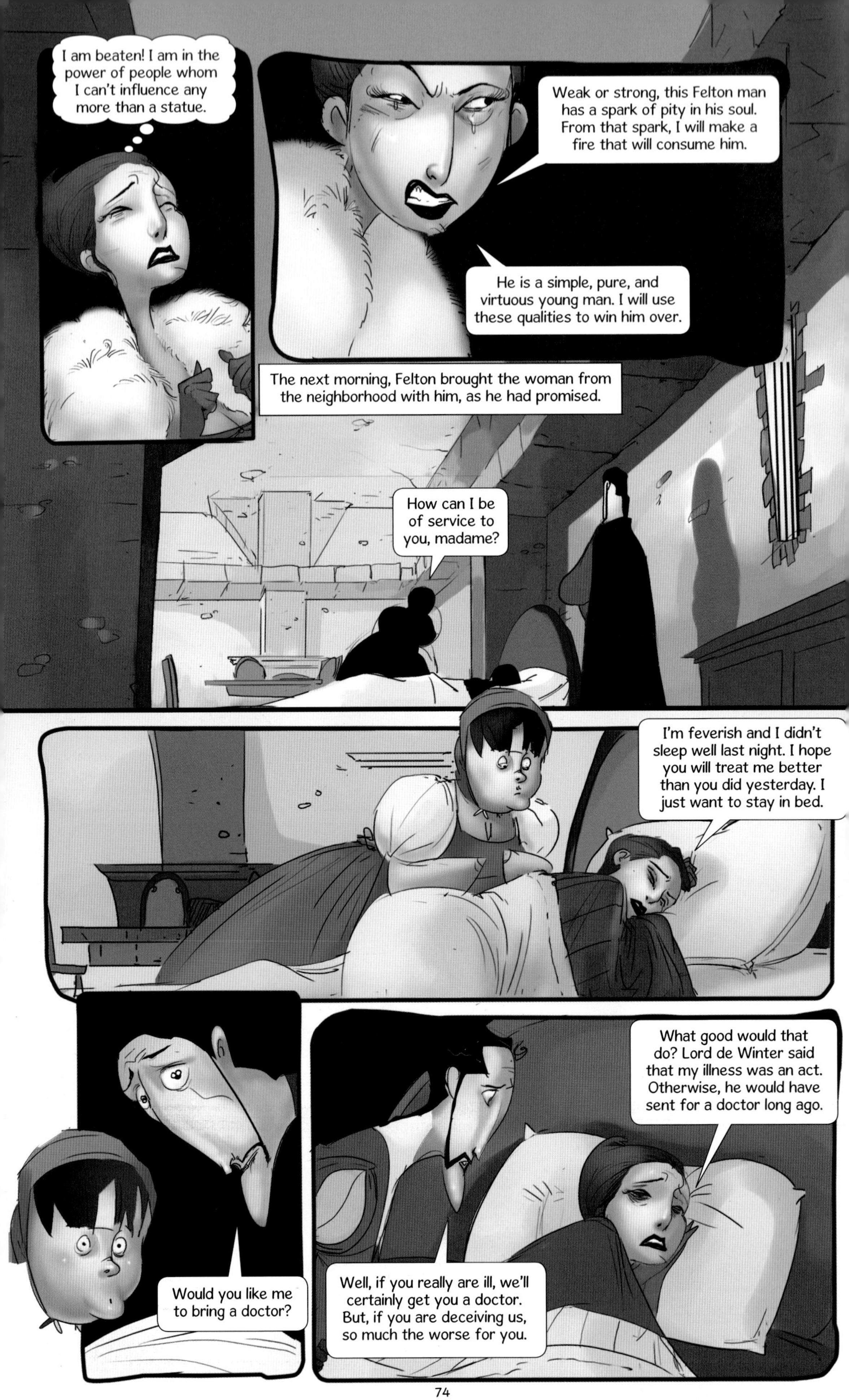
I am beaten! I am in the power of people whom I can't influence any more than a statue.
Weak or strong, this Felton man has a spark of pity in his soul. From that spark, I will make a fire that will consume him.
He is a simple, pure, and virtuous young man. I will use these qualities to win him over.
The next morning, Felton brought the woman from the neighborhood with him, as he had promised.
How can I be of service to you, madame?
I'm feverish and I didn't sleep well last night. I hope you will treat me better than you did yesterday. I just want to stay in bed.
Would you like me to bring a doctor?
Well, if you really are ill, we'll certainly get you a doctor. But, if you are deceiving us, so much the worse for you.
What good would that do? Lord de Winter said that my illness was an act. Otherwise, he would have sent for a doctor long ago.

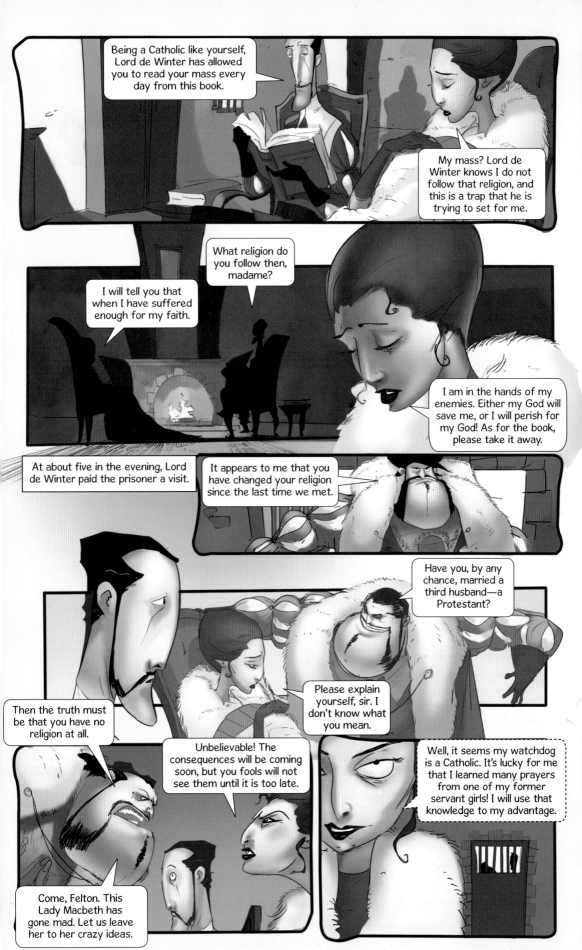

Being a Catholic like yourself, Lord de Winter has allowed you to read your mass every day from this book.

My mass? Lord de Winter knows I do not follow that religion, and this is a trap that he is trying to set for me.

What religion do you follow then, madame?

I will tell you that when I have suffered enough for my faith.

I am in the hands of my enemies. Either my God will save me, or I will perish for my God! As for the book, please take it away.

At about five in the evening, Lord de Winter paid the prisoner a visit.

It appears to me that you have changed your religion since the last time we met.

Have you, by any chance, married a third husband—a Protestant?

Please explain yourself, sir. I don't know what you mean.

Then the truth must be that you have no religion at all.

Unbelievable! The consequences will be coming soon, but you fools will not see them until it is too late.

Well, it seems my watchdog is a Catholic. It's lucky for me that I learned many prayers from one of my former servant girls! I will use that knowledge to my advantage.

Come, Felton. This Lady Macbeth has gone mad. Let us leave her to her crazy ideas.

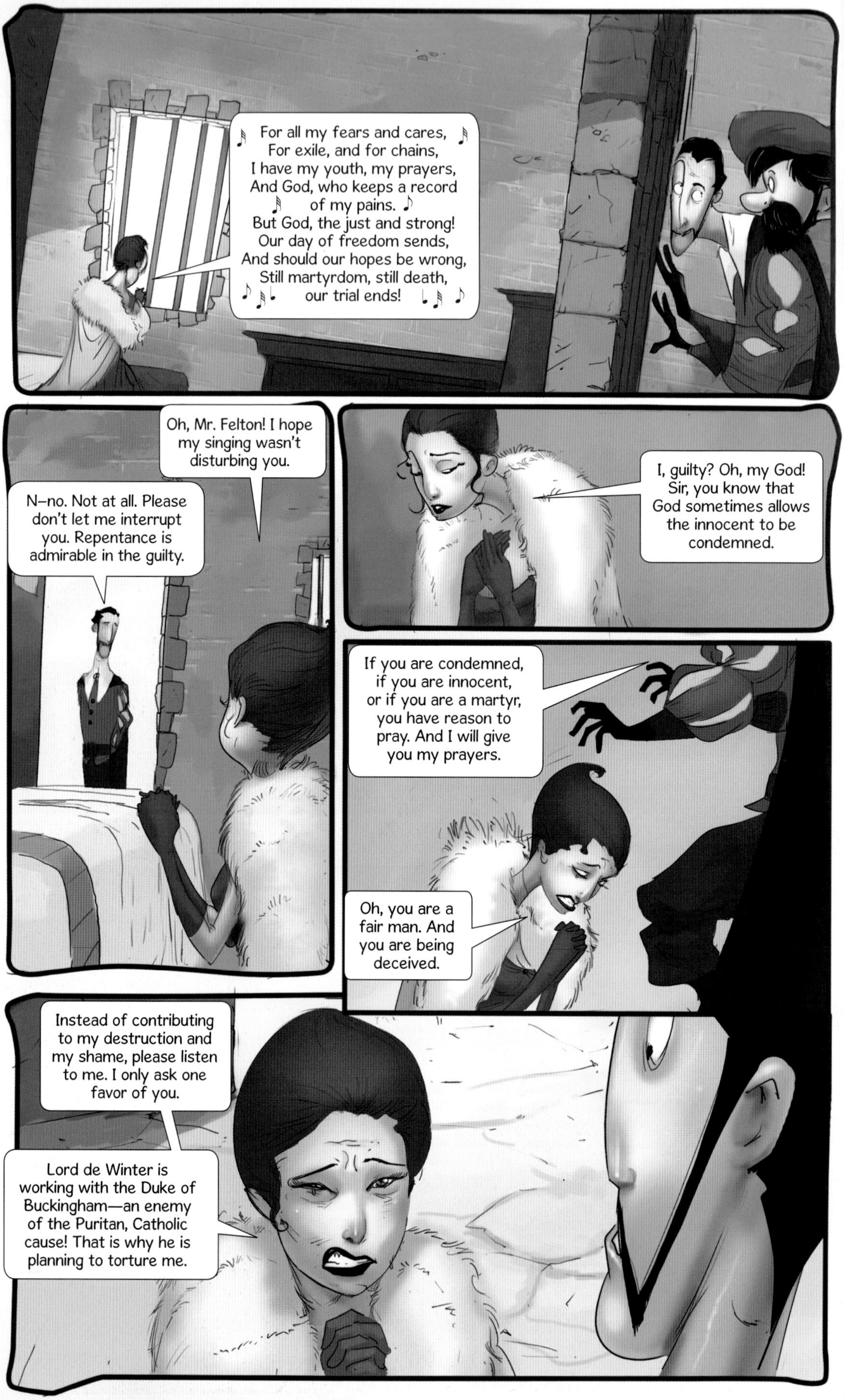

For all my fears and cares, For exile, and for chains, I have my youth, my prayers, And God, who keeps a record of my pains. But God, the just and strong! Our day of freedom sends, And should our hopes be wrong, Still martyrdom, still death, our trial ends!
Oh, Mr. Felton! I hope my singing wasn't disturbing you.
N–no. Not at all. Please don't let me interrupt you. Repentance is admirable in the guilty.
I, guilty? Oh, my God! Sir, you know that God sometimes allows the innocent to be condemned.
If you are condemned, if you are innocent, or if you are a martyr, you have reason to pray. And I will give you my prayers.
Oh, you are a fair man. And you are being deceived.
Instead of contributing to my destruction and my shame, please listen to me. I only ask one favor of you.
Lord de Winter is working with the Duke of Buckingham—an enemy of the Puritan, Catholic cause! That is why he is planning to torture me.

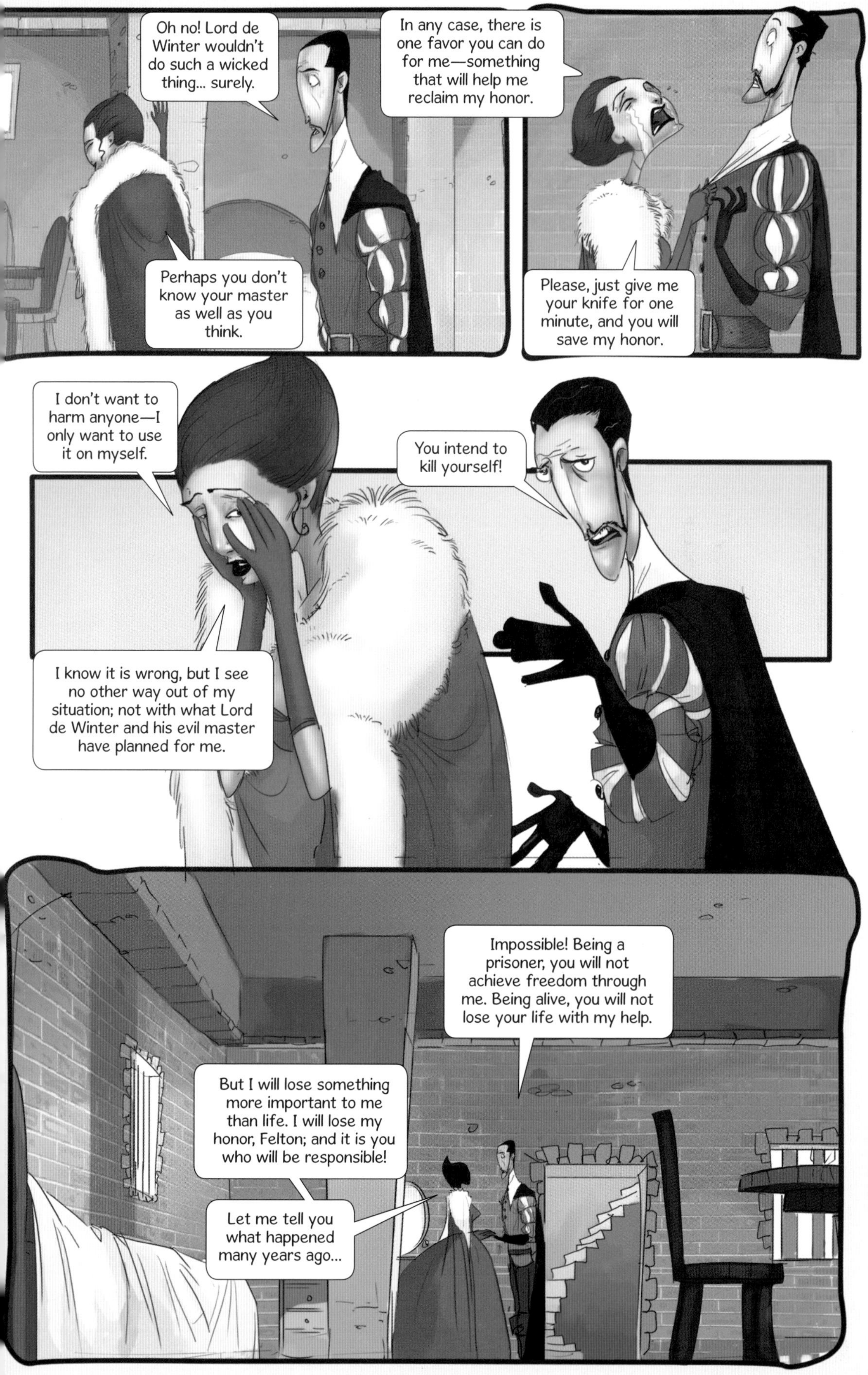

Oh no! Lord de Winter wouldn't do such a wicked thing... surely.
Perhaps you don't know your master as well as you think.
In any case, there is one favor you can do for me—something that will help me reclaim my honor.
Please, just give me your knife for one minute, and you will save my honor.
I don't want to harm anyone—I only want to use it on myself.
You intend to kill yourself!
I know it is wrong, but I see no other way out of my situation; not with what Lord de Winter and his evil master have planned for me.
Impossible! Being a prisoner, you will not achieve freedom through me. Being alive, you will not lose your life with my help.
But I will lose something more important to me than life. I will lose my honor, Felton; and it is you who will be responsible!
Let me tell you what happened many years ago...

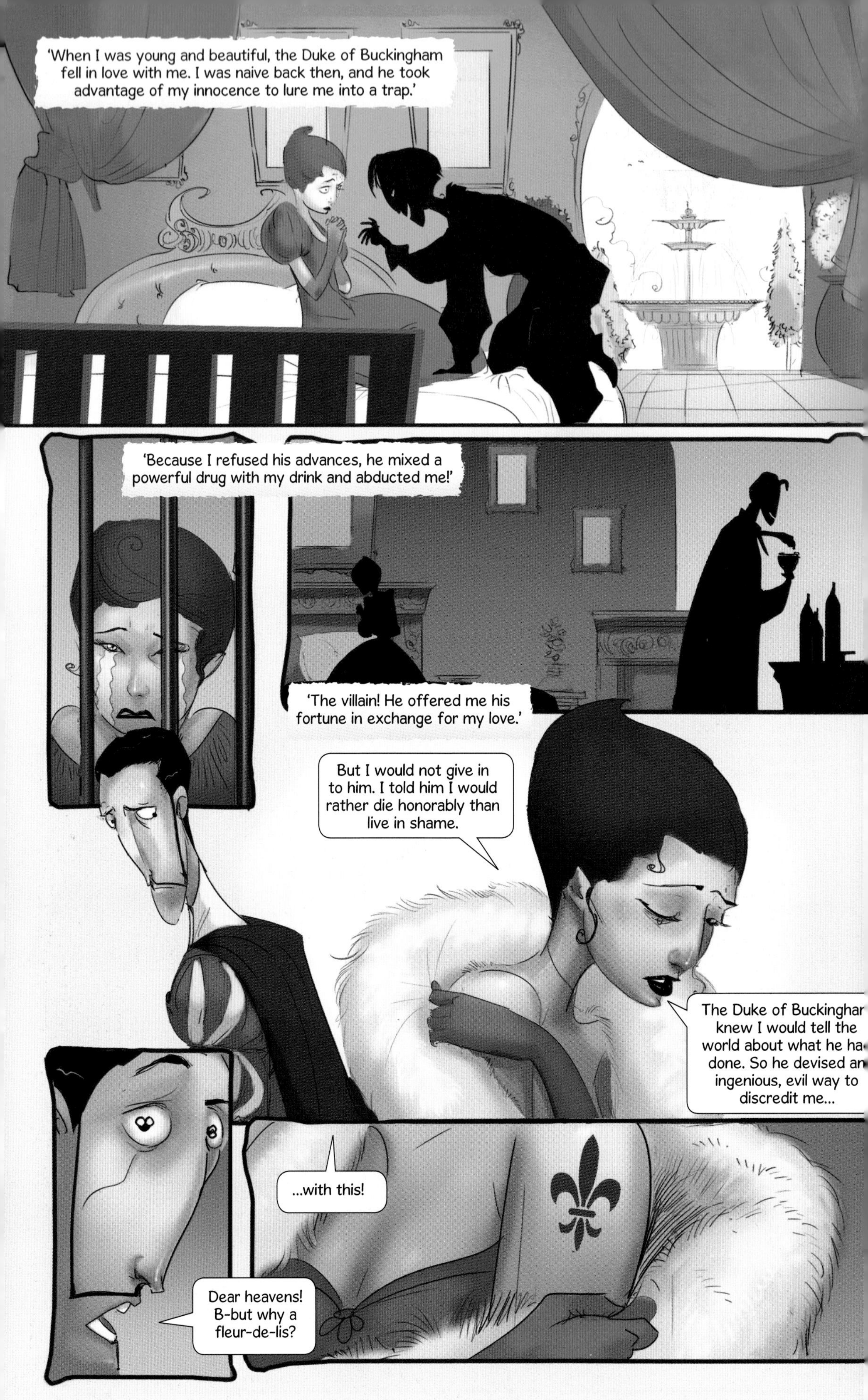
'When I was young and beautiful, the Duke of Buckingham fell in love with me. I was naive back then, and he took advantage of my innocence to lure me into a trap.'
'Because I refused his advances, he mixed a powerful drug with my drink and abducted me!'
'The villain! He offered me his fortune in exchange for my love.'
But I would not give in to him. I told him I would rather die honorably than live in shame.
The Duke of Buckinghar knew I would tell the world about what he ha done. So he devised an ingenious, evil way to discredit me...
...with this!
Dear heavens! B-but why a fleur-de-lis?

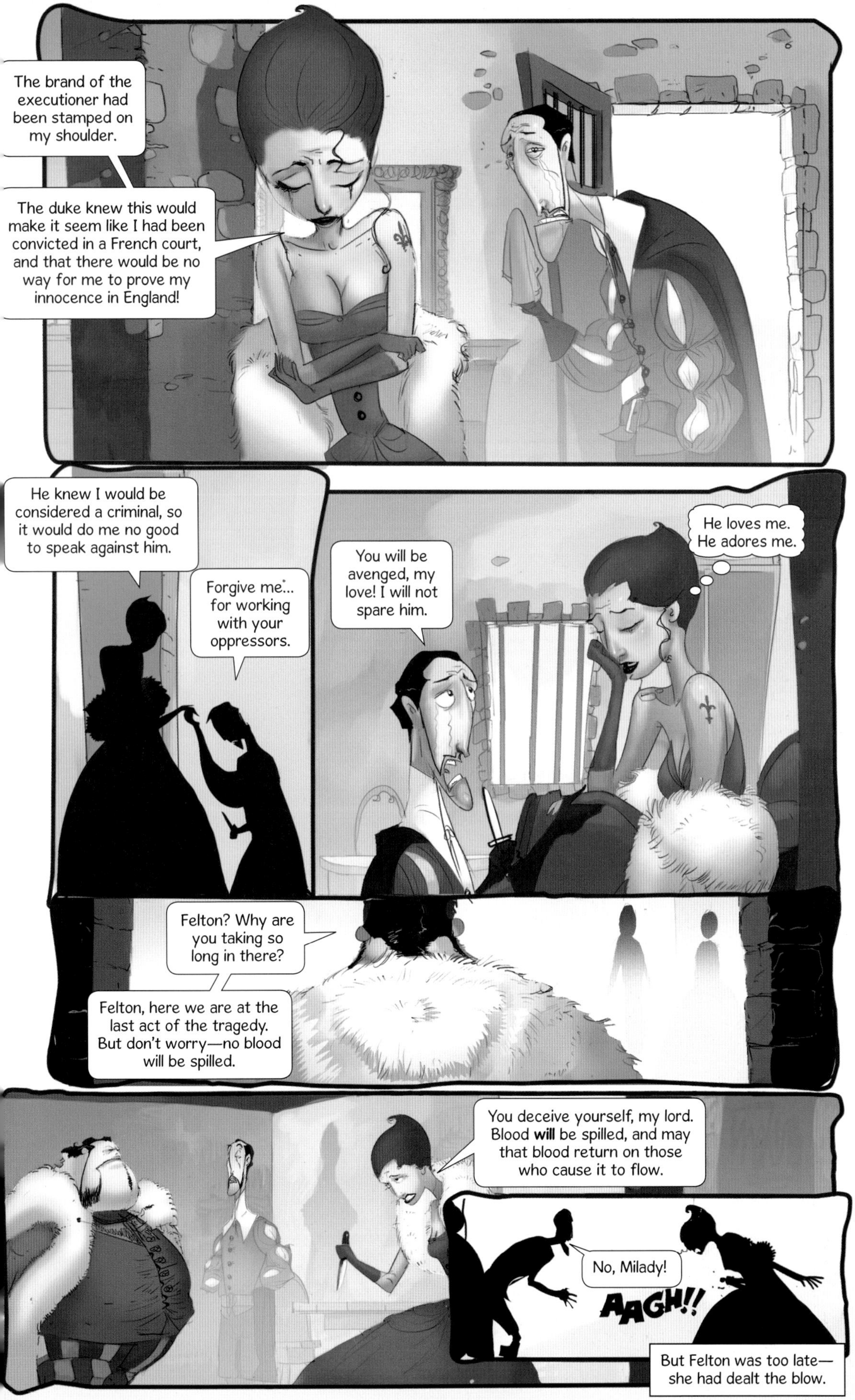
The brand of the executioner had been stamped on my shoulder.
The duke knew this would make it seem like I had been convicted in a French court, and that there would be no way for me to prove my innocence in England!
He knew I would be considered a criminal, so it would do me no good to speak against him.
Forgive me... for working with your oppressors.
You will be avenged, my love! I will not spare him.
He loves me. He adores me.
Felton? Why are you taking so long in there?
Felton, here we are at the last act of the tragedy. But don't worry—no blood will be spilled.
You deceive yourself, my lord. Blood **will** be spilled, and may that blood return on those who cause it to flow.
No, Milady!
AAGH!!
But Felton was too late—she had dealt the blow.

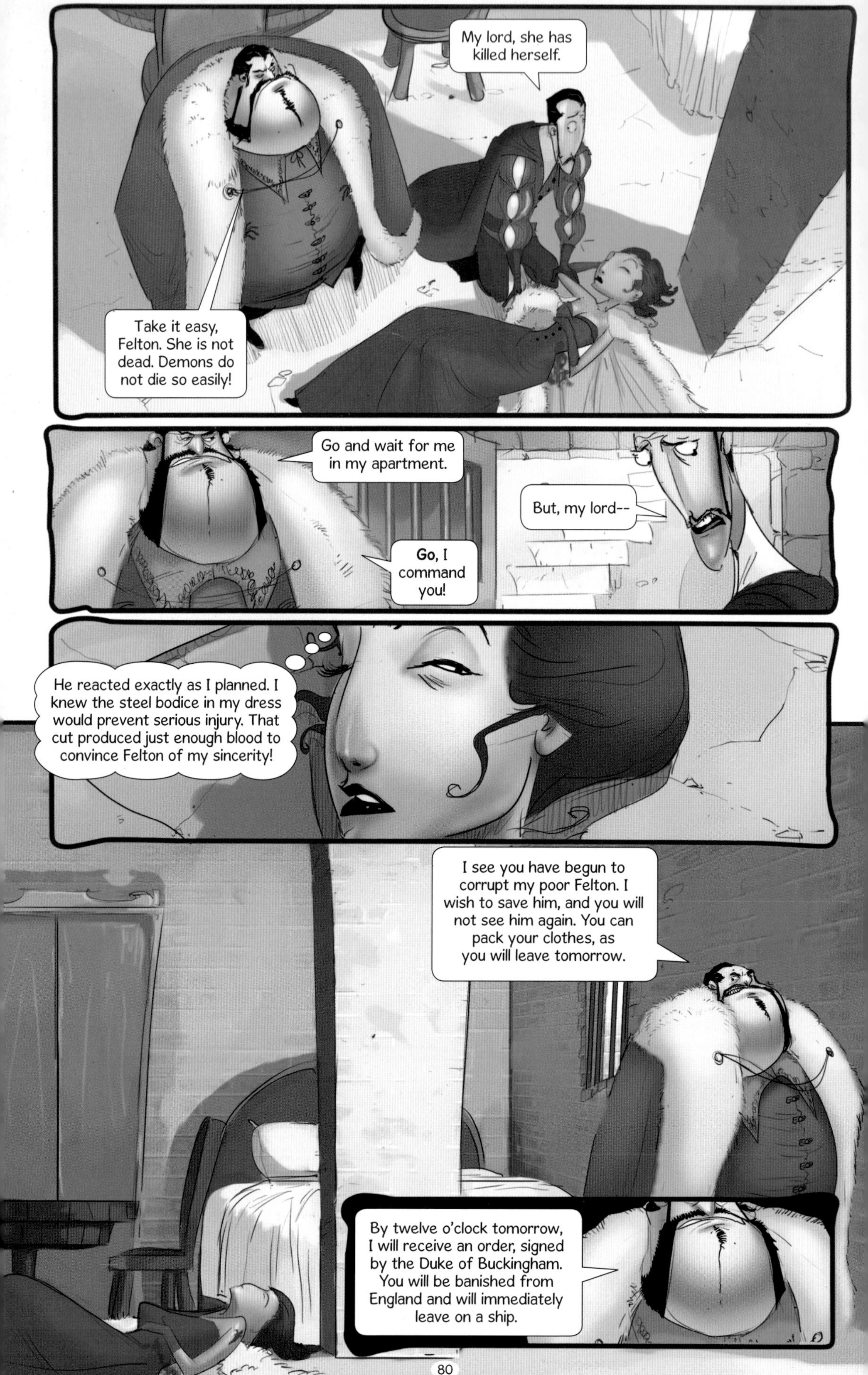

My lord, she has killed herself.
Take it easy, Felton. She is not dead. Demons do not die so easily!
Go and wait for me in my apartment.
But, my lord--
Go, I command you!
He reacted exactly as I planned. I knew the steel bodice in my dress would prevent serious injury. That cut produced just enough blood to convince Felton of my sincerity!
I see you have begun to corrupt my poor Felton. I wish to save him, and you will not see him again. You can pack your clothes, as you will leave tomorrow.
By twelve o'clock tomorrow, I will receive an order, signed by the Duke of Buckingham. You will be banished from England and will immediately leave on a ship.

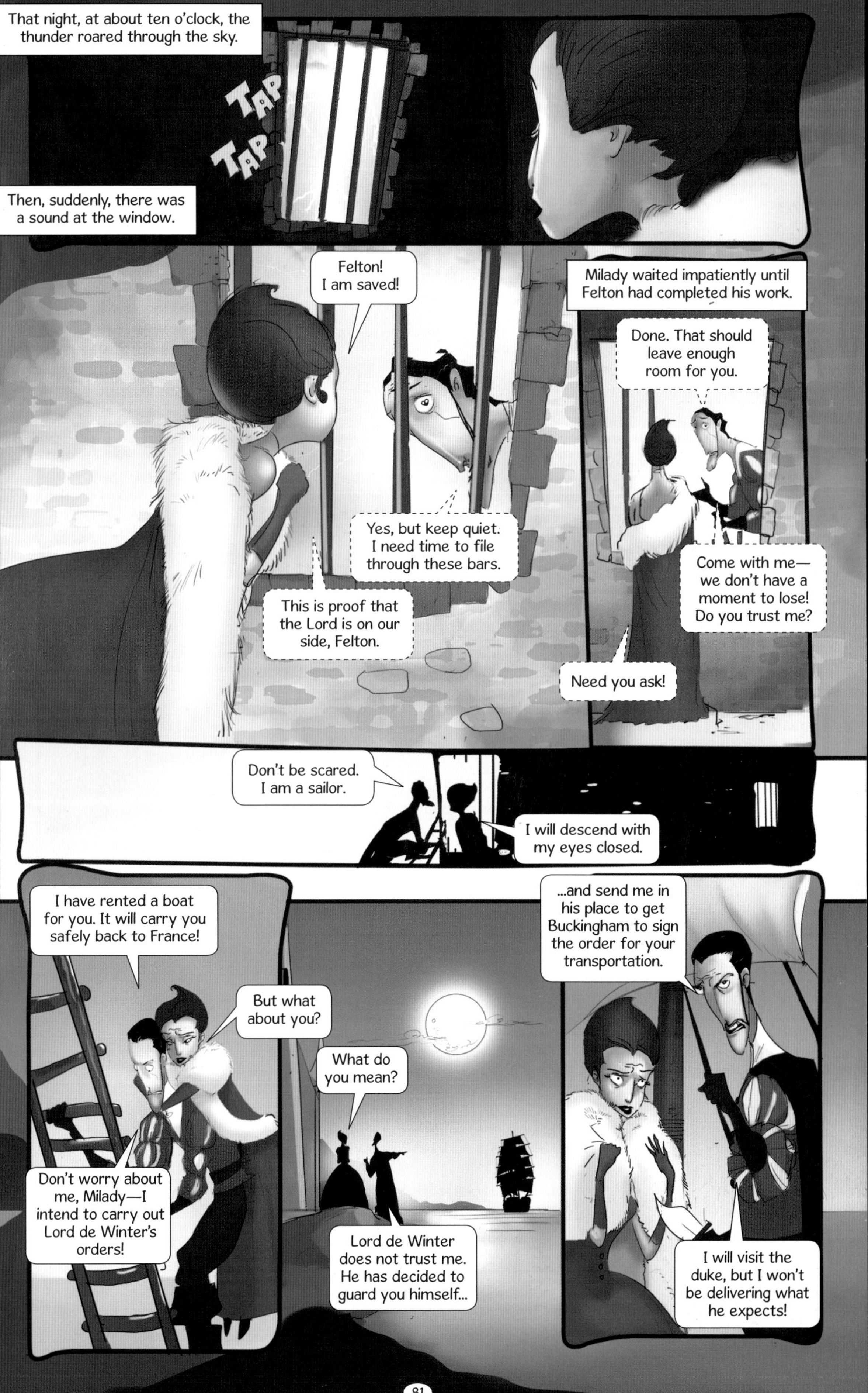
That night, at about ten o'clock, the thunder roared through the sky.
TAP TAP
Then, suddenly, there was a sound at the window.
Felton! I am saved!
Yes, but keep quiet. I need time to file through these bars.
This is proof that the Lord is on our side, Felton.
Milady waited impatiently until Felton had completed his work.
Done. That should leave enough room for you.
Come with me— we don't have a moment to lose! Do you trust me?
Need you ask!
Don't be scared. I am a sailor.
I will descend with my eyes closed.
I have rented a boat for you. It will carry you safely back to France!
But what about you?
Don't worry about me, Milady—I intend to carry out Lord de Winter's orders!
What do you mean?
Lord de Winter does not trust me. He has decided to guard you himself...
...and send me in his place to get Buckingham to sign the order for your transportation.
I will visit the duke, but I won't be delivering what he expects!

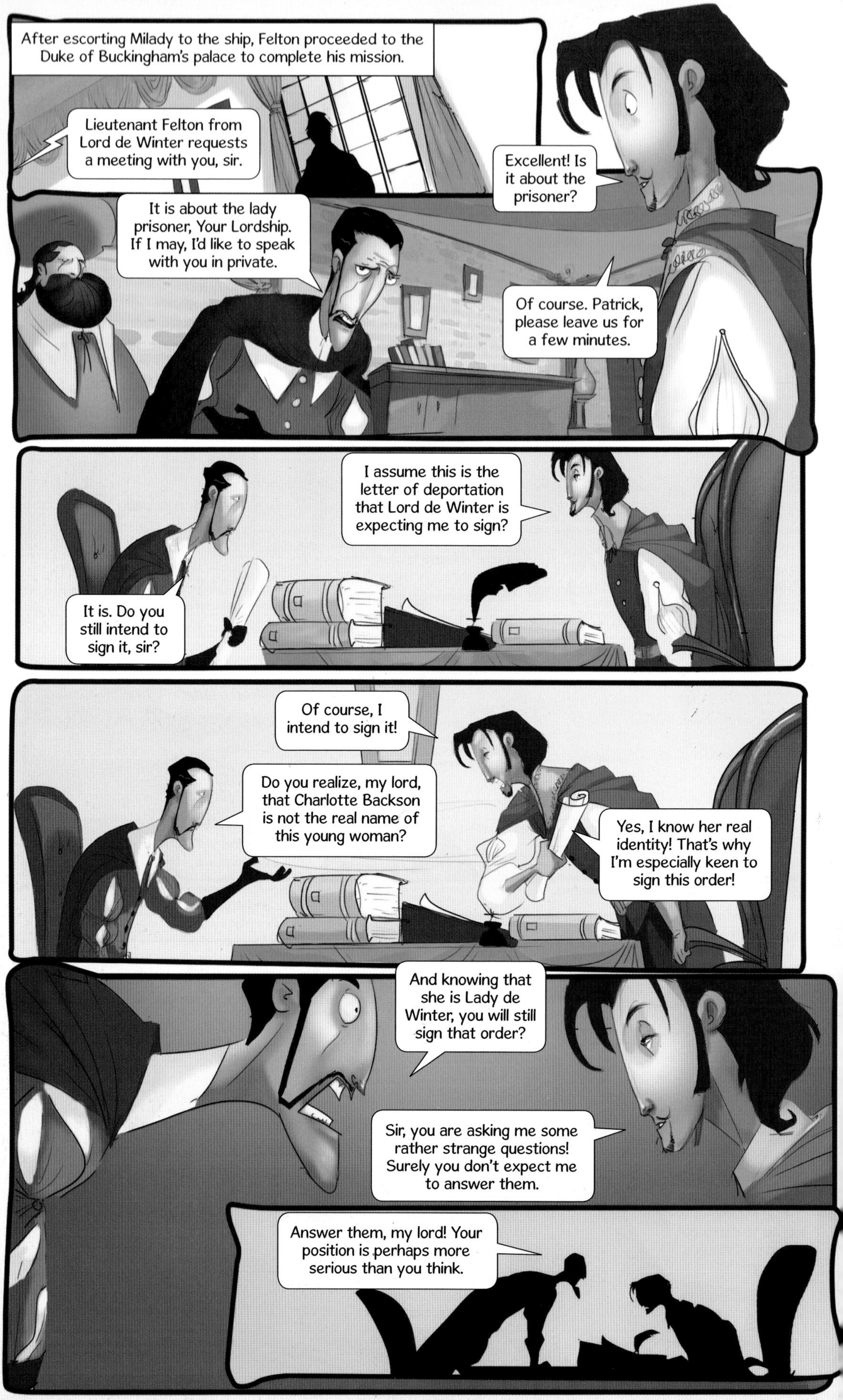
After escorting Milady to the ship, Felton proceeded to the Duke of Buckingham's palace to complete his mission.
Lieutenant Felton from Lord de Winter requests a meeting with you, sir.
Excellent! Is it about the prisoner?
It is about the lady prisoner, Your Lordship. If I may, I'd like to speak with you in private.
Of course. Patrick, please leave us for a few minutes.
I assume this is the letter of deportation that Lord de Winter is expecting me to sign?
It is. Do you still intend to sign it, sir?
Of course, I intend to sign it!
Do you realize, my lord, that Charlotte Backson is not the real name of this young woman?
Yes, I know her real identity! That's why I'm especially keen to sign this order!
And knowing that she is Lady de Winter, you will still sign that order?
Sir, you are asking me some rather strange questions! Surely you don't expect me to answer them.
Answer them, my lord! Your position is perhaps more serious than you think.

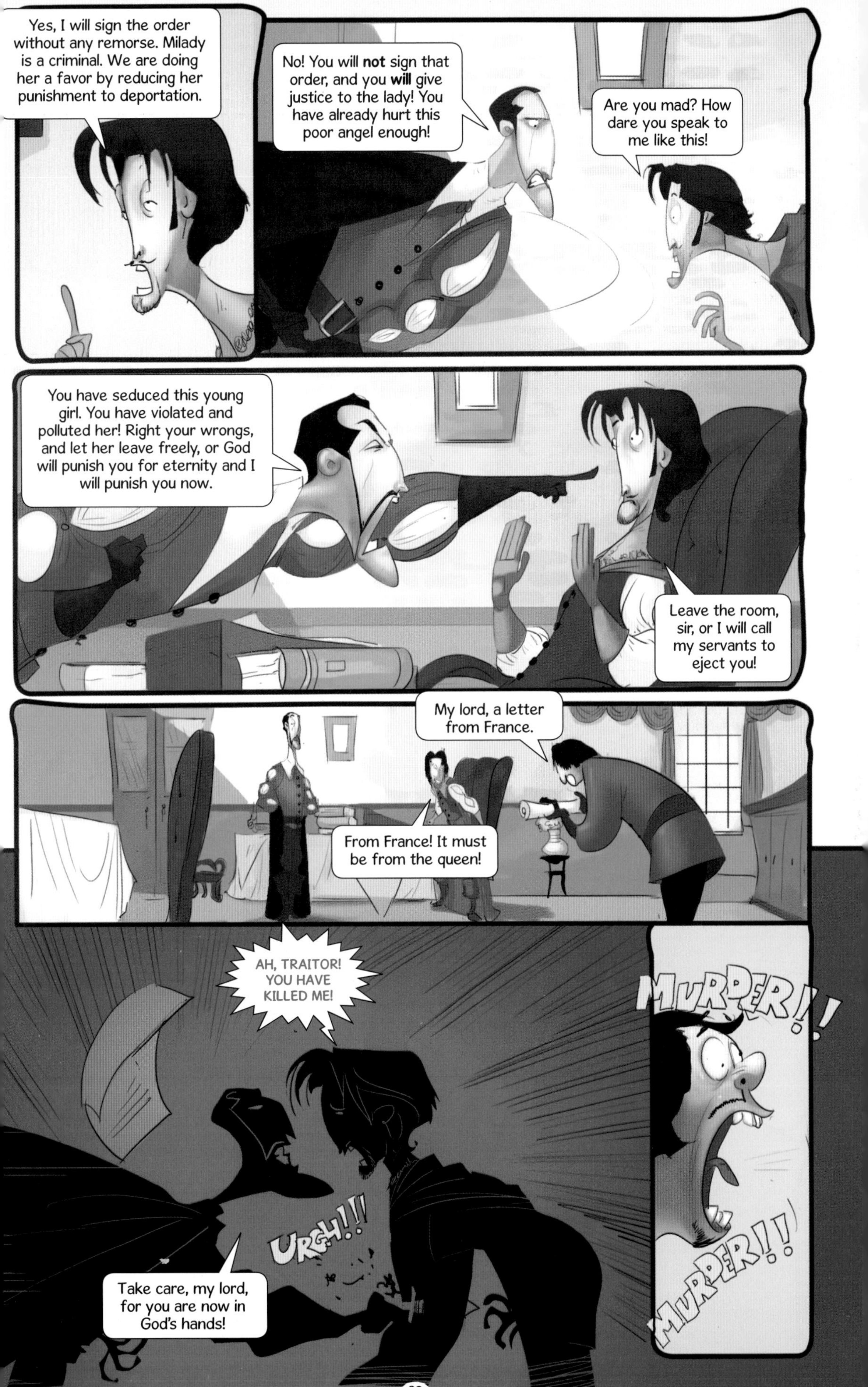

Yes, I will sign the order without any remorse. Milady is a criminal. We are doing her a favor by reducing her punishment to deportation.
No! You will **not** sign that order, and you **will** give justice to the lady! You have already hurt this poor angel enough!
Are you mad? How dare you speak to me like this!
You have seduced this young girl. You have violated and polluted her! Right your wrongs, and let her leave freely, or God will punish you for eternity and I will punish you now.
Leave the room, sir, or I will call my servants to eject you!
My lord, a letter from France.
From France! It must be from the queen!
AH, TRAITOR! YOU HAVE KILLED ME!
URGH!!!
Take care, my lord, for you are now in God's hands!
MURDER!!!
MURDER!!!

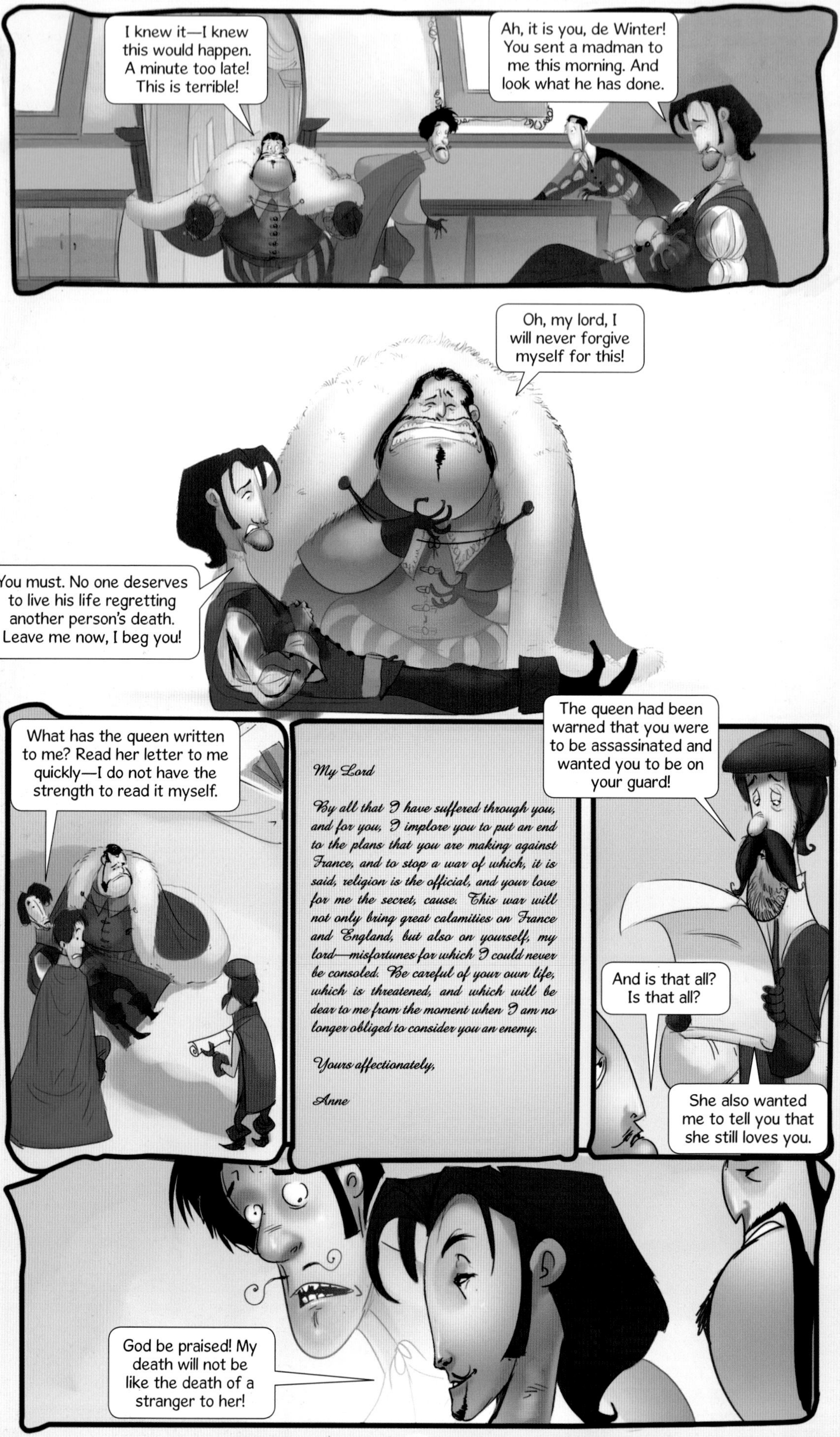
I knew it—I knew this would happen. A minute too late! This is terrible!
Ah, it is you, de Winter! You sent a madman to me this morning. And look what he has done.
Oh, my lord, I will never forgive myself for this!
You must. No one deserves to live his life regretting another person's death. Leave me now, I beg you!
What has the queen written to me? Read her letter to me quickly—I do not have the strength to read it myself.
My Lord
By all that I have suffered through you, and for you, I implore you to put an end to the plans that you are making against France, and to stop a war of which, it is said, religion is the official, and your love for me the secret, cause. This war will not only bring great calamities on France and England, but also on yourself, my lord—misfortunes for which I could never be consoled. Be careful of your own life, which is threatened, and which will be dear to me from the moment when I am no longer obliged to consider you an enemy.
Yours affectionately,
Anne
The queen had been warned that you were to be assassinated and wanted you to be on your guard!
And is that all? Is that all?
She also wanted me to tell you that she still loves you.
God be praised! My death will not be like the death of a stranger to her!

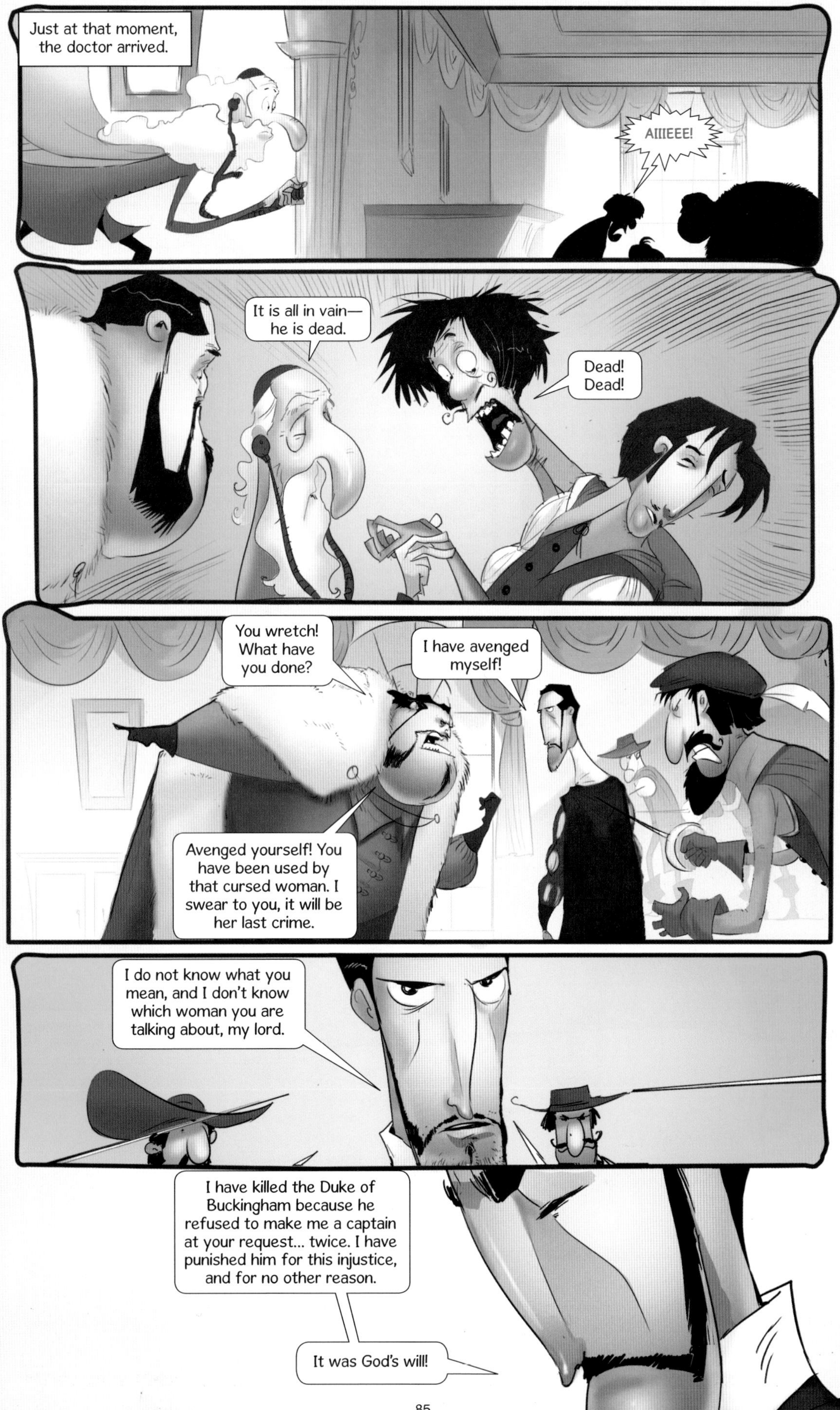
Just at that moment, the doctor arrived.
AIIIEEE!
It is all in vain— he is dead.
Dead! Dead!
You wretch! What have you done?
I have avenged myself!
Avenged yourself! You have been used by that cursed woman. I swear to you, it will be her last crime.
I do not know what you mean, and I don't know which woman you are talking about, my lord.
I have killed the Duke of Buckingham because he refused to make me a captain at your request... twice. I have punished him for this injustice, and for no other reason.
It was God's will!

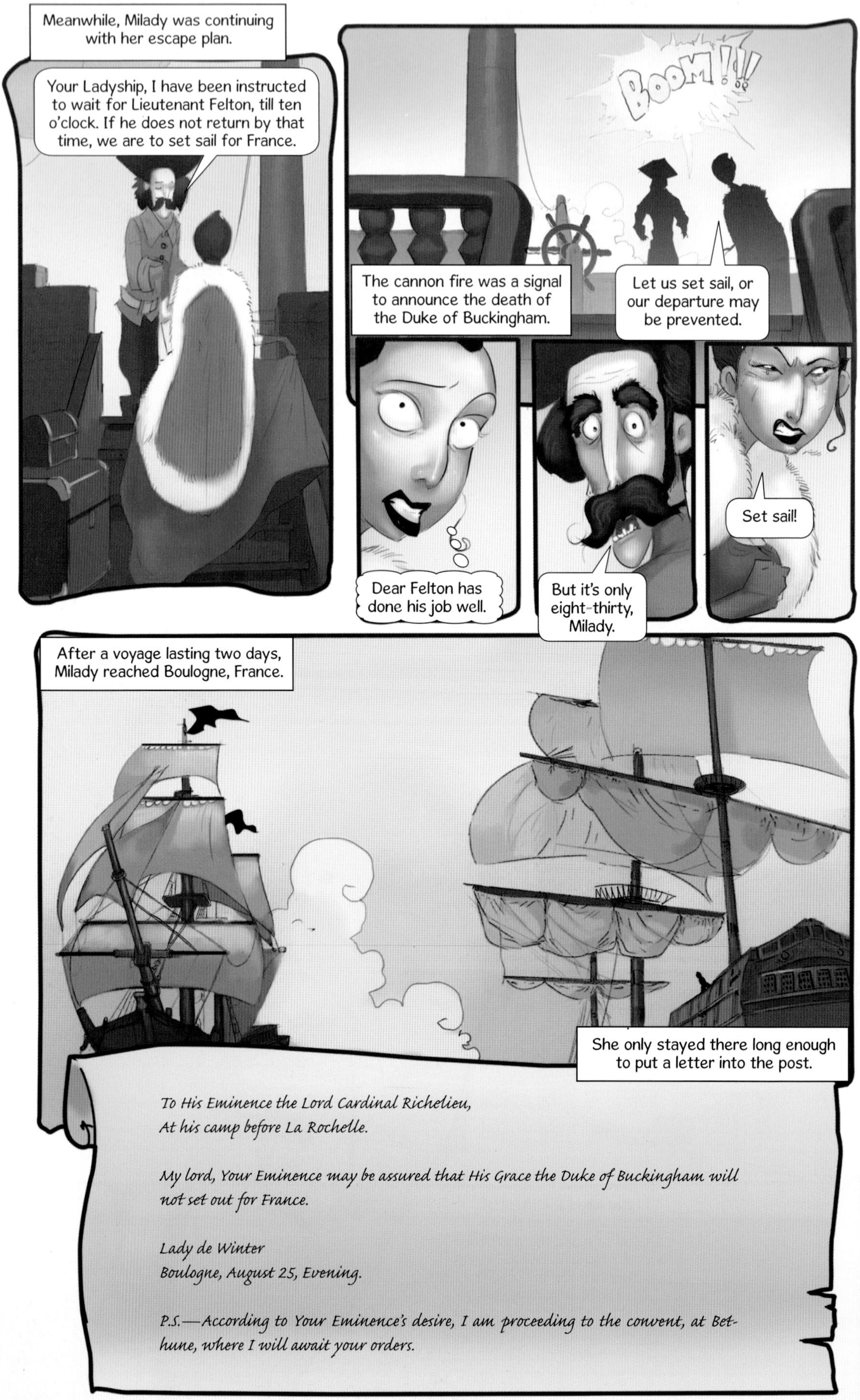
Meanwhile, Milady was continuing with her escape plan.
Your Ladyship, I have been instructed to wait for Lieutenant Felton, till ten o'clock. If he does not return by that time, we are to set sail for France.
BOOM!!!
The cannon fire was a signal to announce the death of the Duke of Buckingham.
Let us set sail, or our departure may be prevented.
Dear Felton has done his job well.
But it's only eight-thirty, Milady.
Set sail!
After a voyage lasting two days, Milady reached Boulogne, France.
She only stayed there long enough to put a letter into the post.
To His Eminence the Lord Cardinal Richelieu,
At his camp before La Rochelle.
My lord, Your Eminence may be assured that His Grace the Duke of Buckingham will not set out for France.
Lady de Winter
Boulogne, August 25, Evening.
P.S.—According to Your Eminence's desire, I am proceeding to the convent, at Bethune, where I will await your orders.

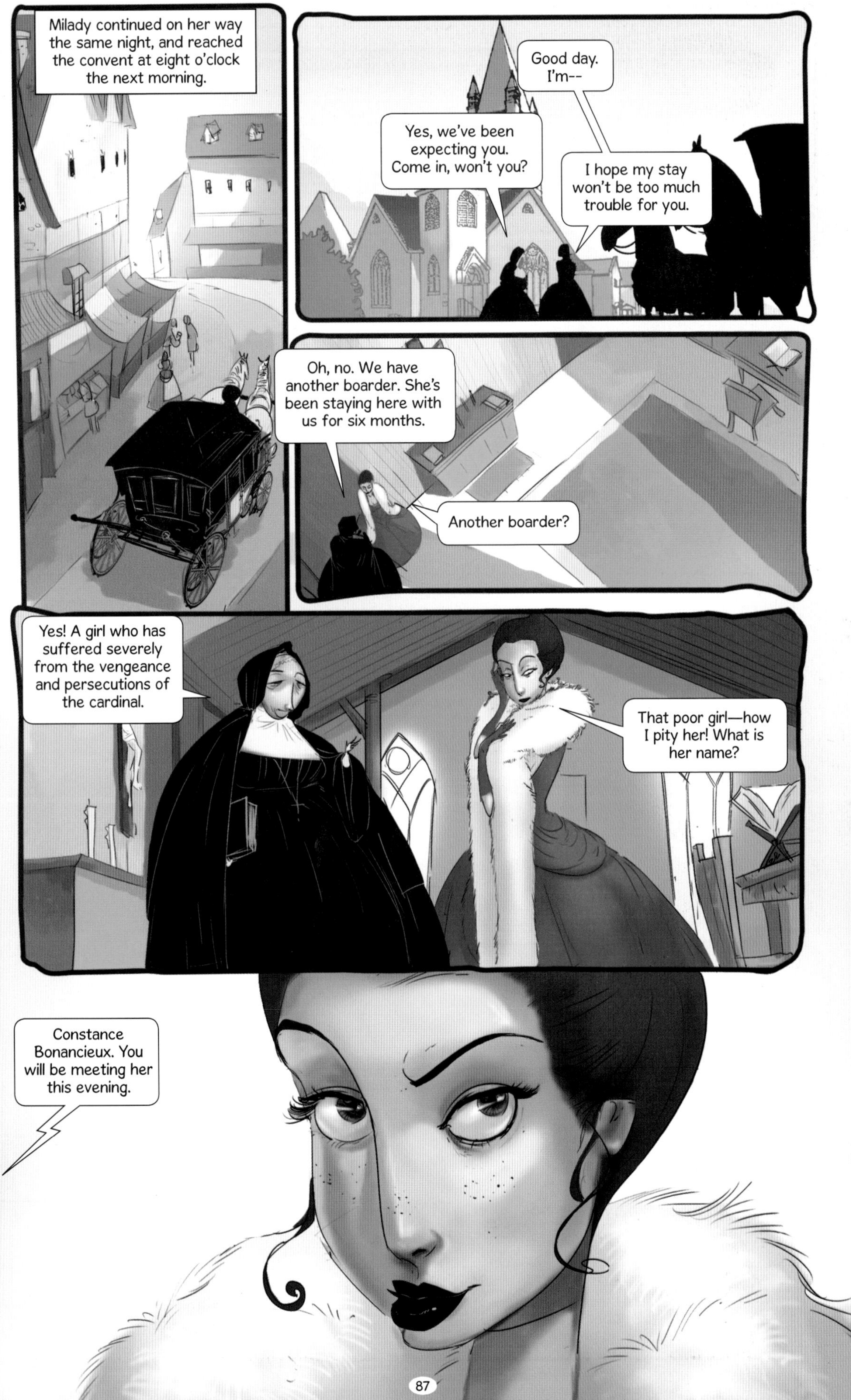
Milady continued on her way the same night, and reached the convent at eight o'clock the next morning.
Good day. I'm--
Yes, we've been expecting you. Come in, won't you?
I hope my stay won't be too much trouble for you.
Oh, no. We have another boarder. She's been staying here with us for six months.
Another boarder?
Yes! A girl who has suffered severely from the vengeance and persecutions of the cardinal.
That poor girl—how I pity her! What is her name?
Constance Bonancieux. You will be meeting her this evening.

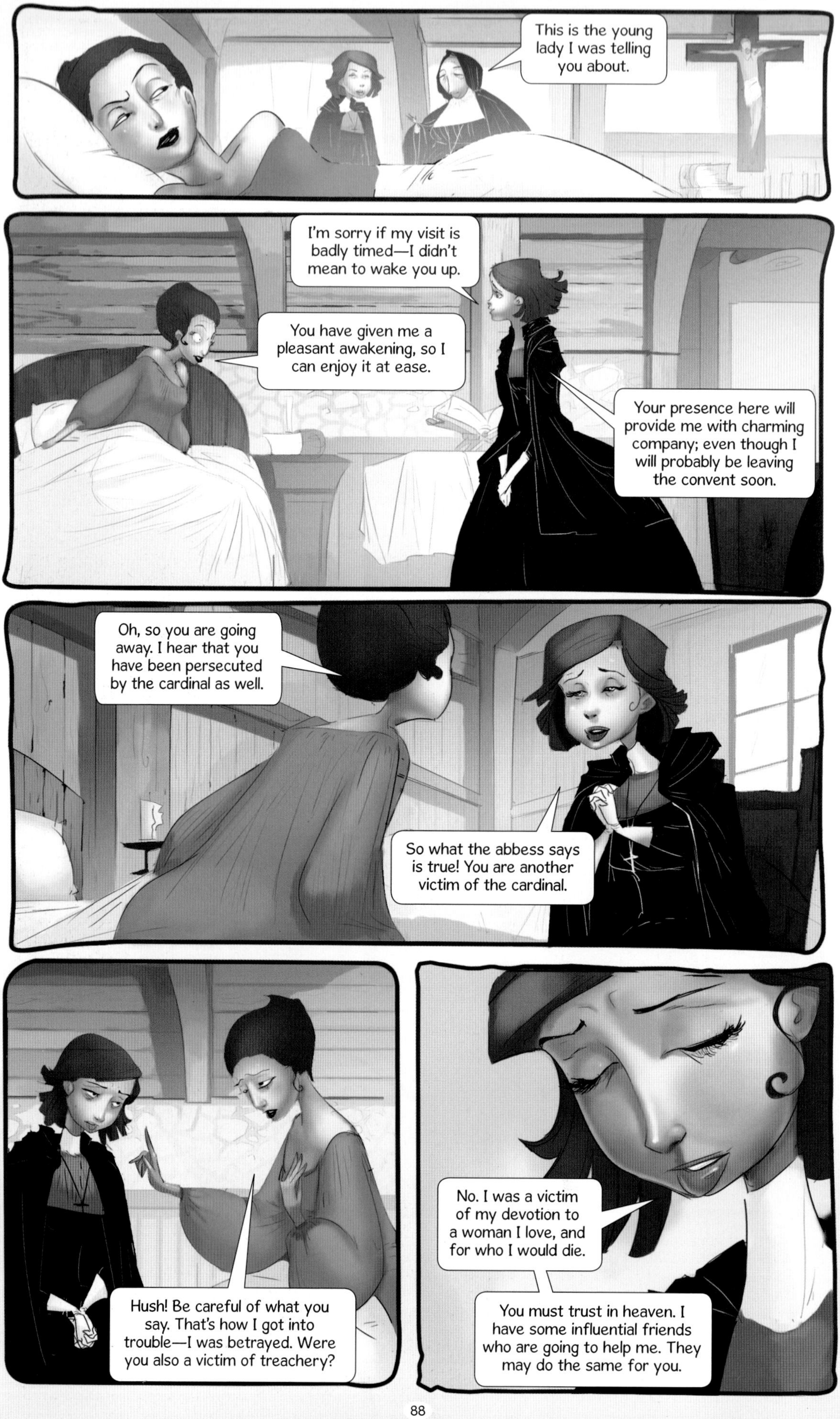
This is the young lady I was telling you about.
I'm sorry if my visit is badly timed—I didn't mean to wake you up.
You have given me a pleasant awakening, so I can enjoy it at ease.
Your presence here will provide me with charming company; even though I will probably be leaving the convent soon.
Oh, so you are going away. I hear that you have been persecuted by the cardinal as well.
So what the abbess says is true! You are another victim of the cardinal.
Hush! Be careful of what you say. That's how I got into trouble—I was betrayed. Were you also a victim of treachery?
No. I was a victim of my devotion to a woman I love, and for who I would die.
You must trust in heaven. I have some influential friends who are going to help me. They may do the same for you.

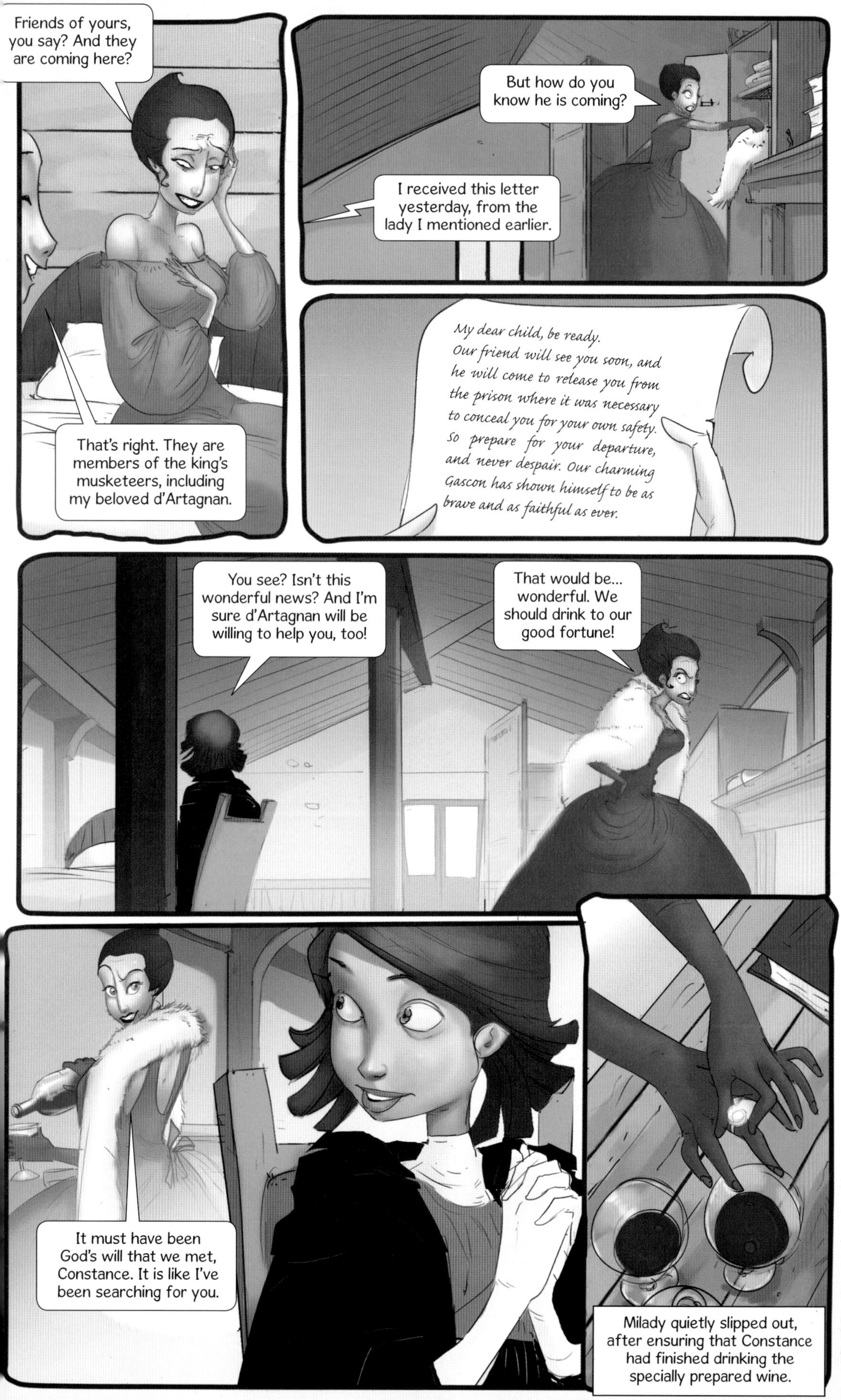
Friends of yours, you say? And they are coming here?
That's right. They are members of the king's musketeers, including my beloved d'Artagnan.
But how do you know he is coming?
I received this letter yesterday, from the lady I mentioned earlier.
My dear child, be ready. Our friend will see you soon, and he will come to release you from the prison where it was necessary to conceal you for your own safety. So prepare for your departure, and never despair. Our charming Gascon has shown himself to be as brave and as faithful as ever.
You see? Isn't this wonderful news? And I'm sure d'Artagnan will be willing to help you, too!
That would be... wonderful. We should drink to our good fortune!
It must have been God's will that we met, Constance. It is like I've been searching for you.
Milady quietly slipped out, after ensuring that Constance had finished drinking the specially prepared wine.

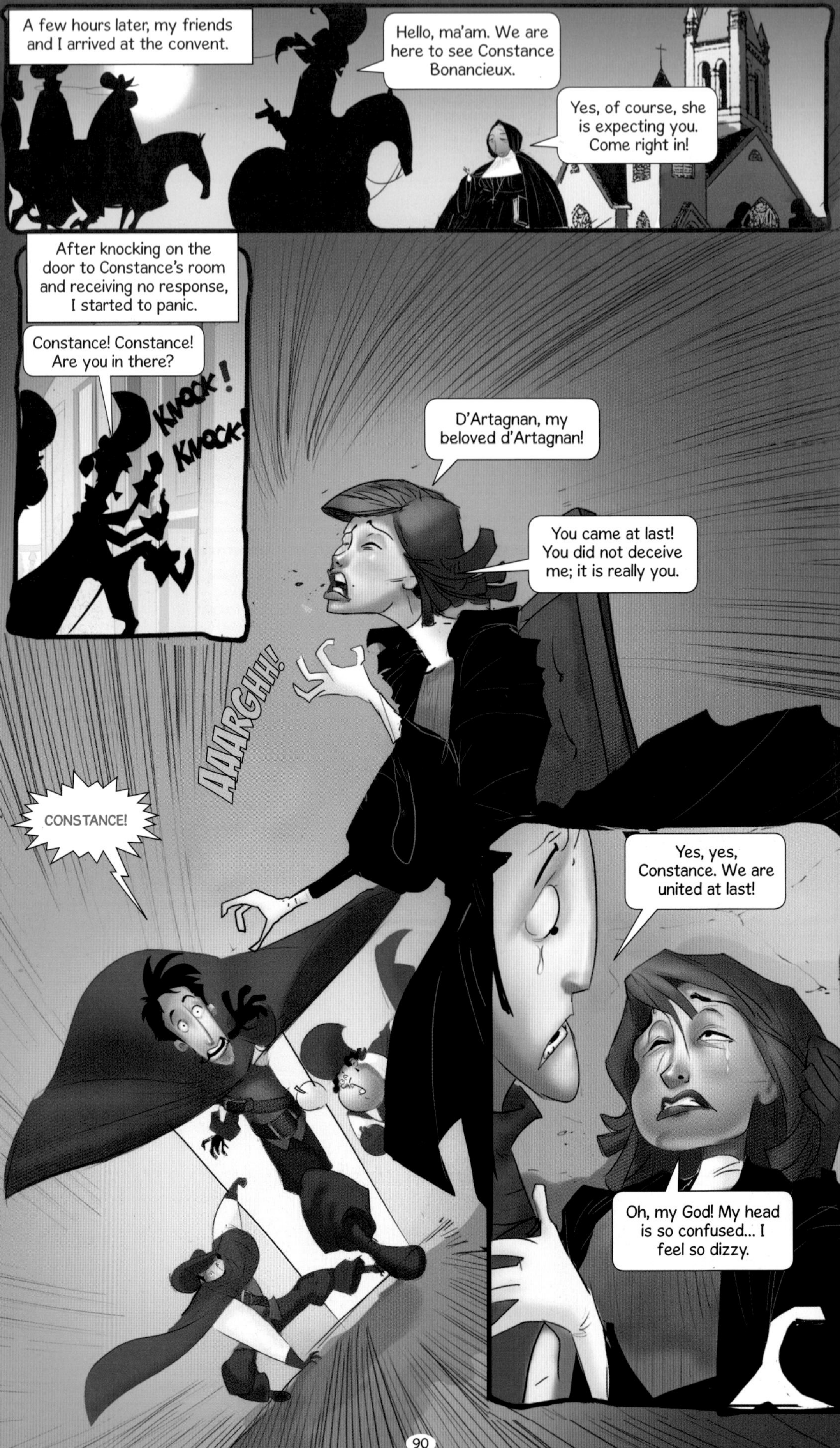

A few hours later, my friends and I arrived at the convent.
Hello, ma'am. We are here to see Constance Bonancieux.
Yes, of course, she is expecting you. Come right in!
After knocking on the door to Constance's room and receiving no response, I started to panic.
Constance! Constance! Are you in there?
KNOCK! KNOCK!
D'Artagnan, my beloved d'Artagnan!
You came at last! You did not deceive me; it is really you.
AAARGHH!
CONSTANCE!
Yes, yes, Constance. We are united at last!
Oh, my God! My head is so confused... I feel so dizzy.

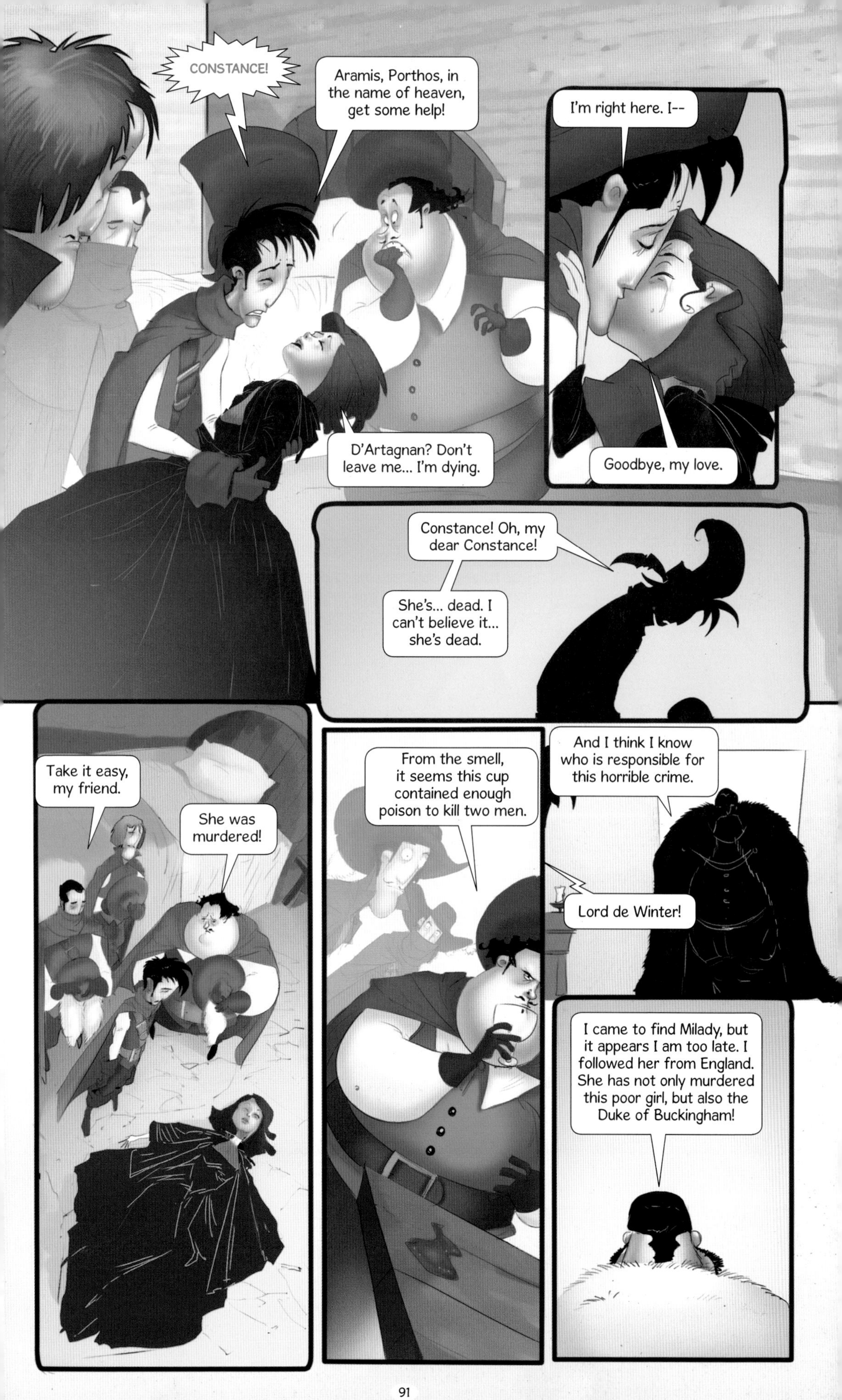
CONSTANCE!
Aramis, Porthos, in the name of heaven, get some help!
D'Artagnan? Don't leave me... I'm dying.
I'm right here. I--
Goodbye, my love.
Constance! Oh, my dear Constance!
She's... dead. I can't believe it... she's dead.
Take it easy, my friend.
She was murdered!
From the smell, it seems this cup contained enough poison to kill two men.
And I think I know who is responsible for this horrible crime.
Lord de Winter!
I came to find Milady, but it appears I am too late. I followed her from England. She has not only murdered this poor girl, but also the Duke of Buckingham!

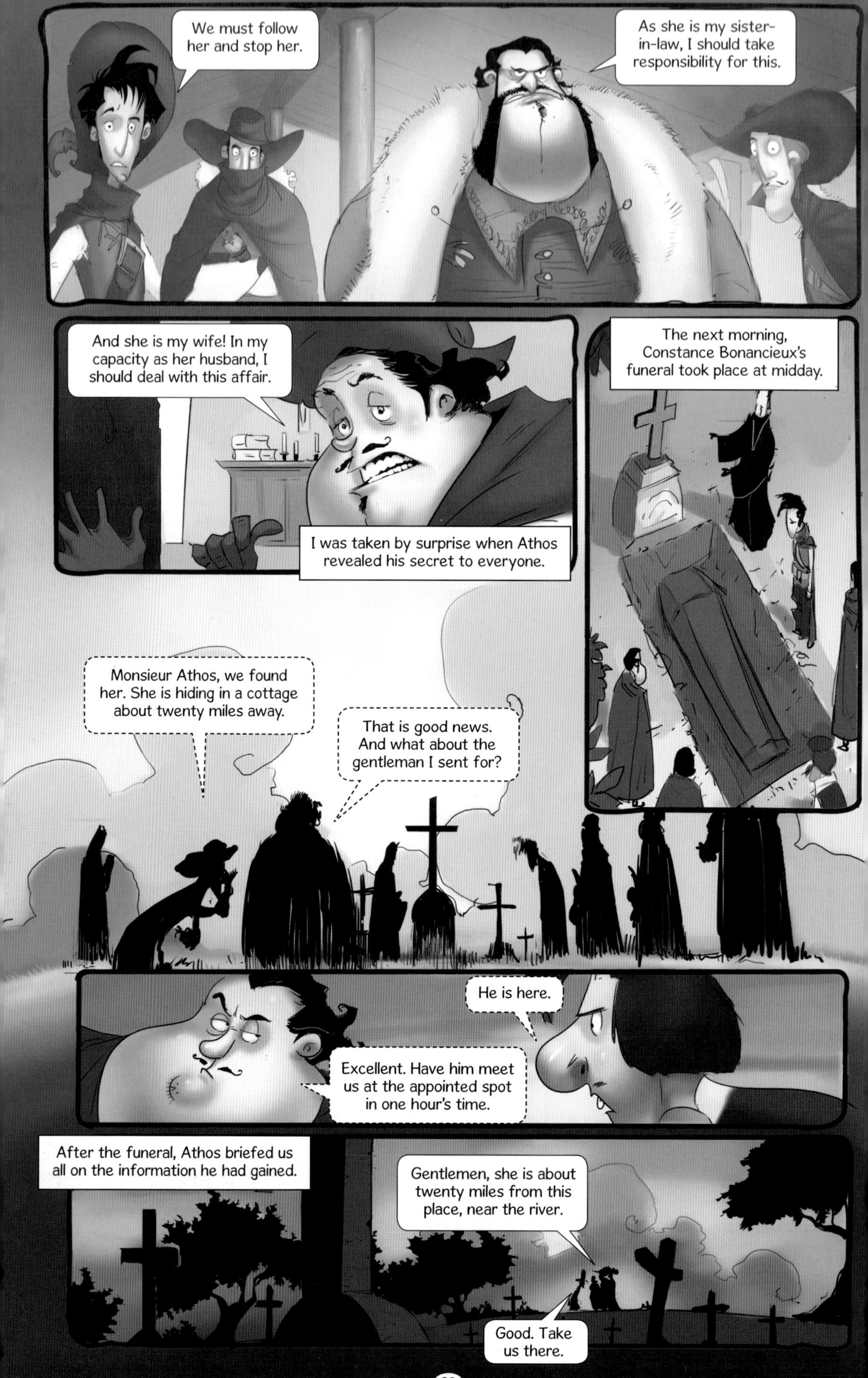

We must follow her and stop her.
As she is my sister-in-law, I should take responsibility for this.
And she is my wife! In my capacity as her husband, I should deal with this affair.
I was taken by surprise when Athos revealed his secret to everyone.
The next morning, Constance Bonancieux's funeral took place at midday.
Monsieur Athos, we found her. She is hiding in a cottage about twenty miles away.
That is good news. And what about the gentleman I sent for?
He is here.
Excellent. Have him meet us at the appointed spot in one hour's time.
After the funeral, Athos briefed us all on the information he had gained.
Gentlemen, she is about twenty miles from this place, near the river.
Good. Take us there.

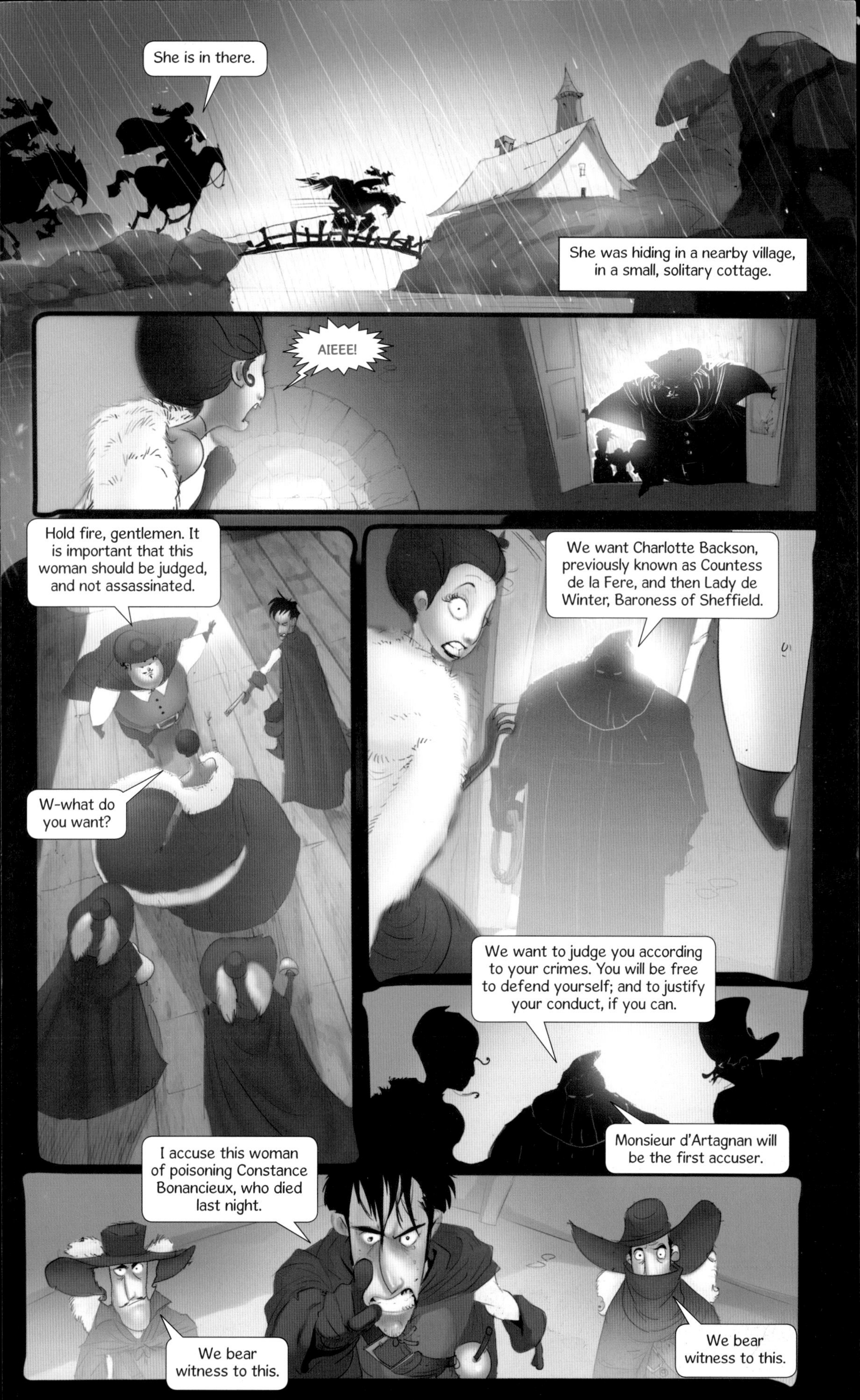
She is in there.
She was hiding in a nearby village, in a small, solitary cottage.
AIEEE!
Hold fire, gentlemen. It is important that this woman should be judged, and not assassinated.
W-what do you want?
We want Charlotte Backson, previously known as Countess de la Fere, and then Lady de Winter, Baroness of Sheffield.
We want to judge you according to your crimes. You will be free to defend yourself; and to justify your conduct, if you can.
Monsieur d'Artagnan will be the first accuser.
I accuse this woman of poisoning Constance Bonancieux, who died last night.
We bear witness to this.
We bear witness to this.

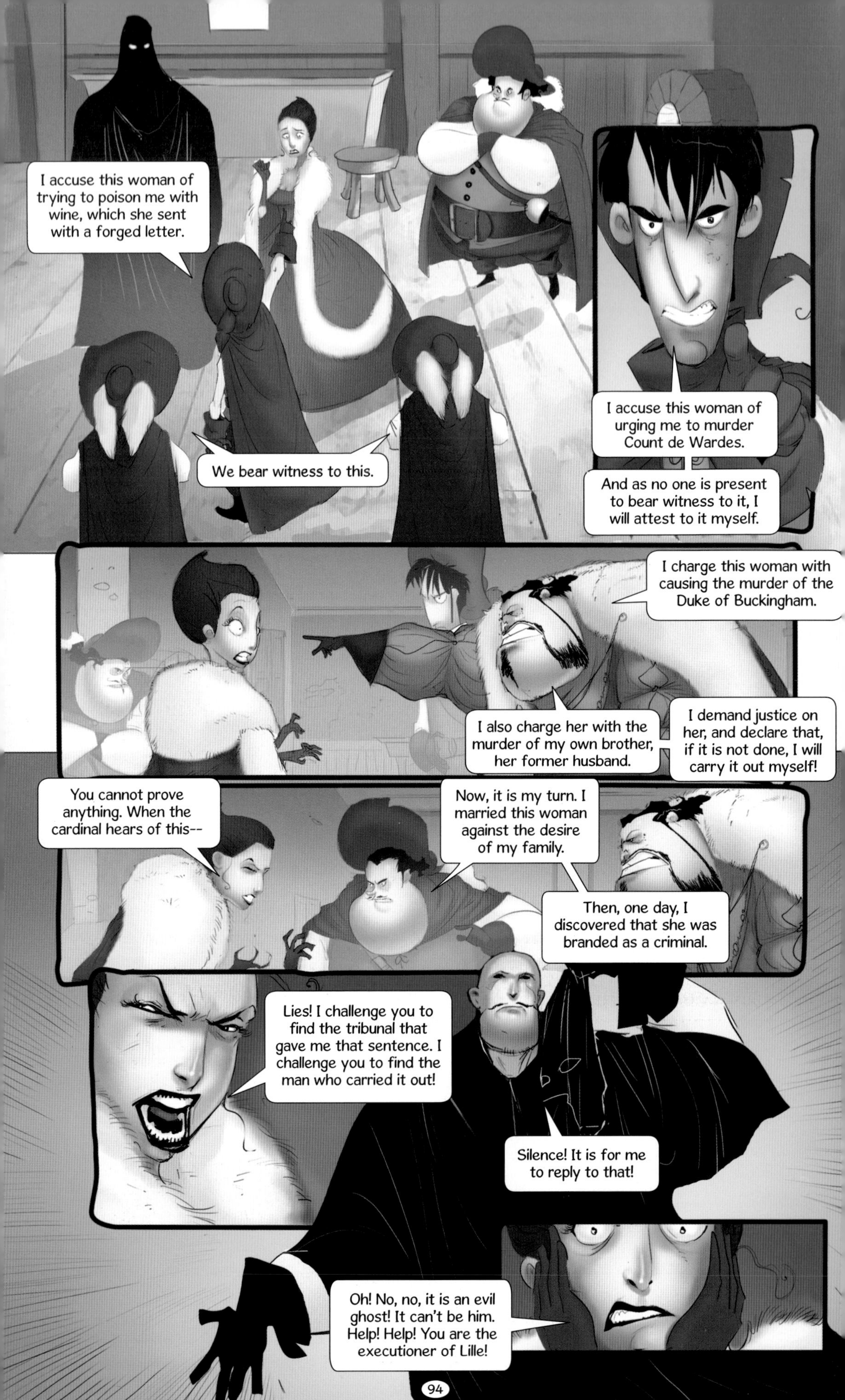
I accuse this woman of trying to poison me with wine, which she sent with a forged letter.
We bear witness to this.
I accuse this woman of urging me to murder Count de Wardes.
And as no one is present to bear witness to it, I will attest to it myself.
I charge this woman with causing the murder of the Duke of Buckingham.
I also charge her with the murder of my own brother, her former husband.
I demand justice on her, and declare that, if it is not done, I will carry it out myself!
You cannot prove anything. When the cardinal hears of this--
Now, it is my turn. I married this woman against the desire of my family.
Then, one day, I discovered that she was branded as a criminal.
Lies! I challenge you to find the tribunal that gave me that sentence. I challenge you to find the man who carried it out!
Silence! It is for me to reply to that!
Oh! No, no, it is an evil ghost! It can't be him. Help! Help! You are the executioner of Lille!

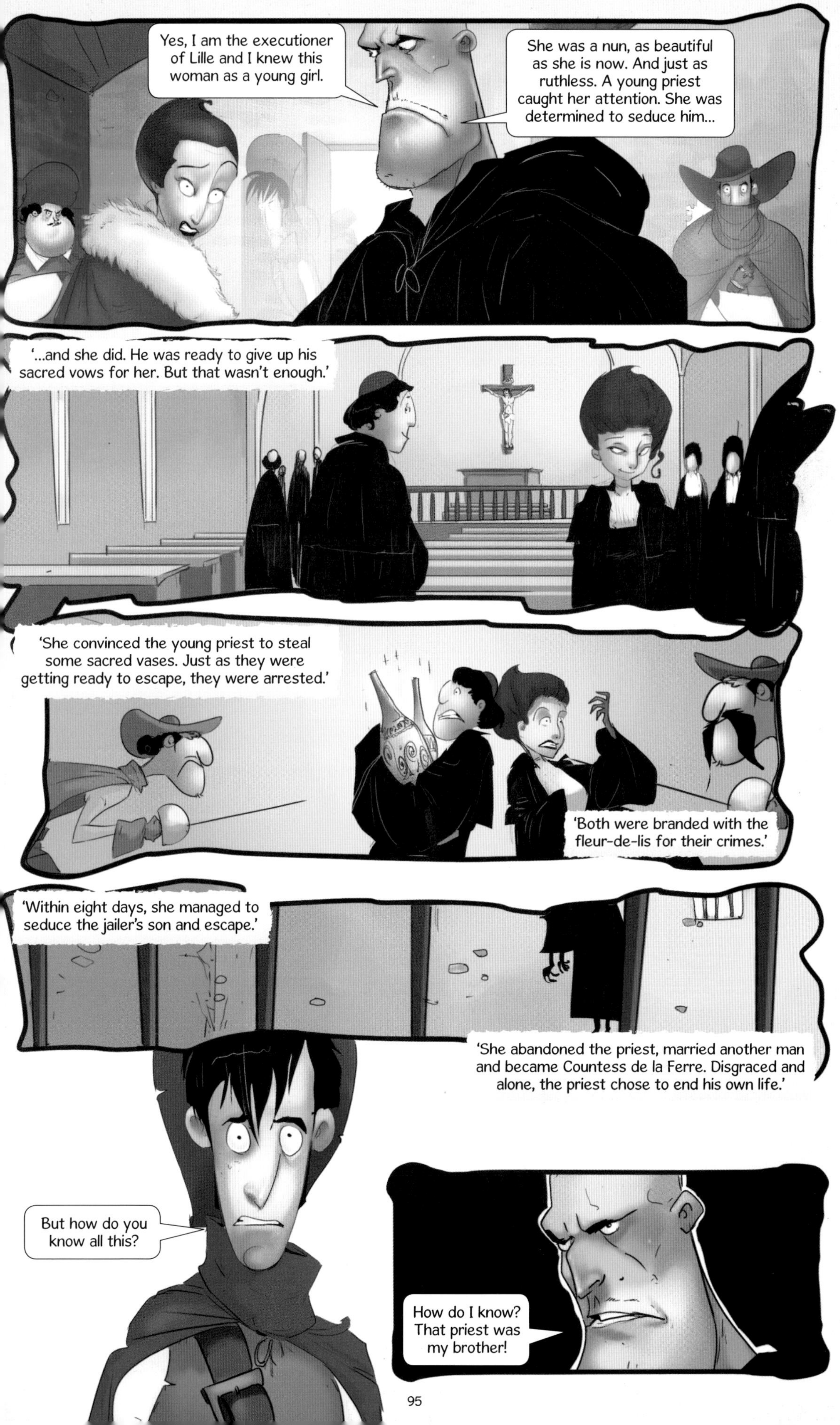
Yes, I am the executioner of Lille and I knew this woman as a young girl.
She was a nun, as beautiful as she is now. And just as ruthless. A young priest caught her attention. She was determined to seduce him...
'...and she did. He was ready to give up his sacred vows for her. But that wasn't enough.'
'She convinced the young priest to steal some sacred vases. Just as they were getting ready to escape, they were arrested.'
'Both were branded with the fleur-de-lis for their crimes.'
'Within eight days, she managed to seduce the jailer's son and escape.'
'She abandoned the priest, married another man and became Countess de la Ferre. Disgraced and alone, the priest chose to end his own life.'
But how do you know all this?
How do I know? That priest was my brother!

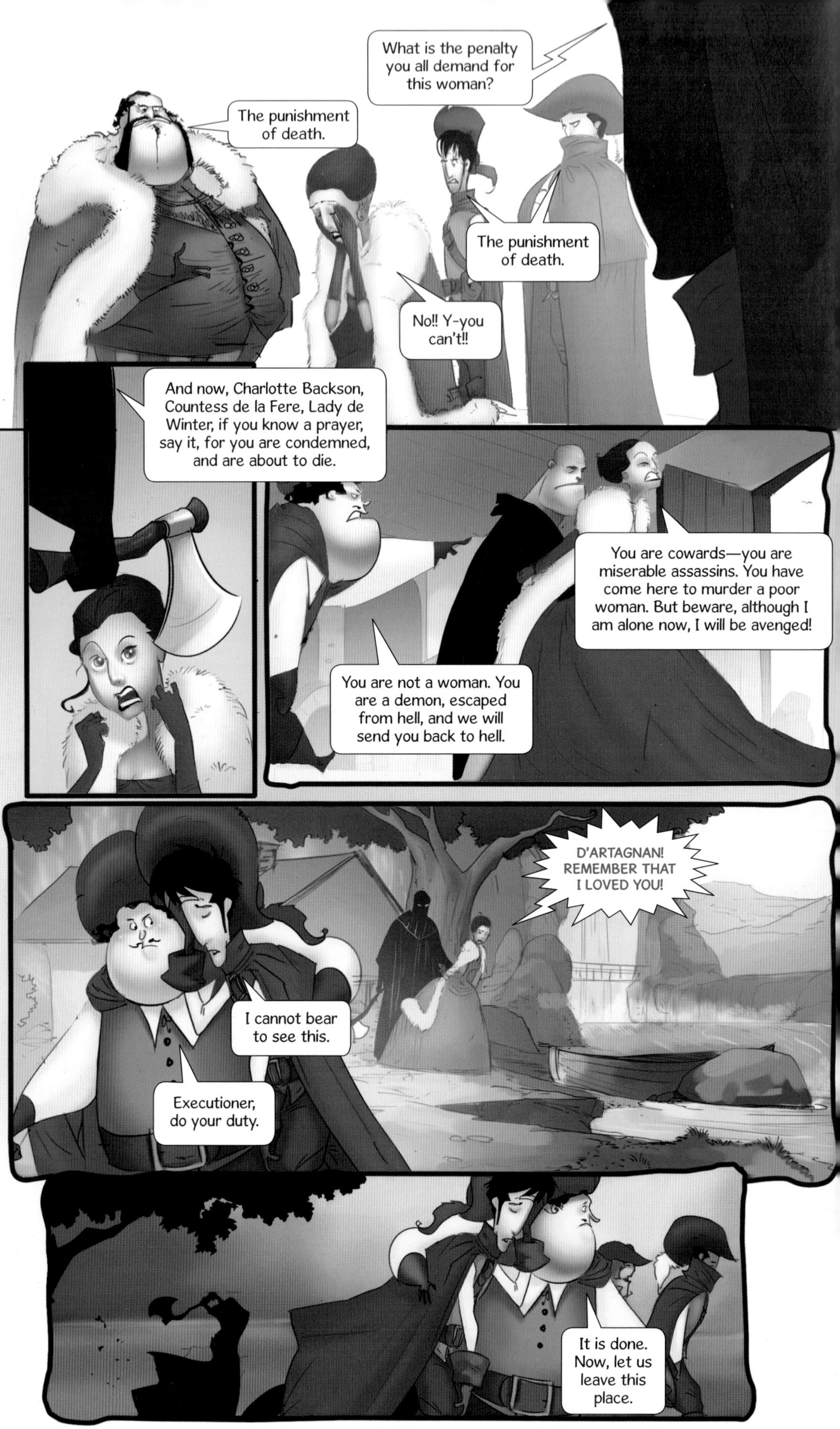
What is the penalty you all demand for this woman?
The punishment of death.
The punishment of death.
No!! Y-you can't!!
And now, Charlotte Backson, Countess de la Fere, Lady de Winter, if you know a prayer, say it, for you are condemned, and are about to die.
You are cowards—you are miserable assassins. You have come here to murder a poor woman. But beware, although I am alone now, I will be avenged!
You are not a woman. You are a demon, escaped from hell, and we will send you back to hell.
D'ARTAGNAN! REMEMBER THAT I LOVED YOU!
I cannot bear to see this.
Executioner, do your duty.
It is done. Now, let us leave this place.

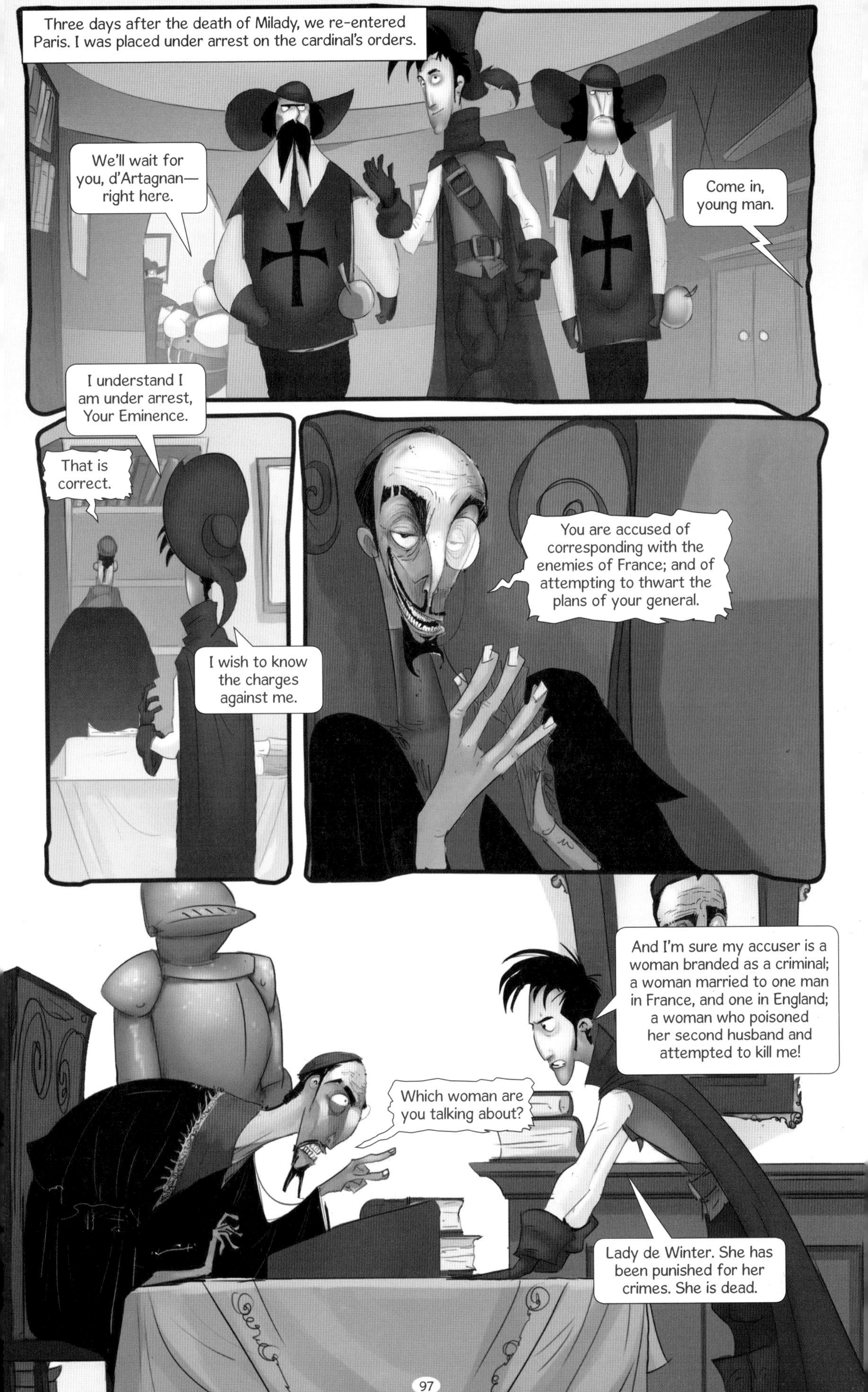

Three days after the death of Milady, we re-entered Paris. I was placed under arrest on the cardinal's orders.
We'll wait for you, d'Artagnan— right here.
Come in, young man.
I understand I am under arrest, Your Eminence.
That is correct.
I wish to know the charges against me.
You are accused of corresponding with the enemies of France; and of attempting to thwart the plans of your general.
And I'm sure my accuser is a woman branded as a criminal; a woman married to one man in France, and one in England; a woman who poisoned her second husband and attempted to kill me!
Which woman are you talking about?
Lady de Winter. She has been punished for her crimes. She is dead.

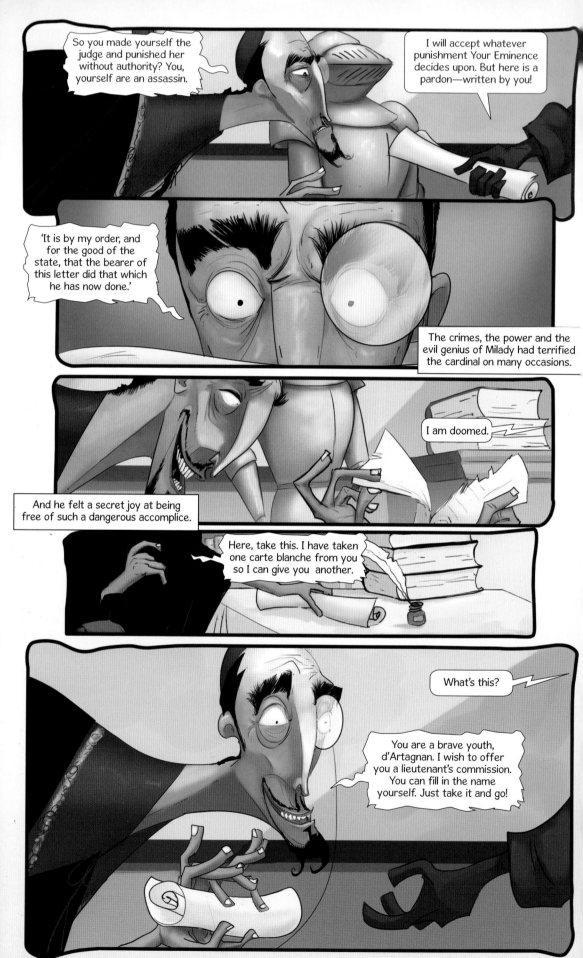

So you made yourself the judge and punished her without authority? You, yourself are an assassin.

I will accept whatever punishment Your Eminence decides upon. But here is a pardon—written by you!

'It is by my order, and for the good of the state, that the bearer of this letter did that which he has now done.'

The crimes, the power and the evil genius of Milady had terrified the cardinal on many occasions.

I am doomed.

And he felt a secret joy at being free of such a dangerous accomplice.

Here, take this. I have taken one carte blanche from you so I can give you another.

What's this?

You are a brave youth, d'Artagnan. I wish to offer you a lieutenant's commission. You can fill in the name yourself. Just take it and go!

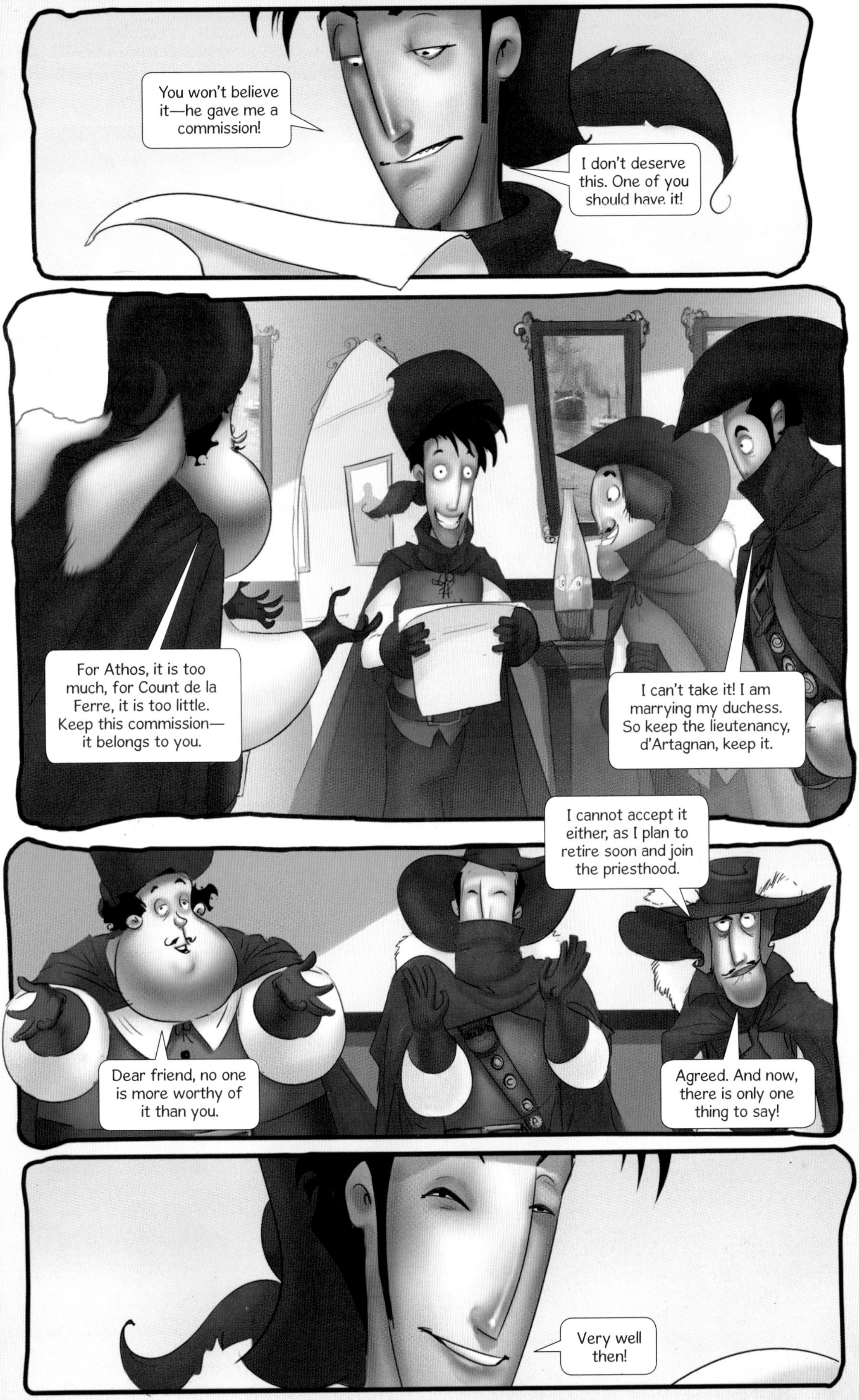
You won't believe it—he gave me a commission!
I don't deserve this. One of you should have it!
For Athos, it is too much, for Count de la Ferre, it is too little. Keep this commission—it belongs to you.
I can't take it! I am marrying my duchess. So keep the lieutenancy, d'Artagnan, keep it.
I cannot accept it either, as I plan to retire soon and join the priesthood.
Dear friend, no one is more worthy of it than you.
Agreed. And now, there is only one thing to say!
Very well then!

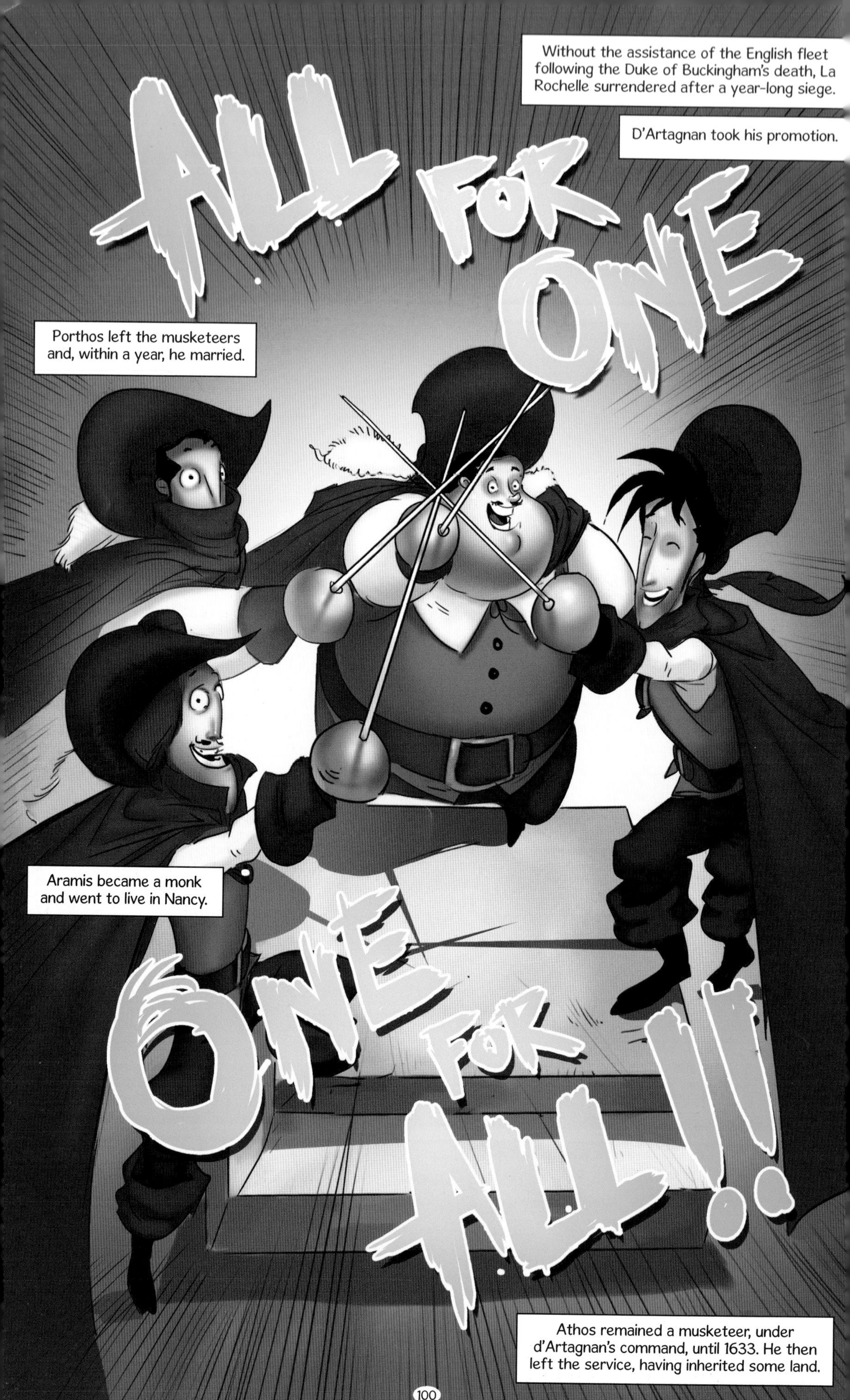

Without the assistance of the English fleet following the Duke of Buckingham's death, La Rochelle surrendered after a year-long siege.
D'Artagnan took his promotion.
ALL FOR ONE
Porthos left the musketeers and, within a year, he married.
Aramis became a monk and went to live in Nancy.
ONE FOR ALL!!
Athos remained a musketeer, under d'Artagnan's command, until 1633. He then left the service, having inherited some land.

Miguel de Cervantes
DON QUIXOTE
PART I
ADAPTED BY LLOYD S. WAGNER
ILLUSTRATED BY RICHARD KOHLRUS

Miguel de Cervantes

DON QUIXOTE

PART I

Adapted by Llyod S. Wagner

Illustrated by Richard Kohlrus

A delightful tale filled with humor, adventures... and misadventures!

Don Quixote—the name is universally known for the idealistic, possibly insane, wannabe knight as much as a masterpiece of literature. *Don Quixote*, the book is widely regarded as the first modern novel while Don Quixote, the character, is among the most recognizable and loveable ever created.

The author, Miguel de Cervantes, once said of Don Quixote that he was created so 'that children may handle him, youths may read him, men may understand him and old men may celebrate him.' Truly, the misadventures of Quixote and his faithful squire, Sancho Panza, are comic and entertaining to readers of all ages. At the same time, they speak deeply of man's place in the world and his aspirations.

This Campfire graphic novel adaptation is the ideal introduction to a story that readers will return to again and again throughout their lifetime—to read it, revel in it, and love it.

CAMPFIRE™
www.campfire.co.in

HISTORY OR REALITY?

Filled with adventure, spies, intrigue, romance, and humor, *The Three Musketeers* is one of the most celebrated adventure stories ever written. Many of the characters were real people who Dumas adapted to fit into his storyline. This is one of the reasons why *The Three Musketeers* is referred to as a historical novel.

WHAT IS A HISTORICAL NOVEL?

A novel in which the plot is set around real-life events from the past is called a historical novel. The author can take liberties and may add fictional characters or sub-plots to historical events. Sir Walter Scott was the first to popularize this genre with his novels on Scottish history.

Let's learn more about the real lives of these intriguing characters and the days of adventure long past.

WHO WERE THE MUSKETEERS REALLY?

Born sometime between 1611 and 1615, d'Artagnan became a member of the king's musketeers by the age of twenty. The characters of Athos, Porthos, and Aramis are based on real-life musketeers who were comrades of d'Artagnan. They are the three musketeers referred to in the title of the book. The musketeers were engaged in cloak-and-dagger operations for Kings Louis XIII and Louis XIV. Louis XIV, the Sun King, appointed d'Artagnan leader of the musketeers in 1658. He was eventually killed in an attack led by the Duke of Monmouth, who was at the head of an English contingent allied to France.

DID YOU KNOW?

1. Dumas did not write his novels by himself. He had many assistants who helped him with research. Some even made rough sketches of the plots of his novels and wrote early drafts. Dumas then added dialogue and other details.

2. Dumas's last novel, *The Knight of Sainte-Hermine*, was published in parts but not quite finished at the time of his death. The last two chapters were ghost written by the Dumas scholar, Claude Schopp. It was only in 2005 that the complete novel was published in France.

OTHER CHARACTERS

Anne of Austria—King Louis XIII was betrothed to Anne at the age of eleven, and married her at fourteen. Anne was the daughter of Phillip III of Spain and Margaret of Austria.

Cardinal Richelieu—He was considered to be a confidant of the mother of King Louis XIII. He was made the chief minister under King Louis XIII in 1624, and was the de facto ruler till 1642. He played a major role in transforming France into a strong nation.

Milady, Duchesse de Winter—It is believed that Milady's character was actually the Countess of Carlisle, who was, in fact, an agent of Cardinal Richelieu. It is said that she actually did steal two diamond studs from the Duke of Buckingham!

DID YOU KNOW THAT THE TERM 'MUSKETEER' CAME FROM THE WORD 'MUSKET'?

The musketeers were the king's personal guards, and were supposed to be armed with muskets. However, in reality, they rarely used muskets. To use a firearm instead of a sword was considered unthinkable for these men of honor. Only musketeers from the lower ranks would have ever used muskets to kill their enemies.

The motto of the musketeers

'ALL FOR ONE, ONE FOR ALL.'

Available now

Putting the fun back into reading!